I0831287

Starchasers:
The Stars Are calling

By Kay Hawkins

Cover art by Leah Keeler

Starchasers: The Stars Are Calling

Kay Hawkins

Published by Kay Hawkins

First Edition 2018

ISBN: 978-0-9959794-4-4

Dedication

To Lois McMaster Bujold,
whose journey of miles
has blazed a trail for me.

Chapter 1

Skyler rolled over and glared at the alarm clock buzzing and flashing 7 a.m. in bright green. Summer was officially over. *Damn.* He glanced around the powder pink room with a window facing the courtyard above two single beds and a desk. Very similar to his room, the one he had the year before and would have again this year. Skyler Therris was getting ready to start his second year in the United Galactic Forces Academy.

Last night, the final one before fall classes started, had been a wild night for Skyler. It had been a wild week, for that matter. He spent every day going to the bar and staying up late. He was 19 now and his friends were all over the place. Michael took the summer off to tend his ailing father. Kax was on a space station improving her piloting skills. Skyler had no family worth visiting. It was just him and his summer roommate with all the time in the world. But it was all coming to an end this morning. Time to stop goofing off and get back to work. A woman's hand crept over his shoulder. The long fingers danced along his bicep. "Could you turn that alarm off and get back to what really matters—pleasing me?"

He rolled over to face her and raised an eyebrow. The hand belonged to Roxanne, the girl Skyler had been seeing over the summer. He had stayed over in her dorm room, identical to his except neater, with girl stuff like makeup and curling irons on the dresser. She was going to be a sixth-year as a security cadet. He had started seeing her at the end of his first year. She was his raven-haired beauty.

"Oh, is that really what matters? I thought going to class and sticking to studying was what 'Really matters?' When did the rules change?"

She gave him a juicy kiss on the lips.

As she kissed him, he couldn't help but think how important this year was. He was one year closer to graduating with a war on the horizon. They could make him graduate early and go to the front lines. He was walking into a minefield. Skyler broke the kiss and let out a deep sigh and rubbed his brow. But in the end, it should all be worth it, as this was the path to becoming a captain. Being a captain was his dream ever since he could remember. His father was a captain, and he was going to be just like him one day. She gave him a stern look.

"You're overthinking again. I thought I told you to stop that?"

He dismissed those deep thoughts and cast his winning smile. "You're right and you're the only thing that should be on my mind." He caressed her sides and kissed her neck.

She moaned, rubbing her hands through Skyler's hair. "I'm falling in love with you," she mumbled through another kiss.

Not another one. Skyler raised his head and narrowed his eyes at her. "Really, you think you love me, Roseanne?"

She pushed him away playfully. "It's Roxanne, remember and, of course, I love you. We have been together all summer."

Well I'm not in love with her. He laughed and turned his head away from her. "Has it been that long?"

He watched and admired her naked body as she got out of the bed.

She picked her clothes off the floor and got dressed. She took a pen off the desk and wrote something on scrap piece of paper, then handed the paper to him. "Just put your shirt on and I'll see you later."

He took the paper and shrugged. He put on his black undershirt. He brushed back his wavy blond hair with his hand before he slipped on his green pants and left her room fully clothed.

As he walked down the halls, he saw a few familiar faces and few new ones. He headed to his dorm and saw his summer roommate packing his bags. Skyler sat on his unmade bed. "You're leaving already? I thought you were here for the rest of the year?"

Perry lifted his curly brown head from his suitcase. "I thought so too but turns out my transfer to Orion Four was accepted so I'm spending the fall in space. I will be back later in the year."

Skyler got off his bed and patted his roommate on the back. "Well it's sad to see you go, but hey, I hope you enjoy the station."

"I hope so; I don't see much fun in watching how seeds grow in colder space climates."

Skyler laughed. "You applied to watch grass grow?"

Perry closed his suitcase and stood up. His golden-brown eyes stared at Skyler. "I applied to work on the space station in the science department. I applied for a few of them and that's the one I got. No idea grass is what I would get. It's work with plants, at least, but humans have been trying to get seeds to grow in cold climates for centuries, and it just doesn't work. They just go dormant."

Skyler gave his roommate a hearty man hug. "I told you, don't talk to me about your plant stuff, it makes no sense."

"Sorry. You know it's just a habit." Perry rubbed the back of his neck.

They fist bumped and Skyler watched Perry leave the room in his orange uniform.

Skyler laid on his bed, rolling onto his side. He reached for the second drawer on his desk that was in between the two beds and pulled out a plain wooden box. He took the piece of paper Roxanne gave him out of his pocket. He placed it in the box with a bunch of other similar papers with sets of letters and numbers on them.

The door opened, and Skyler sat up. He grinned when his previous year's roommate Michael entered, dragging a large suitcase. He smiled at Skyler. "Long time no see."

Skyler hopped off his bed and flung his arms around his close friend, almost knocking him over. "Damn, I missed you! glad to see you again Michael."

Hesitantly Michael gave Skyler a pat on the back. "It's great to see you again too." He stared at the door. "When did they install touch pads in the dorms and why is ours the only one still with a lock and key?"

Skyler helped Michael with his bag and went back to sitting on his own bed. Michael brushed his tousled brown hair out of his orange oval eyes and tucked it behind his cropped shaped ears.

"They upgraded the system for security reasons, but day one I got fed up with trying to remember the code coming home from the bar, and—well, long story short, I sort of busted it. Also, we're not the only ones still using keys. A few others broke theirs too. But anyway, how was your summer?"

"It was a nice summer with my dad. He is doing better." Michael placed his suitcase on the bed and started to unpack his neatly folded clothes. "It was a bit boring without you and Kax. How about you?"

"Well there were a few chicks but really all I did was command simulators. All kinds of boring stuff."

"I guess that would be boring." Michael fixed the messed sheets before setting down a pile of handkerchiefs, "Did you have a roommate in the summer?"

"Yup. His name was Perry Ryan Xyrik. Fun guy but nothing compared to you. He just left." Skyler furrowed his brow. "How did you get the same room as last year? I know I applied to stay here, and this was the only building that they were letting the summer cadets in, so I could keep my room. But you would think they would've paired me with another second year."

Placing his clothes in the dresser, Michael said, "Well, I wouldn't doubt if Fleet Admiral Cane had something to do with it."

"Ya, I bet you are right about that. Hey, how is your dad's recovery from the attacks last year going?"

Michael let out a long sigh. "Better. Well, enough to be on his own, but I'm only going to be here part-time. Till he gets better. He's on medical leave, but if he isn't better soon they're going to reassign him, and for a Squallite he has a pretty decent job. It wouldn't be right for him to be reassigned to a lesser job with his years of experience."

"Now that sucks. Send him my best wishes." Skyler lowered his gaze to the floor. Michael's dad was a great guy. He envied their close relationship but hoped things would return to normal soon. Michael finished unpacking and placing things in his drawers. "So, any news about Kax?"

Skyler shook his head, reflecting on the fiery Catillion he'd spent so much time thinking about this summer, even when he was with Roxanne. "I heard she's coming back. Just that her group is delayed so we won't see her till next week."

Michael put his suitcase away under the bed. "Well now, that is a bummer. It's ok, though. We can have our own fun.

Want to head to the bar and get a few drinks to celebrate the new school year?"

Skyler stared at Michael in amazement. "Sounds great to me! But since when do you want to go to the bar willingly?"

Michael rubbed his temples. "Like I said, rough summer, so I believe I have earned a few drinks."

Skyler's eyes popped. "Wow. You did have a rough summer."

Chapter 2

A few days into the semester, Michael followed Skyler back into the room. Skyler peeled off his cadet jacket and flopped down on his bed onto his stomach with an exaggerated sigh. It looked like he was having one of his dramatic moments.

"What's up?" Michael asked.

Skyler moaned and buried his head in his pillow. "I forgot how hard class was. I miss the summer courses."

Michael laughed. "It's only been three days. You will be fine. I'm finding it quite fun being back here learning again. And this year is harder than my years before."

"I can't handle these dumb drills. They're pointless! Why do I have to memorize all the codes? Why should I care what the crew does in a code Thirty-Two-B?"

Michael went over to the rumpled bed and perched on the edge. He raised his eyebrow at Skyler. It always amazed him what a talented leader his friend was despite his reluctance to follow protocols. "You want to be a Captain, but you don't want to learn the codes? You do realize those codes are the things that tell headquarters and the other personnel what is going on. So, you don't say, 'Hey, there is a purple swirly thing shooting at us.' You say Thirty-Six-G, then everyone knows what's going on. We all have to memorize them."

Skyler rubbed his temples and groaned. "I know, but it's so boring, having so many tests, memorizing the codes. I wish you could just pick them up as you go along. Like a Forty-Five-Z, no one is ever going to use that one." He grunted in frustration. "This isn't fair. The forces shouldn't make my head hurt."

Michael picked up Skyler's command codes book off the shared desk. He flipped through a few pages. "Forty-Five-Z? Isn't that the code for 'An officer on another ship is mooning me?' I agree that one seems a bit pointless. Might be why it's at the bottom of the list."

"I guess you got to do what you got to do." Skyler turned onto his back and stared up blankly at the ceiling.

Michael let out another small laugh. Skyler's moments of drama always amused him as it was such a stark contrast to his boisterous personality "Is there something else going on? It's not like you to get this frustrated over school."

"No, I just like to think of space when I'm stressed."

"I see, so what just happened there? You were talking about codes, and now you want to not talk. All I can say is that I am surprised you almost never shut up."

Skyler brushed back his honey blonde hair. "I'm sorry. My mind just wandered there."

Michael shook his head. "No problem, I just found it odd. May I ask why you love space so much?"

As Michael had anticipated, his roommate's green eyes lit up at the mention of space, one of his favorite topics besides women. "I'm not sure it's someplace I have always felt I was meant to be, if you understand that."

"I never really felt that way about anywhere," said Michael. "I have been many places but not yet felt at home." *There was the base when I was a child, then my dad's house and his cousin's place on Squall. Now I'm back on base again and continually switching dorms. It's my third year, I won't be here much longer, so no point in getting settled. Wonder if there really is a home for me out there.*

Skyler took a deep breath and a peaceful look came over his face. "As far back as I can remember I've wanted to go to space. Space is so beautiful. The stars are so much closer. You have the hollow blackness and silence and that makes it so peaceful. And seeing a planet from orbit is just amazing. It's hard to describe. You feel like you can hold this one powerful ball of so much life." He glanced at Michael. "Space is so beautiful. You know, I was even conceived in space. But my mother wanted to raise me on Earth. She said no to raising her child on a starship.

That's one of the reasons I'm an only child. Once I came around, my father stayed working and mom stayed on the ground. They rarely saw each other after that."

"So, you want to stay in space because your father was there?"

Skyler continued to stare at the ceiling. "No, I used to think that. But it was just a feeling that I was meant to be out there. It's where I belong. It until last year when I went to space for the first time on my own. So, I know it's not just a fantasy."

"Really? You don't mind the nothingness? The entrapment of being confined to a starship?" Michael paused to think, *being a captain would be great, but I don't know if I could stand being on a ship for an extended period.*

"No, because the ship is an extension of yourself, and all who are in it are part of this great being. When I'm in times of trouble, the thoughts of space come to me and that tell me it will be okay."

Michael shook his head and stood up. "You are weird, you know that?"

Skyler turned to Michael, who was heading out of the room now. "Hey, where are you going?"

He checked back at Skyler. "Study hall. It might be just the beginning of the year, but I still need to study."

Skyler snorted at Michael. "Fine. Suit yourself."

***

Michael left the room and made his way down the hall. As he walked, he kept his eye on his feet, pondering his conversation with Skyler. Despite the difficulties with classes, Skyler always managed to have everything figured out and know exactly what he wanted. Michael wished some of that confidence would rub off on him. Still looking at his feet, he didn't notice when someone bumped into him. "Long time no see," said a woman's voice.

He raised his head to find Kax standing right in front of him. He gave her a wide smile. Michael didn't get attached to many people, but Kax and Skyler were the rare exceptions. He'd come to rely on them last year, and when things were rough with his father this summer, he'd often wished he could talk to Kax. She was a terrific listener and always knew how to cheer him up. "I missed you so much," Michael told her, surprised he was admitting it.

Kax hugged Michael, squeezing him tight. "I missed you too Michael how was your summer?"

"Not as fun as you summer I bet," he said when they separated.

Kax's cat-like ears drooped. "Aw, is your Dad not doing well?"

"He could be doing better, but he is doing well enough, I was able to hire a health care worker, so that I was able to come back. Tell me about yours."

Kax twisted a lock of her strawberry blonde hair. "It was just piloting routines and such, nothing great."

Michael didn't buy that. From what he understood, it should have been a fantastic experience for a budding pilot like Kax. She must be downplaying it out of respect for his own depressing summer. You sure about that? Come on, I want to hear the details."

"Well..." Kax flashed a big grin. "It was great, it was amazing, I never thought I would get so close to things. Far away stars, I mean, it was amazing, I have been to space before, but nothing like this and I was in total control. They got us to pilot our own shuttles. And they had a crew on the station who watched. This way if anything went wrong they could call us back."

"I'm glad you did have a fun summer, and now you're back."

"That's right, I'm back. And the funny thing is the room they assigned me to is right above yours from last year." She had only been back for a few minutes and he was already feeling better. "Really? Neat. Skyler and I have the same room again. You do realize there's a vent that goes from our room to the upstairs."

She nodded. "Yup."

"Then I suggest you seal your vent and buy earplugs."

Her eyebrows curved. “That’s an odd thing to say, why would I do that?”

Michael gritted his teeth, his face flushing. He hoped he didn’t have to elaborate. “One word. 'Skyler'.”

Her eyes widened, and she slapped her forehead. “How could I forget Skyler’s libido? Is he still after me, by the way?”

“I'm not sure, but I'd say yes. His feelings for you seemed deeper than what he feels for other girls.”

She blushed, startling Michael. Kax wasn’t a girl who blushed easily. “You want to go to the cafeteria for lunch?” She asked quickly, changing the subject.

“I was heading off to the study hall, but I could do lunch.”

Michael followed her toward the cafeteria, now dealing with a new worry. While Kax and Skyler were his two best friends, he wasn’t convinced they belonged together. Or that he wanted to be a third wheel.

Chapter 3

Down at the cafeteria, Michael rushed to the line. Kax ran to catch up. She’d never seen Michael excited to see replicated food. When she got in the line, she demanded, “Michael, what’s gotten into you?”

Michael smiled like a child in a candy store. “Look.” He pointed to a digital red glowing sign. “The sign says: Replicator Is Broken. So, that means they are serving real food.”

Kax’s eyes popped in amazement. “Wow, we did pick a good day to come.”

They both excitedly followed the line and went up to the counters and got food off the racks. All the electricity seemed to be down in the kitchen area. The robot lunch workers were powered down and not serving. Actual people in select powered areas of the steel kitchen had prepared the food. When they had their pasta and salads on the trays, they used their swipe cards and exited the line.

They took their trays to the table. “Anything interesting happen to you this summer besides the obvious?” Michael asked, and began to eat ravenously.

Kax played with her food for a bit before looking up at Michael. “Not much. There were only a few people there. Thirty in total and mostly older cadets.”

Michael frowned. “Thirty people? But you were on a space station. Shouldn't there be more?”

Kax shook her head. “Not this one. It was being rebuilt. So, they had Cadets train and used us for small missions back and forth, to supplies to the new space station. A few times we got to go to the new one and shop for a bit, but there’s nothing big there yet. All this summer felt like extra credit training, nothing more, nothing less.”

Michael examined his seven-vegetable pasta. “Still better than mine.”

She could see the sadness in Michael’s drooping orange eyes. “So, you mentioned before. But what exactly is wrong with your dad?”

Michael sighed. “Typhidalendia, it's a rare illness that he got when he was younger but stays dormant till you start to enter old age. He should have gotten it maybe about twenty years from now, but the attack with the Cassiopaeans caused it to activate. He got it when his ship was attacked. The crew got weird spores all over their skin that go in and mutate your DNA. Dr. Kelley is working on removing the spores, but they’re alive and grow inside, so they’re hard to stop. Typhidalendia causes your organs to change into another species still alien to us. Even when we have let others go through the change, no one lives.”

Kax listened closely to Michael’s story. It left her almost speechless. “That sounds horrible. So, it stays dormant to take advantage of our bodies when we become seniors.”

Michael bit his lower lip. “Yeah, kids have been known to fight it off, but not adults. Dr. Kelley can't cure it, but he is trying to manipulate it to somehow stop the degeneration. My father will be feeling fine, on his way to recovery, then boom, he is sick again. The good thing is both the spores and the disease don't affect the vital organs till the end.”

Kax’s jaw dropped. “Oh my, that sounds even worse. I mean it's like his body is saying change or die, but both will be slow and painful. Is there a chance another planet knows how to treat it?”

Michael shook his head. “The ship was lost when they found it in that area of space. They have tried to get back there, but more just seem to get sick. There is no answer from the dead planet or the ship it came from. It seems hopeless, but if my Dad stays in shape, he might fool the illness to thinking he is young or something.”

“So, I guess his fate is sealed?”

He fiddled with his fork. “Mostly, they don't know yet. I would say yes, but I’m hopeful they find something. All I know is when my father dies, I'm on my own and alone.”

“You’re going to make me cry this is so sad I have my dad, siblings and distant relatives I can contact. But you have no one. When you have kids, have lots of them.” Tears glimmered in her eyes. He pinched the bridge of his nose. “Well that’s another problem...”

“Kax,” Skyler interrupted, “don’t you know Michael won’t be having kids? He likes sausage.” He sat down next to them with a tray of food. He winked at Kax.

Michael turned his head to see Skyler making an obscene gesture with his hand and mouth.

Michael glared and gave Skyler an angry shove. “It’s not like that at all, and you know that. Even if I did like men, there’re lots of ways for me to still have kids.”

Kax snarled at Skyler, “Michael is a career man! He’s not having kids for a long time. Think about it. We’re not college students, we’re working. How many do you know in our classes who are planning on getting married or having kids? The average says the higher-ranking Officers had their families in their late thirties. That’s close to fifteen years away for us.”

“You have a point Kax, but when it comes to me, both of you are wrong.” Michael got up and left his unfinished food.

Kax and Skyler shared a puzzled expression. Michael ignored them and walked away.

Kax faced Skyler. “What did we say wrong? Do you know the real reason?”

“Something to do with culture, religion or whatever. He told me something about it last year.” Skyler leaned over to steal Michael’s food. “So, you’re back. How was your summer?”

"It was great until you showed up." Kax whacked his hand and moved Michael's tray closer to her. "Michael wanted this food before you showed up. So, I will make sure he gets it." She took her empty fruit cup and started putting in Michael's pasta salad.

"What? You're not happy to see me?" Skyler went back to his spaghetti. "Ya, sure save the food for him, but remember real food goes bad. I prefer replicated food, it tastes better."

"He will eat it, don't you worry. By the way, how was your summer?"

Skyler had a mouth full of noodles and tried to speak.

Oh, Skyler you charming son of a bitch I can't believe I missed this attitude. She rolled her cat-like eyes. "Swallow, then speak."

Skyler finished his bite and with a grin answered. "That's what I told the girls all summer."

"And I told the guys, not in my hair." She grinned. 'Ha take that, two can play that game.'

"That's gross." His face twisted in disgust.

Kax leaned on the table. "Then tell me what you really did."

"Simulation tests is all. How would I react in certain situations? Testing my loyalty to the ship and Captain." He went back to eating his food.

"Ugh, done that. It's easy in theory, but hard when you get the asshole Captains. I have been tempted to fly the ship into the sun because of some of them." She went back to picking at her food.

Skyler laughed. "Ya, there was one I had for a month. They put you at the pathetic rank of Petty Officer and made you work with the worst Captain. Who you know yourself is breaking rules, but he is your superior, so if he tells you you're supposed to fly the ship into the sun, you do it. But some are to test if you will stand up to him."

"Good thing it's just a simulation, but it's preparing you for the worst."

"I haven't failed a simulation yet. I'm doing so well they're advancing me in a few of my classes. Maybe we will have a few together." He spoke with confidence.

Kax jaw dropped. “Not failed one? How did you manage that? Some of them are no-win. Also, I just got in, I don’t know my classes.”

He brushed his hair back wearing a smile of confidence. “No test is no-win, there’s a right way and a wrong way. If you think it’s no-win you’re doing it wrong.”

‘Well now that can’t be right? Could it be?’ She raised an eyebrow and finished her food.

On the way back to the dorm, Kax walked next to Skyler carrying the food for Michael. She sensed Skyler was trying to walk a little closer, making her feel slightly uncomfortable. His hand caressed hers, and she jerked it away. “Keep your hands to yourself.”

“Sorry.” Skyler jammed his hand into his pocket.

As they continued own the corridor, an older Squallite cadet with light brown hair, orange eyes and pale skin made his way over to them. “Hey Kax, you’re back! I was wondering when I would see you again.” He moved closer to her, ignoring Skyler’s glare.

Oh no, he’s back. She manufactured a false smile. “Hey, Rantra, I just got back today. It’s nice to see you again. How was your summer?”

He smiled and leaned close, cupping her chin as if he was going to kiss her. “I was lonely without you.”

Kax turned her head just in time and his kiss landed on her cheek.

“How about we catch up, say, in my room tonight? Around seven o’clock?”

She reluctantly accepted a piece of paper with his room number on it. “I’ll see you then.”

He kissed her on the lips, this time. “I’m looking forward to it.”

He walked away, leaving Kax’s heart pounding out of control. *Dammit, I should have broken up with him sooner.* She assumed he would forget about her over the summer. Skyler had been scowling the entire time. “Who was that and how did you meet him?”

Kax kept walking. “Remember that night before finals you took us out to Diamandis to try out your new pants?”

Skyler's eyes widened in shock. "I can't say I'm not impressed, but you don't seem to like this guy."

Rantra is a jerk, but Skyler is nice and always there for me. She shook her head, giving Skyler a small hug. "It's complicated, but I don't want to talk about it right now."

"I understand." He hugged her back. "You know, you don't have to do anything you don't want to."

She broke the hug. "I know."

***

When they got to the room, Skyler saw Michael laying on his back reading a book about the codes of command.

"If you can make any sense of the codes, let me know." Skyler sat down on his unmade bed.

Michael shot him a glare. "Twenty-Four-R, leave me alone."

Kax went over to his bed and handed Michael the plastic container of food.

He sat up and took his container. "What's this?"

Kax gave him a kind smile and sat down on the end of his bed. "It's your leftovers. I know how much you love real food."

Michael let a small smile out. He placed the container on the desk by the bed. "Thank you, Kax. You are always a good friend."

"And what about me?" Skyler asked.

Michael shot him a glare and answered. "You are, and always will be, a pain in my side."

Skyler put his hand over his heart and widened his mouth. "After everything I have done for you." He got up off his bed and grabbed the textbook out of Michael's hand.

"Why did you do that?" His jaw dropped.

Skyler acted all smug. "If living with me is such a pain, then you can't use my books anymore."

Michael surrendered in defeat. "Fine then. Take the book. You'll just have to worry about studying without my help."

Kax's lips curved down. "Michael, what is wrong with you? You are never this way. What's going on? I want to know now."

Michael took in a deep breath. "I don't want to talk about it, but since you're making me, it's the stress coming back to class. All my personal feelings being mixed with ones at home, I don't know what else I can say. There is too much you know and too much you don't. But I don't think I can solve this easily."

Skyler and Kax both shared a look. Skyler knew they were all going through a stressful time. This year would not be easy for all of them if they couldn't find a way to put this stress all behind them. There was still a war on the horizon and no one knew yet how that would affect all of them.

Kax rested her hand on Michael's shoulder. "I understand. We will let you be. I do want you to know if you want to talk to someone I'm here for you. If you want to talk to someone else, um, there're lots of councilors on site for you to see."

"I know I have an appointment next week. Dr. Kelley is sending me to someone."

Kax leaned over and hugged Michael. "We are your friends. We care about you."

Michael hugged Kax back.

Skyler handed Michael the book back. "Here, you can still use my textbooks. I was just trying to get a reaction."

"I know, and thank you."

Kax smiled as if a new idea popped into her head. "Hey, how about we get this off our minds and go do something, any ideas?"

The guys looked at each other.

Michael shrugged. "Not sure what there is to do. I have been looking at the activities they have for us but they're not till the weekends. Not much to do."

"We could go to the common room. There's lots of games and people to hang with there."

"Oh ya, I forgot about the common room," Skyler said with a spring in his voice. He shot Kax a wink. "There are games, snacks, TV, a jukebox. We really don't go there enough." Skyler stepped away from his bed and went towards the door when he heard a knock. He opened the door and standing there was Roxanne. *Oh right, I'm still seeing Roxanne. I wonder if Kax will get jealous? Oh well. She isn't my girlfriend yet.* He smiled. "Hey there, I didn't think you were coming by today."

She smiled. "I know we didn't have plans, but I thought we could go out and have some fun?"

Skyler grinned. "Sounds good to me. We were just about to go to the common room together."

Roxanne leaned in and whispered into Skyler's ear. "That's not what I was talking about."

A bigger grin came over Skyler's face.

Kax cleared her throat.

Skyler looked over his shoulder at Kax and Michael. "Hey, I know we were going to hang, but my girl needs me. I will catch you later." Skyler left the room with Roxanne on his arm. *Will Kax ever say yes?*

Chapter 4

Michael pretended to not be conscious when Skyler came back to the room late into the evening. Michael watched Skyler place a piece of paper in a box in the third drawer, climb into bed and fall asleep. He didn't say anything and tried to meditate once again.

After an unsuccessful attempt, his thoughts drifted to the paper. What was on that? *Skyler is always bothering me; why can't I bother him?* He rolled over in the bed and spoke loudly. "So, what was that piece of paper you put in the box?"

Skyler jerked awake. "It's nothing dude, go to sleep."

Michael got out of his bed and flicked on the light. "I know it's not nothing. You have been doing it every time you have come back from Roxanne's."

Skyler placed his hand over the drawer. "It's my business. Leave it alone, okay? I'm going to have a bad hangover soon, so I want to get some sleep."

"Fine, then. I will go back to sleep." Michael went back to his bed, lay down and closed his eyes, leaving the light on.

"Dammit, Michael, turn the light off. It's hurting my head."

"I will turn them off if you tell me what's in that box," Michael said with a smirk.

Skyler paused for a moment. "You can be a jerk sometimes, you know that, right?"

Michael heard him but pretended to be in full meditative state and ignored his groans. He watched as Skyler tossed around in the bed. He saw him reach his arm out to the light, but it was too far away, and groan in defeat. Finally, Skyler gave up, taking a pillow and covering his face, and tried to get some rest.

***

In the morning, the boys were awakened to Kax making a loud entrance. "Hey guys, time to wake up! Classes will be soon!"

Michael opened his eyes and gave Kax a smile. "Morning Kax. You're real cheery this morning."

Skyler woke up squinting, trying to cover his eyes. "Kax, get out of here. I'm not feeling so good. Just leave."

Kax busted out in laughter. She turned to Michael. "Wow. Never thought I would hear him say that."

Michael got up and started getting dressed. "Yes, he had a late night. I think it's only been three hours of sleep for him. By the way, you're bright and cheery this morning, may I ask why?"

Kax smirked. "No reason. I just got a well-needed rest last night."

Skyler covered his head with the blankets. "Could you stop making noise? It hurts, okay? Just get out of here, I don't want to hear about you getting laid."

She grabbed the pillow off Skyler's head and tossed it across the room, "For your information, I didn't meet with Rantra last night. I really did just get a good night sleep."

Michael narrowed his eyes at Kax, not sure if he should say anything or what it was all about. "You're dating Rantra? What would make you do something like that? He's not that nice of a guy."

She widened her eyes at Michael. "Why would you say something like that? Who I date is my own business."

"Sorry if I stepped out of bounds," Michael said. "It's just we Squallites know each other, and he has a reputation."

"Thanks for the warning." She rubbed her arm.

He saw a look of doubt in her eyes.

"Shut up, both of you!" Skyler called out, burying his face into his mattress.

"What do you think we should do?" Kax asked.

Michael picked up his tablet and checked his schedule on the screen. "I don't have classes till noon, we can drag him down to the infirmary and get him a cure?"

Kax watched Skyler suffering on the bed. "There is a little bit of a pleasure I get from seeing him suffer, but come on, let's put the poor guy out of his misery. Can you carry him?"

Michael laughed. "He's a lightweight." He went over to the bed and lifted Skyler over the back of his shoulder. "Come on, dude, you should have gotten this taken care of before you came back. You do know there is a cure for pre-hangovers now."

Skyler swatted at Michael as he was picked up off the bed.

***

Michael had Kax help him get Skyler out of bed. They headed out of the room and down the hall. They carried Skyler with one arm around each shoulder.

Kax struggled to carry Skyler. "So why are your classes so late today? I thought the fourth year and higher have full time, so they can get most of the training in at once?"

"You're right, but I don't want to go to war so I'm lightening up my schedule, in hopes they will say I'm not ready," Michael answered, carrying Skyler with no difficulty.

"How long do you plan to keep that up?" Kax inquired. "You know the war with the Cassiopaeans is inevitable and only stopped for a short ten years. They want to go to war again and may not be willing to make peace again."

Who am I kidding? With a heavy heart Michael replied, "I know, but the election is next year, and when the changing of the world leaders happens, that could change Earth's position."

Kax bit her lip. "True, but if the Cassiopaeans decide to bomb Earth, you would have to be an idiot not to try to stop them."

Skyler jerked his body and shouted. "Stop talking! My head hurts, and your words are making it worse!"

Michael and Kax shared a laugh.

"Okay, we will be quiet for you, sweetie." Kax said and gave him a kiss on the cheek.

Michael raised an eyebrow. "Why did you give him a kiss?"

Kax smirked. "Because he's too sick to enjoy it."

Skyler made a sour face and groaned. "You guys are so mean."

They laughed with each other. As they walked down the halls to the infirmary, Fleet Admiral Cane in his gold uniform came running down the hall to catch them. "Cadets Tillion, Jones and Therris, I need you." The greying haired, ageing, one-eyed fleet admiral focused on the limp Skyler. "What's wrong with Cadet Therris?"

Michael stood at attention with Skyler on his side. "Hangover, sir."

Cane rolled his eye towards Skyler.

Skyler stood up on his own at attention and stared right at the Fleet Admiral with his bloodshot eyes. "Fleet Admiral ready duty I am." They all stared at Skyler.

Fleet Admiral Cane examined Skyler up and down then peered over at Michael. "You sure he is well?"

Shaking his head, Michael scoffed. "I'm amazed he can stand on his own right now, Sir."

Fleet Admiral Cane groaned. "Good grief, seriously? And Jones, you don't always have to be so formal. Get his hangover cured. Before you start this mission. I need you three to go to security room four and tell them your clearance code is 4623B. They will hand you three uniforms and IDs. Do what they tell you. I can't tell you much more, just do it, understood?"

Michael pushed his hair back and pointed to his docked-like ears. "Security rooms are off limits to Squallites. Also, we don't have special ops training."

The Fleet Admiral waved his hand. "Don't worry about your race, with that code it doesn't matter if you're space sludge. This is a mission that I know you kids can do and I can't have it fail. Now get going." Cane pulled out his cell phone and typed in a code. Beams of light appeared and transported him out of the hall.

Michael looked over at Kax. “Do you remember that code?”

“4623B, and let’s get going,” Skyler answered instead. He started to walk away on them.

Michael and Kax stared at each other.

Skyler made his way down the hall, but he was going the wrong way.

Kax went over and grabbed him. “We're going to get your hangover fixed first, then go to security room four.”

Skyler shook his head. “No, we have to get to the room and do the mission. Now, you heard him.”

Michael grabbed Skyler’s arm. “Yes, I heard him. You need to get your hangover cured first. Even if you don’t want to, that’s the wrong way to the security room.”

Skyler glared at his friends. “You don’t get it, we need to do the mission now!”

Kax rolled her eyes. “We understand but let’s do this, go and get your hangover cured and I’ll give you a kiss you can enjoy.”

Skyler turned in the direction of the infirmary and headed through the doors.

“Power of seduction, huh?” Michael turned to Kax and laughed.

She tossed her hair and wiggled her hips. “It works every time.”

Skyler walked up to the counter ignoring all others who might be in his way and blocked the counter. He spoke to the secretary. “I have a hangover, get me a cure.”

The secretary lowered her brow and sharply responded. “You have just pushed aside ten people for a hangover cure? I don’t think so.”

Skyler peered over his shoulder and saw the line-up. “Huh when did they get there?” He faced the secretary again this time he leaned on the desk and widened his bloodshot eyes as far as he could. “Look at my eyes, lady. Do I look like I can notice much?”

Oh Skyler. Michael went to the counter and put his arm on Skyler’s shoulder. “I’m sorry for my friend, but may I ask why there is such a big crowd here today?”

The secretary pointed to all the sickly people in the room. “Kesepian flu, if you don’t have it, you’re on the list for inoculations. Please take a number and leave me alone.”

That doesn’t make sense. Michael rubbed his chin. “I thought the Kesepian flu vaccine was unstable and not allowed to be given out?”

She handed them two blue tickets with numbers. “The orders were approved by Fleet Admiral Davis, please leave me alone.”

Michael clenched his fist while taking a deep breath. He spoke calmly. “Listen, is there any chance we can get to see Dr. Kelley specifically?”

She didn’t even look at her screen or chart. “No, get out.”

Michael’s fist was shaking but he thought he would give it one more shot. He spoke calmly again. “I know my friend Skyler was rude, but since we are not here for the flu shot, there should be no problem with us getting in to see Dr. Kelley. We are sort of in a rush.”

She hit the security button. “You’re a Squallite. You have no right to speak to me like that. Now get out of here before the security comes.”

He went to raise his fist. The anger boiled in his eyes.

Kax grabbed his arms. “Let’s just get out.”

Michael took a deep breath and turned around with Skyler and left.

Once out of the room Skyler looked at his friends. “Now what? I still have a hangover.”

Kax took a deep breath, placed her hand on her chin. “How well can you function in this condition?”

Skyler studied the off-white hallways. “It’s starting to fade. A few things are fuzzy. But point me in the right direction.”

“Well then it will just have to do, buddy.” Calmer now, Michael headed down the hall and glanced over his shoulder. “Are you guys coming? Options are low, and we need to get this mission started.”

Kax and Skyler followed Michael down the hall. As they walked, Skyler turned toward Kax. “So, what about my kiss?”

Kax pushed Skyler away making him stumble. “You didn’t get your cure.”

Chapter 5

The security corridor was different from the other corridors in the academy. It had dark walls with a few light strips on them, and there were no windows. To Michael, it felt as if they were in a hallway during a power failure with the emergency lights on. They wandered around trying to figure out which door was security room four. All the doors were the same heavy metal grey slate with no numbers. Michael kept his ears open in hope he could notice anything different about the rooms. He frowned and halted.

"This is ridiculous. I know the Fleet Admiral sent us on this mission and we have to find security room four, but I tell you: this might be a long corridor, but there is no security room four. There are three and the rest are backup maintenance rooms that rarely get used."

Kax ran her fingers through her hair. "I know, but he wouldn't have sent us on a wild goose chase. There must be something. Is it possible it's hidden or disguised?"

Michael paused to think. "We could try the maintenance rooms. I have the passcodes to access them."

They walked down the hall to the first maintenance room. The backup maintenance room's doors were clearly labeled, with a plastic sign above the door stating, 'Maintenance Room.' Michael began to type in his passcode and the pad illuminated green. He was almost finished when a green scaled alien popped his head out of storage room two.

The alien called out, "Jones, Therris and Tillion, over here."

All three followed the alien into the room. At the back of the storage room, there was a door. They trailed him into a dark hidden room full of black chrome controls and other electronics with only the controls and view screens lit up.

Skyler looked around. "Can we get some light in here? It's so dark."

A tall dark-haired woman in the back called out. "Dim lights, please!"

As the lights brightened up, they could now see at least fifteen Security Officers. All three of them stood there looking at the officers in the room. The officers looked back at them. The green alien spoke up from behind the control panel. "I need you three to get on the Cortez and follow the flight plan. Therris, you will be in command till you reach your destination, then you will hand over command to Admiral Casey. Tillion, you are going to be the pilot. I hope you know your advanced meteor moves and the Shiloh maneuver. For you, Jones, you are to make sure the engines work the entire time and will pose as a Security Officer. This is a top-secret mission. Do not tell anyone. There is a list of instructions in the logs; follow them to a T. Be back as soon as you can."

They all followed the alien security officer to the loading bay of the cloaked ship.

Once they were on the ship there were a couple of other security officers. Obviously, this ship was designed to run on a skeleton crew.

Skyler and Kax headed to the bridge. Michael made his way to engineering. They were soon ready for takeoff.

Skyler read over the private mission log and saw they were on a rescue mission of the Admiral who had been held prisoner on the Cassiopaean prison planetoid. The message told him to keep this mission a secret. The officers were told only what they needed to know.

Chapter 6

Kax found the coordinates of the planetoid to be a bit odd not sure why the federation wanted to go into Cassiopaean space. Her hands trembled, and her ears curled when she saw the list of jumps and where she would have to make the Shiloh maneuver. It was a hard thing to do on a small ship and on a large ship like this. It was designed for small fighters escaping from combat in dire situations. She was not sure how it would be possible. She had aced her test on the Shiloh maneuver. Was that why she was chosen for this mission?

***

In the back, Michael examined the engines, huge and powerful and designed to go an extremely far distance in a short time. The ship appeared to be made for long-distance travel and combat. It was an odd combination Michael had never seen before. To try doing both the ship would have issues. It was almost like this ship had been made as a prototype. His eyes narrowed. *This might be a death mission.* He knew what the Shiloh maneuver was and hoped it was on the way back because there was no way they could do it and live right now. It worried him that they were the ones sent on this mission. *Why us? This ship needs too much work to be able to do everything it was built for.*

***

It wasn't long before they were off. Skyler was full of excitement about his first legal mission, not to mention secret. The hangover was strong, but not as bad as it had once been. He could do this. He had to concentrate and focus on the plan. Knowing this could be dangerous, he kept looking over the mission plan, wondering why Cane chose them for this risky mission.

Chapter 7

The trip down to the planetoid was fine. It was a simple couple of hours. Skyler spun in his captain's chair, Kax navigated the ship, and Michael was busy maintaining the engines.

Skyler felt amazing sitting in this comfy black gold captain's chair. The interior of the ship was a gold chrome, which really was a new thing because most were silver or a rusty copper. He knew it was temporary, but his heart was telling him this should be permanent. He looked around the bridge noticing that it was small and oval, with the pilot seated in front of the Captain.

"It's going to be OK," he heard her mutter. She had no problem going through the gates, and seemed comfortable with the ship's speed. This was the first ship they had been on that could make ten jumps at one time. She had never piloted for this long and the strain was starting to show on her. But she could do it; he had no doubt in his mind.

In the back and on the left side, there was not much room for anything but the Communications Officer. It was quite cramped. He knew the ship was bigger because of the walk he had on his way to the bridge. *A very odd design.* Looking around, he had never seen a ship built like this. Either the Federation was building these new ships for war, or it wasn't a Federation ship at all. He wondered who lent them the ship. More likely it was Federation though, because nothing showed signs of other languages. He was glad about that because he would not be taking Alien Linguistics till next semester.

***

Three hours into the trip they only had one more jump before they reached their destination. When a loud alarm clanged, the Communications Officer hollered out. "Captain! incoming message from the Cassiopeians. they want us to decloak."

Skyler's eyes widened at the news. *This couldn't be right. There was nothing about this in the mission log.* He spun towards Kax. "How far are we from Cassiopaean space?"

She checked her viewscreen. "We shouldn't be there until after this last jump, sir."

He rubbed his chin. "Message on screen."

She transferred the message, and the lights flickered off in the control room.

Skyler was puzzled. Lights didn't just shut off like that. He wouldn't let on that he was having issues with his ship, so he said nothing. A Cassiopaean Legate came on the screen. "Please identify yourself, and what are your orders?"

Skyler didn't want to say the name of the ship was classified, then it hit him what kind of ship they were on. *We're on a Cassiopaean freighter modified for the Federation.* He smiled and added in his best Cassiopaean accent, "We'res just a ssmall freighter that's ssupposed to drop offs ssupplies to the norths planetoid." The Legate's nose twitched with suspicion, then he checked his computer. "Yous ares cleared. Ifs I were yous I would sstop at local maintenance sstation befores you leave. Your ship is leaking fuel."

Skyler nodded. "Will do so, sir."

The communication cut. They all took a deep breath and continued their course. Who knew that would happen? It was about as close as they hoped they would get to the Cass.

Skyler leaned over and hit his intercom and asked, "Officer Jones, I have reason to believe that we are leaking fuel. What is going on?"

Michael came to the Com. "Yes, Captain, I wanted it to make it look like we had some problem in case they said that we were in the wrong location."

"Good job. But do we have enough to get us back?"

"Yes, Captain, we have lots. That's not what we should be worried about. We need to make sure the engines don't fail if we must use the Shiloh Maneuver."

Kax put the helm on auto and got up. "Officer Jones, can't you just reinforce the engines with the power from the life support?"

"That sounds like the logical thing, but if I do that it leaves us with little to no air. We might be intact, but we would be dead in space."

The ship went silent. Skyler took a deep breath and thought, it had to be a test. Why would the Fleet Admiral send them on a suicide mission? They were too young; they weren't even finished school. If one of them were to die on the mission, it would be his fault. He couldn't let that happen. He couldn't let anyone die. He spoke into the Com. "Is there any way possible we can do this, and all survive?"

Michael replied. "There is one, but the chances are slim."

Skyler took a deep breath. "What are the chances?"

Jones let out a long sigh. "5% Captain, and that will only work if at the end of the Shiloh maneuver Officer Tillion makes a hard left and not a right."

Kax's eyes popped. "Are you crazy? That might send us to the other side of the galaxy! We do not have the supplies or the time to get home. Michael, you have to find another way."

Skyler lightly pushed Kax away. "Hold yourself, Officer. This is my ship."

He went back to the Com. "We don't have much of an option. We will have to wait for the Admiral to come aboard for the final decision. But if this plan keeps us alive, then do it. I will not lose a crewman on my ship if I can control it."

Jones took a deep breath. "I will do the best I can."

The communications ended.

Kax scrunched her face at Skyler. He glared at Kax. "You have a ship to pilot, don't you?"

She snarled and went back to her post.

"I understand your feelings, and they are noted," Skyler said. "But I tell you this our job is to get home no matter what comes our way, and I will make sure we do."

Kax, back at the post, took the ship off auto. She was upset with the "Captain's" attitude, but something inside her told her he was right.

***

In the back, Michael was trying to figure out the engines maybe there was another way. Maybe there was another jump gate they could go through. There were so many things to consider. He didn't want anyone to die, but there didn't seem a way out of this, especially with another crewman coming aboard the ship. The ship soon got to their location. Michael changed his uniform to an orange level security uniform and followed Skyler with another officer to the doors. They all knew their orders: get the Admiral and get out. They had their guns with them in case they ran into trouble. This was it, no going back. Skyler held out his hand making a counting gesture, three, two, one. They ran out the door, sticking to the walls, out of the main line of sight. They had a basic map of the prison in their heads. They ran down the halls searching for the room. One long corridor after another, one more turn and they were there. They saw a window in the door of this cold dark gray sterile environment. They scanned trying to find a way in. The door seemed to be sealed as if it was part of the wall.

Michael listened to see if he could hear anything. He didn't, but he did notice a vent he could climb through. "Captain there's a vent. It will take you to the Admiral's room. I'll go in and bring him out."

Skyler examined the vent on the ceiling. "You do that. Make it quick."

The vent was seven feet above them on the ceiling. Michael placed his hands in the sides of the vent and pulled himself up inside. It was nearly impossible for a human to manage, but Squallites could do it. He climbed up and crawled making as little noise as possible. He opened the vent in the Admiral's cell and called out. "Admiral, come with me."

The Admiral was almost unrecognizable. He was covered in bruises and cuts, he had been badly beaten, and he didn't at first look like he had the strength to get up. Once he lifted his head and saw Michael and a chance to make it out of there, a burst of energy came over him.

Michael leaned down out of the vent and hoisted up the overweight Admiral and lifted him into the narrow vent. Skyler heard footsteps coming from down the hall. He sent the other Officer to check it out while he quietly called into the vent. "Stay still. Someone is coming."

Michael and the Admiral waited patiently in the vent.

***

Skyler waited for the signal from the orange security officer to find out what was going on. He stepped forward when he heard shots. He closed the vent. "Whatever happens to me, finish the mission."

He bolted ahead and saw two Cassiopaean guards come toward him. One took a shot. Skyler shot back. He tried to hold the two of them off. They came within arm's reach. Skyler swung a few punches. One guard kicked Skyler in the back. He scanned for the Security Officer. His stomach dropped, and a look of horror crossed his face when he saw her dead on the ground. One of the Cass wrenched the gun from Skyler and the two of them pinned him in the corner. He had lost all hope. His heart sank. He would rather die than betray his friends. This was his mission, he was the Captain, and he was not going to let anyone else die on this mission.

The taller Cass asked. “What’s ares yous doings here?”

Skyler refused to answer.

The other Cass pointed the gun at Skyler’s head. “Whats ares yous doings here? Tell uss or dies.”

Skyler refused to say anything, *If this is how it ends, then let it be.* He didn't want to die, but it would be better than watching his friends die. He closed his eyes. The taller Cass picked him up by his hair and bashed him into the wall. “Sstupid Human! Tells uss why yous ares heres, and wheres ares the otherss?”

He winced in pain as the Cass tightened his grip, but he wasn’t going to break. He was going to die; this was the end. He thought of all the people in his life and the places he had been, and how he would miss them all. But he was doing the right thing. The short Cass held the gun to Skyler’s head. The tall one said. “Ones lasts chances to lives. threes, twos...”

Bang! Two shots were fired.

Skyler opened his eyes, exhaled and patted his body, “I’m still here.” He continued to check himself. He was intact. He peered over his shoulder and saw Michael and the Admiral in front of him holding guns. They shot the Cass dead where they stood. Skyler took a deep breath, still shaken up and in shock. He stared down at his trembling hands.

Michael grabbed Skyler’s hand. “Come on, we have to go now!”

The fire in his eyes returned. “Right, let’s get going.”

Michael released Skyler’s hand. Skyler went over to the body of the fallen comrade. He picked up her heavy dead weight body and carried her into the ship. Before Skyler went to the bridge, he hit the intercom. “Tillion, full power, out of here, now!”

He didn’t wait for anyone and took the body of the girl to a bed. He glanced at the manifest. There wasn’t a doctor on board. He knew she was dead, but it didn't matter. He was going to bring her body home to her family. He knelt and examined her soft round face. Her once bright green eyes had now faded; they would never shine again. He smoothed her long brown hair and lightly touched her light tan face.

He closed her eyes. “I'm sorry.” As he watched her laying there motionless he murmured, “Have I met you somewhere, maybe? Could you have been one of the girls from the bar? If you died so easily, how many others have I met or slept with who are now dead?” There was a long silence. “You know you’re the first one I lost under my command? Even in the simulations I never lose anyone. I was responsible for you. Look at me, I’m talking to a dead corpse.” He folded her hands over the wound on her belly and cried.

***

Back on the bridge, the Admiral had taken command. He quickly glanced over the mission logs. He leaned toward Kax. “You look a bit young to be a pilot.”

She hit auto and spun around. Cuts and bruises were scattered across the aging white-haired admiral’s face. His uniform was torn and covered in blood stains. He needed a doctor more than he needed to be in command. “I'm the third year advanced Cadet studying with Thomas and Cane, sir!”

He rubbed his bruised temples. “I'll take your word, just make sure you get us home.”

***

Back in engineering Michael was getting ready to rig the engines to work for this next hurdle. How could he get this to work? *Maybe I could move these wires around and try to maneuver this over here.* He played with the wires. “Eureka!” He shouted.

A message came on the engineering intercom. “We are being followed,” warned he Admiral.

“Understood, sir.” Michael replied. *Now we’re going to need that Shiloh maneuver.*

Michael knew that the Shiloh Maneuver was the best way to lose an enemy ship when traveling through wormholes. He’d learned in class that when you enter the wormhole, you spin the ship in a barrel roll twice and speed up. You are so inconsistent none of the sensors can pick you up till you are too far away.

Only problem was that a ship in unstable flight during a wormhole jump would have almost no way of knowing what was on the other side. Michael spoke over the intercom, "Tillion, get ready to do the Shiloh Maneuver at the next wormhole."

***

The Admiral said, "Officer Tillion, I don't want you to do the Shiloh maneuver. It will kill us all! Just try to take us to the Zingiber neutral zone. You're too young and inexperienced to make it work, anyway."

Kax turned in her chair, eyes wide. "I'll have you know on my exams I have aced the Shiloh maneuver and I know what I'm doing. And why the Zingiber neutral zone? You will kill us! We are not at peace; they will shoot us down."

The Admiral frowned. "We are not at war. We have a non-aggression pact. They will attack the Cass first."

Kax retorted. "But we're in a Cassiopaean ship. They won't know or care to find out the difference."

"I am your commanding officer. You will do what I tell you!"

Kax rolled her eyes. "Yes sir." She turned back around in her chair. She didn't care if there was less than 1% chance of surviving. She wasn't going near the Zingibers. She didn't alter course. She didn't care if the ship was ready or not. She turned the life support down to the minimum and typed in the command.

They headed for the wormhole when the Admiral got out of his chair. "I gave you an order, don't go through that wormhole!"

Kax hit the engines. She then got up and turned around and punched the Admiral in the face.

He fell cold on the floor.

"Don't tell someone how to save your life!" Kax sat back at the helm and hoped for the best. She programmed the loops and prayed they had time to get the energy they needed to the engines. She reduced the life support a bit more until they were out of the wormhole. This would give them five minutes before they passed out. With no one to guide her, she figured this was the best option. As they entered the wormhole they sped out of control. She held her breath, she needed to stay awake to make the ship's first spin, and she was about to pass out when she used her last ounce of strength and jerked the ship to the left. Kax hoped Michael was right. She could hear the hull failing. *This better not be the end for me and my friends.*

She closed her eyes, holding her breath. She didn't want to end up on the other side of the galaxy with no way to get home. Kax liked her life, and she didn't want to be stranded on a planetoid with Skyler. The two Cassiopaean ships were out of range and they were about to leave the wormhole.

It all went black.

Chapter 8

A few hours went by. Michael made it to the bridge of the ship to make sure Kax and the others were safe. He saw Kax on the floor and picked her up, trying to wake her. *She doesn't seem to be breathing.* He did CPR, hoping it was not too late.

Skyler entered the room and saw Michael holding Kax. His heart sinking, he rushed to their side. He crouched down on the floor and picked Kax up. He held her tight in his arms. "Please, not you too." He brushed the hair out of her face and caressed her soft cheek.

Michael moved closer to Skyler. "Is everyone ok?"

Skyler scanned the room. The others were starting to wake up, but not Kax. Skyler clamped his hand on Michael's shoulder and they both began to shed tears.

A loud gasp from Kax's lungs came up. She coughed and stared up at the two. "What's wrong?"

Michael and Skyler hugged Kax.

Skyler eyes glistened with tears. "You weren't breathing. We thought you were dead."

Kax smiled. "Well I'm glad you two were here to save me. Where are we? Did we make it home?"

Michael lowered his gaze. "No Kax. We are in the Alpha Quadrant, 640,000 light years from Earth."

Kax's heart dropped and she held her head down. "Really? So, we're never going to see our home again?"

Skyler laughed and hit Michael in the arm. "Don't say that! You will scare her. We made it home just fine. We're at the docking port at headquarters."

***

Dr. Kelley examined the cadets to make sure they were fine and weren't unconscious too long. Kax, Michael, and Skyler sat in the infirmary on their own beds. The walls were a powder blue and there were three levitating beds per room.

"Well besides for minor physical trauma, you all should be fine in a couple of days. I would prefer if you all took it easy." Dr. Kelley faced Skyler. "Especially you, Skyler."

Skyler put on a cocky smile.

Dr. Kelley glanced at Skyler's chart. "You, mister, are a mystery. You really did all that with a hangover?"

Skyler grinned. "I'm just that stubborn is all. You can't keep me down."

Dr. Kelley frowned. "Your brain was very active. I'm surprised you could do any of it. Probably most of it was psychological."

"What do you mean, doc? I think I was drunk. I drank about twenty beers and got like three hours of sleep and got lucky. I didn't make it up?"

The Doctor laughed. "No, you were ill, but you managed to convince yourself you weren't. Your determination is impressive—a lot stronger than I would have expected."

Skyler grinned, all proud of himself.

The doctor jotted notes on Skyler's chart. "Oh, and fifteen beers? I would cut back, or you will be back here sooner than you think with liver poisoning."

Skyler laughed. "Doc, can't you just give me some pills and make my liver regenerate?"

He shook his head. "Medicine might work miracles, but you have to suffer first."

Skyler shrugged. "Seems worth it."

Kax got up and smacked him across the face. "Dammit, grow a brain."

Michael laughed.

Skyler turned to the doctor. “Hey, she hit me! I might get brain damage.”

Dr. Kelley shined a light in Skyler’s eye. “You’ll be fine. Remember you’re missing your brain, and before you ask, medical science can’t grow you one of them.”

They all laughed and heard a stern ‘Harrumph’ come from the doorway. The room went quiet; it was Fleet Admiral Cane. The Fleet Admiral went over to the doctor. “Have you finished their physicals?”

“Yes, sir. They are in fine health. A day’s rest and they will be good as new.”

Cane looked satisfied. “Thank you, Dr. Kelley, now may I have some privacy with my Cadets.”

The doctor nodded and left the room.

***

Kax began to tremble when Cane’s cold eye met with hers.

Cane faced his Cadets. “I would like to thank you all for being so brave and all the hard work you did. I have heard some interesting stories in your reports. Care to explain?”

They all put their heads down in shame.

Her body tensed and froze as Cane focused his attention on her. “Why did you feel it was necessary to punch a senior officer?”

Oh, crap I’m in trouble. Kax swallowed with worry. *Here goes nothing.* She answered, “Because he was giving me an order I thought would put the crew in danger. Michael and I had already talked about a plan with Skyler on how to get us home.”

The guys stared at her with awe.

The Fleet Admiral kept his firm look. “Oh, so what? His idea wouldn’t have worked? You defied orders from a senior officer, a man who has been doing his job from before you were born. You think that was okay because you didn’t like his orders?”

Kax’s face started to sadden. *Stay strong Kax you can do this.* She was having a problem holding back tears. “I’m sorry, sir, but my orders were in the log. From you. You knew I would need to use the Shiloh Maneuver, and the way the Admiral told me it would have taken days, maybe weeks to get home, and a less guaranteed chance of survival."

The Fleet Admiral kept an emotionless expression, purposely being hard to read. "It is your job to listen to your commanding officer, and you defied him and almost ended up on the other side of the Alpha Quadrant."

Kax let out a long sigh in defeat. "I know I broke the rules, but when I joined this academy, I took an oath as a pilot to protect my ship and all the crew. I was just as responsible as the Captain and had to follow the highest orders. The orders to make it home safely came from you sir, a Fleet Admiral. His orders did not appear to care if we made it home."

The Fleet Admiral did not acknowledge Kax and turned his attention to Michael. "What made you use the vent?"

Michael paused and spoke. "Well sir the door to the room seemed to be fused to the wall. There was no way to get in without setting off an alarm, and I'm quite good at climbing vents."

Oh no what did Michael do? She held her clenched fist in her hand.

The Fleet Admiral examined Michael. "And what about how you configured the engines? Where did you get that idea? Do you think someone with more experience could have done better?"

He stared straight back into Cane's eye. "I did my best sir. Maybe a more experienced engineer could have but there was only a security and communications officer available, and with this new hybrid ship it was hard to do anything. It was down to the basics of engineering to figure out how to create this. I have no idea how we managed to survive, but I kept the ship intact as long as I could."

The Fleet Admiral nodded, not letting on whether he was pleased with Michael's answer. "Were you aware of the Admiral's orders to go into Zingiber space?"

"Yes, sir." Michael kept his cold stance.

Wow Michael is so serious. How can he be so calm while I'm a nervous wreck?

Cane frowned. “And you still chose to modify the engines to the original plan?”

Michael nodded. “Yes, because I wasn't sure if the plan was really changed. Even if we had gone into Zingiber space, what was done to the engines wouldn't have mattered unless we were fired upon.”

The Fleet Admiral finally shifted his attention to Skyler. “And you, Cadet Therris, where were you during the second half of the mission?”

Here we go. Skyler is never worried about talks with Cane. She watched Skyler’s response.

Skyler put his head down. “I was in the cabin with my fallen Officer, sir. I felt the need to pay my respects to her since it was my fault she died.”

The Admiral raised an eyebrow. “What did you do to cause her death?”

“She went ahead to check on the noise and got shot. I should have been on lookout first. I was her commanding officer.” Sadness came over Skyler’s face.

Kax watched in awe as her strong Skyler broke down.

The Fleet Admiral broke his emotionless gaze to let out a mournful sigh. “She was a Security Officer. Her job was to protect the crew at whatever the cost, even her life. You as a Captain are responsible for your crew’s lives but she knew the risks, and she did her job. Just don't put them in any unnecessary danger. But unfortunately, sometimes deaths can occur through no fault of your own.”

Skyler nodded. “Sir, can I ask what her name was?”

The Fleet Admiral lowered his head. “Officer Mary Grey. She just graduated from the academy. I’ll have her file sent to you along with any other info. Your first is always the hardest.”

Skyler whispered, “Thank you.”

The Fleet Admiral regained his stern attitude and looked at the group. “I am very proud of all of you. I was very impressed with your performance. You all did amazingly well. Still have lots to learn, but I am glad you made it home.”

The Fleet Admiral turned away to leave the room when Michael spoke. “Why did you send us? You have so many more qualified officers. Why would you send us? We are Cadets.”

The Fleet Admiral took a deep breath. "Because you three show exceptional skills and are always trying to be heroes, this way I could show you with a simple mission what it was like and what was involved to be a real hero. I thought it would be a good experience for you."

Kax frowned. "Simple? You know how damn hard the Shiloh maneuver is! You could have killed us all!"

"You almost killed them all with your stubbornness," Cane snapped back. "I gave you the suggestion to use the Shiloh maneuver. You could have tried to outrun them till you made it into Federation space! Or you could have gone to Zingiber space like ordered. Getting home didn't mean you had to do it in that ship. There were so many other things that could have been done!" He calmed himself and smirked. "You decided to try an almost impossible attempt and risk all your lives because you wanted to get it done quicker. Think about it. But only a great officer would have faith in the impossible." Cane left the room, with the three of them feeling uneasy.

It was not what she expected. It was both praise and discipline at the same time. *What am I to do? Maybe I'm not cut out to be a pilot and put up with this kind of pressure.* Uncertainty filled the room.

Chapter 9

The end of the week came, and Skyler, too sad to leave his desk, put his head down after class. *I've always wanted to be a captain, but it was harder than I expected. How did my dad deal with losing a crew member?* Skyler had been here for two years and thought he was prepared. Maybe he was just rushing things. *It was a small simple mission, and I screwed it up.* He let out a small whimper. *Maybe I'm not cut out for this.*

He rubbed his head on his forearms burying his head deeper into the desk. Skyler wished his dad was here now, so he could ask him what to do next. He'd just lost one, but his father lost many.

Her funeral is tomorrow. What am I going to do? Cane said I didn't have to go. He groaned in misery.

He sat there, his legs paralyzed with sadness. *Maybe if I just stay right here time will stop. Just for me, just for this one moment, so I don't have to face the fact I sentenced one of my crew members, a girl who I might have hooked up with, to her death.*

The classroom was empty. Everyone had left, and Captain O'Brien was packing up his things and about to leave and lock up the room when he heard Skyler's groans. He walked up to him and said with his thick Irish accent, "Hey, you got to get going now. class is over."

Skyler shook his head. "I can't, my legs won't let me. They keep telling me I can't get up and face the world."

O'Brien sat in the desk next to him. "What's the matter, son? You have been down this past week, you used to be so passionate about school, and now there is something missing."

Skyler's eyes were filling with tears, but he was unwilling to let himself cry. "I don't think I am cut out to be a Captain anymore. I tried, Fleet Admiral Cane sent me on a secret command mission. I got to see what it was like to be in command and I got a crew member killed. She was only a few years older than me, with a long life ahead, and it was my fault. Now I have to go to her funeral tomorrow morning."

O'Brien listened to what he had to say. "Did you do all you could? Did you make sure no one else was hurt? Could her death have been prevented?"

Skyler nodded. "She was a security officer, and she went first to make sure everything was okay. She was going to check on the noise we heard. I could have gone first. I could have saved her life."

O'Brien put his hand on Skyler's shoulder. "This is your first death, you will always wish there was another way to save everybody but there is not. If you had gone first and died she would feel just as bad. It was her job to protect you and she did. You might have been the Captain, but she was the security officer. It was her job to protect you and die for you. I won't say your life was more valuable than hers, that is not fair, but there was nothing you could have done. Just make sure that you reduce all chances of it happening again and that you live your life to the fullest."

Tears were now pouring from Skyler's eyes. "But what do I tell her family?"

O'Brien smiled. "You tell them, laddie, that she died saving the lot of you. She died a hero to her family. They may be upset but knowing their baby died a hero's death is more than anyone could ask. I know that is what I would want if it were one of my children."

Skyler wiped the tears from his eyes. "I guess you're right, I never thought about it like that. I was thinking I failed."

O'Brien leaned over and gave Skyler a hug. "Listen you can never fail if you are following orders, and you can never give up because you will be a Captain. Most of the lads and lasses in this class will never know what you know till it is too late. You have been there on the battlefield you have been given a gift. You know the dangers now. Don't let it destroy you, let it make you a stronger leader. You hear me?"

Skyler was feeling a lot better as he hugged back. "Thank you, Captain, I will honor your words and be the best I can be."

They both let go and stood up. Skyler left the classroom with a spring in his step. He checked his tablet for messages. He had one from Kax, *Leaving the academy, it's too much for me, goodbye.* His heart shattered into a million pieces. No, she couldn't be serious. He needed Kax. And she needed the Forces. He couldn't let her make this mistake after everything he'd just learned.

Skyler ran down the hall and into the next building toward Kax's quarters, hoping he wasn't too late. He ran through the girl's corridor till he got to her room. He frantically knocked on the door. Her roommate answered, and he could see Kax in the back, packing. Out of breath, he managed to say. "Can I talk to Kax?"

"Um, I guess." The short dark-haired roommate responded.

Kax didn't bother to look up from packing her suitcase. "Go away, Skyler. I don't want to talk about it."

He went to Kax's side. "Kax, don't leave. I care about you and it's going to get better. You and I did all we could. You did what you thought was right. You saved our lives."

Kax started to break into tears pushing Skyler away. “No, I screwed up I almost killed us all, and I almost died.”

Skyler held out his arms offering her a hug. “But you didn't, you made it to live another day. I thank you for that. Who cares how it was done? I gave you the order to. If you didn't feel it was the right thing to do, you wouldn't have defied the Admiral. Kax, I’m nothing without you in this academy. Please understand that I care for you and you are an amazing pilot. Cane even said that if you were any less of a pilot, it couldn’t have been done.”

Tears poured down her face. “I have never disobeyed an order before in my life. I could've killed us all, I trusted you! I thought somewhere in my head that you were right and nothing else could have been done to get us home. I put my faith in your words over the Admiral, a man more than twice your age, how stupid was I? Stuff like this never happens in the simulations.”

He took a step closer. “You’re not stupid. That’s the difference between real life and a simulation. In real life people get hurt. You knew as well as I did that it was the right thing to do.”

She buried herself in Skyler’s open arms. Her sad eyes stared into his calming green eyes. They both leaned in and in the heat of the moment kissed. As they kissed, her tears slowly faded away. He caressed her shoulders and held her close. Kax put her hands on his face. They stayed locked together for a few seconds before letting go. Kax smiled. “I'll stay, not for you but for myself. Because what would I be if I wasn't a pilot?”

Feeling good and proud he had changed Kax’s mind, he held her tight one more time. “Kax you are a wonderful woman, and I know the world needs your piloting skills.”

Chapter 10

During the week Michael had been more distant than usual, spending more time in engineering. *What could I have done differently?* He flipped through the pages of the old engineering textbooks. He pounded his fist on the engineering dashboard. *Dammit, did I do the right thing? Those engines were so modern. They had the same basic makeup as the old ones, but could there have been a way to do the Shiloh maneuver without risking their lives?*

He had sent a request into Cane to obtain a copy of the plans for the ship they were on and it was approved. He almost got everyone killed, even if there wasn't a better way to have done it. *Maybe the problem wasn't with the old but with the new.* He took out his tablet and opened it to engineering. He frantically typed in a few formulas. *If I can't make the old engines work, I will just have to improve them.*

Michael worked hard on his new theories. When he had his proposal done, he went over to commodore Ipinik.

Ipinik was an eight and a half foot Squallite. He had orange eyes and docked like ears. His hair was the same light brown hair as Michael's but with the difference of having faint white streaks. Even with his aging hair, his face was yet to show any age lines. He was your stereotypical Squallite with the one exception of his skin being slightly paler than other Squallites'.

Ipinik studied the plans. "I see a lot of bold ideas here, Jones. What do you plan to do about them?"

Michael smiled. "Sir, I believe that if the forces plan to go to war and defend Earth against the Cassiopaeans, we are going to have to do better than converted ships. We need new ships that will be better. With these plans, I feel I can make this work."

"What about your school work?"

"I can manage both, Sir. You know my test scores."

Ipinik reviewed the plans one more time. "Granted, you may work on these ideas as long as you don't fall behind. Just because you have some ideas for side projects doesn't mean your school work should suffer. Until they are complete and proven, they are just side projects. Understood?"

Michael stood at attention. "Yes sir."

Ipinik handed Michael back his plans. "Good. You may continue with your work. Don't let us down."

***

Skyler and Kax had gone to the dorm to check for Michael. Skyler used his key and opened the door. He checked inside. "He's not here. Must be in engineering."

"Well then, let's go there and find out," Kax suggested.

When they arrived, the place was deserted. The main room in engineering was painted slate grey. There was a deck in the middle of the room with the walls filled with outdated filing cabinets, but they were upgraded with key pads on each drawer. There were four grey leather chairs along the wall. The room was very basic but not too large. Next to the desk, there was a door that led to the rest of engineering. They saw one taller, older Squallite working: Commodore Ipinik. He was typing something on his desk's computer.

Skyler approached him. "Hey, is Cadet Jones still here?"

The man pointed behind him. "Yes, he is in the diagnostics room. Let me take you there." The further they ventured, the more the place began to narrow and curve.

"Dude, this place is like a hedge maze," Skyler stated, stretching his neck, trying to get a good look at the ceiling.

"Well this place was built for and by Squallites," Ipinik explained.

"I have never seen a place built like this," Kax exclaimed.

"We do have a few human engineers and a few other races, but engineering is dominated by Squallites. Unless you have been to Squall, you won't see many places like this." Ipinik continued to guide them. "Your friend is just around this next corner."

They entered a dome-like room. In the center, they saw a man at a ledge with a mask, using a plasma torch with some metal.

"There you go; that's him. He's been working non-stop on this project of his." Ipinik pointed before walking away.

Skyler called out to Michael. "Hey, buddy! Time to quit; let's hang out."

Michael ignored them and kept working.

Skyler started to move closer.

Kax grabbed his shoulder. "Don't. We'll wait. That's plasma, it's very dangerous to be around without protection."

Finally, after waiting a few minutes, Michael got up, put the heated metal in a containment field and went to the control panel near Kax and Skyler. He saw them and said, “Hey guys, when did you get here?”

Skyler frowned. “Really? We have watched you blow that metal forever. How long does it take?”

Kax hit Skyler’s arm. “That’s rude.”

Michael laughed. “That long, huh? Well then, I guess drinks are on me. I will be there in a few minutes. I have to run a few more tests and I will be ready.”

Skyler rolled his eyes at Kax. “Can we just go? He doesn’t seem to need us for anything. He can just join us later.”

“We will wait for him.” Kax scanned around the room. “Also, I don’t know how to get out of here.”

Michael frantically typed things into the controls, not paying attention to his surroundings. He seemed to be concentrating hard on getting the calculations just right.

Kax peered over Michael’s shoulder. “So, what are you working on right now?”

Michael didn’t look away from the monitor. “Making a new metal alloy that is strong enough to withstand any number of blasts. I was testing how it would work breaking the atmosphere. Now, how much pressure it can take before it breaks down...”

His eyes were wide, and the sweat rolled down his face.

“Michael, have you gotten any sleep recently?” Kax said with a concerned voice.

“Squallites don’t sleep, we go into a meditative trance to recharge our bodies. But I think the last time I did that was two days ago.”

Skyler was getting bored. He started looking around at the controls. He couldn't believe how high the control went up; they touched the ceiling. He knew Squallites were tall, but this was crazy. These buttons had to be 12 feet high. He continued to examine the room. *Looking at how these palaces are, Michael must be one of the shorter Squallites. Hmm, I’ll have to ask him about it later.* He continued to admire the controls. First time he had ever been in engineering. He decided to start fiddling with things he shouldn’t. Skyler jumped up, trying to see if he could reach the top of the controls.

"Just a few more keys," Michael whispered to himself. "I just got to finish this sequence." He hit the last button, and bam! The lighting in the containment field changed. Shocks of light flashed like a rainbow thunderstorm; it was something you would want to stay in a containment field. A few minutes later the containment field was starting the breakdown. There was no damage to the metal. "My plan is working." His and Kax's eyes were fixed on the rainbow light show happening in the containment field.

Skyler stopped what he was doing when he saw the rainbow flashing ball out of the comer of his eye. His eyes were captured by the beauty of it all. When it was over Skyler went back to jumping and trying to reach the top buttons.

In minutes, the lights faded, and the containment field turned off and a metal hose came from above and sprayed the alloy.

Michael went over to the alloy and Kax. "Michael are you sure that's safe after all you put it through?"

"Oh, that was just a basic test. We do it all the time, it simulated the pressure of metal going through space."

Skyler made a loud grunting noise when he jumped up.

Michael swiftly turned around. "Stop that, don't touch anything!"

"So, can we go to the bar now?"

Michael shook his head. "No, I have to take this to the range now and shoot at it. You can come along, if you like. But please don't touch anything here."

Kax stared at Michael whose eyes were bloodshot. "You're not going to the range today, you're too tired and overworked. Let this sit or put it away."

Michael glared at her. "I am going to finish it. This is my work; I need to see it through. This could be the breakthrough of the century."

Kax replied, "That might be true, but the discovery can wait till tomorrow, Michael. You look like you're going to burn out."

Michael's eyes were filling with anger, "I'm going to get my work done!"

Skyler went over to Michael. “Dude she’s right, we’re all under stress and I think you have been working too hard. No more waiting; we’re going to go to the room now.”

Michael swung his right arm towards Skyler, pushing him over.

“Hey! What do you think you’re doing?” Skyler got up and grabbed Michael.

Michael pushed Skyler off and snapped. “Get off me and let me finish my work!”

Kax seized Michael’s shoulder, turning him around and said, “Let the experiment rest. Finish tomorrow.”

Michael snarled. “Stay out of this! You don't understand, I need to get this work done!”

Kax sounded frustrated. “We understand that, but you have to know it can wait. No one will touch your work!”

Michael ignored them and went back towards the metal.

Skyler couldn't take it. Nothing they were saying to Michael was getting through. He was ending this. As Michael got closer, Skyler ran over and threw a punch at the side of his head. Michael fell to the ground and didn’t get up.

Kax rushed to Michael’s side. “Skyler why did you do such a thing?”

Skyler shrugged. “He wasn't listening and wouldn't stop. Let it be and take him back to the room, so he can get a good night sleep.”

Kax frowned. “You didn’t have to punch him, you can be such a jerk sometimes.”

Skyler dusted himself off. “Well, at least my way worked.”

Kax shook her head and attempted to pick up Michael.

Skyler clutched Michael’s shoulders and helped Kax. Their dorm wasn’t far from engineering and there were no stairs on the way.

The 200-pound Squallite was heavier than he had expected. Once in the room, Skyler plopped Michael on the bed and then flopped onto his own. “You’re not going to offer me a place to relax?” Kax pouted.

Skyler grinned, raising an eyebrow. “Hey, the invitation to lay in my bed is always open.”

Kax rolled her eyes. "You're a jerk, I didn't mean it that way. But my back does hurt." She went over and laid next to Skyler on the bed.

He rolled on his side to face Kax. "You know, if your back hurts I can give you a massage."

Kax glared, then paused. "Ok, but keep it above the clothes."

"It would be my pleasure."

Kax rolled onto her belly.

Skyler got his magic fingers ready and started slowly rubbing her back. "Wow, your back is so tight. When was the last time you had a massage?"

"It's been too long." She began to purr.

"What are you doing?"

"Catillions purr when they are happy enjoying something, like a massage or sex. We don't moan. So please continue." She purred.

"That's kind of hot." He went back to stroking her back. His figures trailed down her skin, lightly caressing her tense back muscles, making her purr louder and louder. He rubbed her neck sensually and traced his fingers up and down. She purred a bit more before letting out a yawn.

Skyler finished rubbing her back. "Do you want me to leave so you can get some sleep?"

"No, you can stay. It's your bed."

He helped her with the covers and rolled over facing the wall.

She shifted placing her arm around Skyler, spooning him. "Thank you," she whispered into his ear before drifting off to sleep.

Chapter 11

The morning came. Kax woke up and saw Skyler next to her in bed. She smiled and remembered what he had done for her, about the massage and respecting her. She saw him sleeping all peacefully and leaned over and kissed him on the cheek. She got out of bed and went to leave when she heard Michael wake up.

He tried to open his eyes, but he winced. “Skyler, Kax, are you there? I can’t open my eyes!” He shook with panic.

Kax panicked and hurried over to him and sat next to him on the bed. “I’m here, Michael, what’s wrong?” She placed her hand on his shoulder.

“I don’t remember much, when did I pass out? I can’t open my eyes....”

He tried rubbing his eyes. “Kax, did I take my contacts out before I went to sleep?”

“Contacts? I didn’t know you wore contacts. I guess you didn’t.”

“Kax, I’m blind. We have to get me to the infirmary now. I think my contacts went back into my eye and they are stopping me from opening them.” He panted heavily.

Kax nodded. “Oh, I didn’t mean for this to happen. Come on, it’s early, about five a.m., I’ll send a text to Dr. Kelley and let him know we're on our way.”

Michael got up and Kax held his hand and guided him down the hall.

At the infirmary, Dr. Kelley was waiting for them. “Unless I’m on call, I don’t usually get up this early, but from your text this sounds serious.” He let Kax and Michael in the back door to his office. Kax watched as he helped Michael onto the table and grabbed a medical tool. He used a handheld x-ray light to see where the contacts were sitting. “They are really far back. It doesn’t help your eyes are still swollen from being bloodshot. I’m going to give your eyes an anti-inflammatory and that should reduce the swelling. From there I think I can get a tool to pull the contacts out and hope they didn’t do too much damage.”

Michael nodded. “Thank you, Doctor, I didn’t plan to sleep. I was knocked out.”

The doctor took the spray and aimed it into the eyelid, “What were you doing to be knocked out?”

Kax fidgeted with her skirt. *Oh no! Michael is hurt. I never meant for this to happen.* She answered, “Michael was working too hard and was sleep deprived, so we tried to get him to come take a break. He was too delusional, so Skyler knocked him out and we took him back to the room.”

Dr. Kelley narrowed his gaze. "I don't like that story one bit."

Michael bowed his head. "I know, I was a jerk I have just been under a bunch of stress."

The doctor glanced over his chart. "Michael, why are you wearing contacts? You don't have any issues with your eyes."

What's going on? Why would Michael do this to himself? Her stomach became uneasy.

Michael put his fist to his mouth. "This isn't something I'm proud of, but I guess I have to tell you, my eyes are orange, not blue. I wear contacts to cover the fact that I'm a Squallite. I know who I am, but I try to look as human as I can, so people will be less likely to judge me on my appearance. I wear my hair longer to cover my ears and blue contacts to cover my orange eyes."

The doctor nodded. "I understand you're not the first, but might I suggest getting surgery to appear more human? It's very common with people in your situation."

Michael tensed up. "I have considered it, but I couldn't. I am still a proud Squallite. I don't want to be Human; I just do not want people to judge me based on my appearance so if I look like them people will care less."

Kax went over and gave Michael a hug. "Oh, Michael, that's so sad! I had no idea you felt that way."

Michael hugged her back. "I don't tell everyone I feel ashamed, but I wish there was a day when a Squallite could walk down the street and not be second class. I try to cover it up a bit but then it makes me feel like a traitor. It confuses me."

Dr. Kelley ran his aging hand through his light brown hair. He peered at Michael. "If I make you feel better, I never look at you any differently than any of my other patients. you're a person who comes to me when they are not well and needs my help. That's all that matters. Even when we are fighting with the Cassiopaeans, when the few Cass cadets we have come to me, I treat them like anyone else, even if their race is the enemy. Helping people is my job no matter who they are."

"Thank you, doctor, it is nice to hear somebody say that. That is what makes you a great doctor, well that and the fact that you know how to heal people." The doctor laughed and checked

Michael's eyes again. "In time your eyes should hurt less but don't open them yet. I will tell you when. I don't want your eyes moving. This is a difficult part. For the future, Michael, I would consider the surgery to change your eye color. I know you said 'no,' but these colored contacts are unsafe, and if you don't need them there isn't any point in wearing them. They're the wrong size and you don't need them. Then again after this, you just might need them."

"I will consider it. I have to talk to my Dad about that. Being the only Squallite with blue eyes would be a bit odd. Fake blue, that is a bit more acceptable."

I had no idea Michael felt this way.

The doctor opened one of Michael's eyelids and with a set of silver nano tweezers, he pulled one of the contacts out of Michael's eye. He tried to squint. Dr. Kelley fought to keep his eye open. "You're not the only Squallite with blue eyes. I have also done the surgery a few times. There are a few in the Forces, who you wouldn't think were Squallites, but look closely and you will see them, but don't mention it to them."

Michael was shocked then. "I think I know who you are talking about. Not a specific person, but my Dad has told me about a group of Squallites who refuse to admit who they are and cover up their looks and live their life as Humans. That's not me. I just want to look more accepting till the day I can tell someone I am a Squallite and they won't care."

Kax butted in. "Wait a second, Michael. If you do these tricks to make you look human, why are you in engineering? If you look human, couldn't you be in any division you want?"

Michael shook his head, "I wish it were that simple. But when you join you get a physical that will check your DNA. If I lied about my race they would find out. I still have the high bridged nose and light slim bone structure and half ears and wider almond-shaped eyes. It doesn't take a genius to figure out that I would be an odd-looking human." He paused. "If you removed your ears and covered your eyes you would pass for more human than me."

Kax raised an eyebrow. "You're 6 foot 5. You're hardly short. Only the northern Catillions get to be that tall."

Dr. Kelley laughed, "Kax, Michael's race can grow from 7 to 10 feet tall with 8 being their average. Michael is really on the shorter side, but he's only 21. He might still grow but his father is only 7ft. But speaking of Catillions your biology is more complex on the inside than outside. But I need to get back to work." The doctor examined Michael's eyes closely with a light. The doctor removed the second contact from his eye. He took the x-ray light and went over to look for damage.

Wow, Michael is actually short. I guess that explains why engineerings ceilings were so tall.

The doctor mumbled about some minor scraping on the eye and nerves. "Ok, Michael. When I say so I want you to open your eyes and tell me what you see."

Michael nodded, and the doctor pulled up a hologram eye chart on his tablet. "Ok Michael read the first three lines."

"I can't, Doctor. Your hologram is broken."

Kax could see the hologram was a little transparent. The doctor fixed it to make it look more solid like the pieces of paper were really held in the air. The doctor examined Michael. "Now can you read it?"

"It looks like lines to me. I see parts, but other things in my vision are blacked out like black spots."

Dr. Kelley turned off the hologram and pulled out another tool that would stimulate regrowth in all parts of the body. He ran it over the part of Michael's eyes that seemed to be damaged. The doctor wrote him up a prescription. "Get this filled and it should help. Till then you're on sick leave. Your eyes need to get better. I think it's nothing major, but I will make you an appointment with the eye doctor. I think it is just going to take some time to heal from the trauma your eyes have gone through. Have Kax walk you back."

Michael nodded. Kax took the prescription from the doctor and helped Michael off the table. Before she opened the door, the doctor added, "Oh, and Michael, no contacts till the eye doctor says so."

Michael took a deep breath. "Thank you, Doctor."

***

Skyler saw Kax and Michael were gone and figured they left for class early. Skyler didn't mind; he had a hard day ahead of him. He had to go to his second funeral in his life. He didn't want to but what kind of Captain would he be if he ran out on everyone when things got bad. Fleet Admiral Cane told him he didn't have to go, but in his heart, he knew it was the right thing to do. The Fleet Admiral already got him a meeting with the parents before the funeral he tried to think of what he was going to say. He didn't really know her, and he didn't talk to her much, just that she died a hero. He got dressed in his dress uniform and put his medals on and headed out.

They held the funeral in the main hall, so he didn't have to go far. Once he had his uniform all on, all nicely pressed, shoes shined, he looked at himself in the mirror and headed to the door. *No going back*. He walked down the hall. On his way, he saw a few others heading to the funeral. *They must have been her friends*. He entered the hall; it was nicely decorated with chairs on both sides and at the front of the aisle there was a platform bearing her ashes. That made his heart sink. There was no more of her, just the ashes of what had been. He wanted to fall to his knees to cry. Skyler put on the biggest brave face he could. He took a deep breath and held back the tears. He turned away and headed to the office in the back of the hall. There was a desk with her file laid out on top. Her parents weren't due to show up for another ten minutes, so he sat at the desk reading her file again seeing if he could figure out what else he was going to say. *I can't tell them I may have had a one-night stand with their daughter*. It bothered him, the whole thing bothered him. He wanted to cry, but he was an acting Captain; he couldn't. He had to show strength when no one else could. He was a rock.

He read over her file, Mary Grey, oldest of Five, only girl. Age twenty-five excelled at hand to hand combat. A 3.5 GPA. *She was on her way to a bright future*. She wasn't the first, but she was one of the many this war had already claimed, and who knows how many more were about to die. She had graduated the year before she and had a clean record. As he read through the file, a tear ran down his eye and fell on the page. He wanted to cry more, but there was a knock at the door. He quickly wiped the remaining tears off his face. "Come in."

An older couple came in; they were her parents. The mother, skinny with her gray curly hair, was crying. The father had the same look as Skyler. He too was holding back the tears. A tall man of six feet and completely gray hair, he had lots of upper body strength. Skyler stood up and shook their hands. "Hello, I am Cadet Therris. I was the acting Captain when your daughter died. Please have a seat."

They both sat down. Skyler shuffled the paperwork. "I am so sorry, I didn't know your daughter well, but when she was under my command she fought bravely and died a hero."

The mother was crying. Skyler handed her the box of tissues on the desk. The father looked at him. "We always knew being in the security division she would die young. But why was a young man like you acting as captain?"

Skyler took a deep breath. "I am not sure exactly, but all I know is when Fleet Admiral Cane gave me the assignment I wasn't told much. She died defending Admiral Casey, she was brave and did her best."

The mother wiped some tears away. "We don't blame you; she left a message for us before she died. She knew what the risks were."

Skyler took a long breath. "I stayed with her once she died. I was the one who went back to make sure her body made it back home to you. I didn't think it was right to leave her behind."

"How old are you, boy?" Her father asked.

His question shocked Skyler. "Nineteen, sir, I'm a second-year advanced Cadet."

The father nodded. "You are an honorable young man. Like your father. The reason she joined UGF was that Mary wanted to be like her uncle. The used to serve under Captain Therris. Lieutenant Martin Grey, he was a science officer."

Skyler's eyes widened. "Is that so? My father died before I really got to know him."

"Knowing my daughter was under the command of a Therris means a lot. I know you are honorable, and it gives me peace to know you were the Captain and my daughter served you well. Thank you, sir."

The parents stood up and so did Skyler.

The father spoke one more time. “Thank you so much for your time and care. I wish you well in your career. You are very mature for your age.”

Skyler blushed and opened the door for them. “Your daughter was a great officer in the brief time I knew her. I’m happy she was my security officer, and again she is a hero.”

***

Skyler sat in the front row next to Fleet Admiral Cane during the ceremony. He wanted to cry. Cane leaned over and whispered in Skyler’s ear. “Here’s a tissue. It's ok to cry.”

Skyler took the tissue. “Thank you, sir.”

The service was short. Skyler didn't want to stay once the service finished. There was the dinner and Skyler didn't feel like eating or staying. He went to Cane. “Sir, I know I should be here, but I don’t feel much like staying.”

“You can go,” Cane said. “I'll take over. You did wonderfully today. I hope you have a good night. Get some rest. You did better than most their first time.”

The tears were forming in his eyes again. “Thank you, sir.”

Chapter 12

Skyler headed back to the room. He changed out of his uniform and was so upset he didn't realize Michael and Kax were in the room playing cards on the bed.

Kax turned. “How was the funeral?”

Skyler jumped, startled to see Kax and Michael. “Tragic, her parents were proud, and the rest was so nice, but she shouldn't have died she was so young.”

Kax got off the bed and embraced Skyler, “You did a good job you were brave and, by the way, Michael’s blind.”

Skyler frowned and mumbled. “What? I mean how can that be? He’s playing cards.”

Michael laughed at Skyler’s expression. “I'm not blind. I hurt my eyes and was in the infirmary all morning. I can see most things, but I can’t read; it's all fuzzy. I'm on some meds and rest till I see the eye doctor in a week. My eyes should get better, but I'm just confined to quarters till then. As for the cards, they're a little difficult but I can tell what they are. Want to play?"

Skyler rubbed his face in confusion. "Ok that makes little sense to me, but hey, I got the time."

He pulled the desk chair over to Michael's bed. "Deal me in."

They all played cards into the night.

Chapter 13

Monday morning, Skyler woke up feeling much better. Michael was in a deep sleep and class was soon, so he figured he would head off early. An *Early for class that's not like me what's wrong?* He checked the time and didn't know what would make him get up this early, *Oh, well nothing else to do.*

He figured he would see Kax in class later. He walked down the hall thinking about Kax and how he finally got to kiss her and how she let him rub her back. He loved her from the bottom of his heart. The kiss was spontaneous, but it was better than nothing. To him, she wasn't one of the many nameless girls he had so many times over but a beautiful smart young woman he could see settling down with in the future. As he headed to class, he ran into Roxanne. He didn't know what to say to her, he liked her, but he had a weird feeling in his chest that told him not to talk to her and that it wasn't right. He was going to avoid her but unfortunately, she noticed him and approached. "Hey, Captain, nice to see you again. What are you doing tonight? I thought maybe we could spend some time together in my quarters. My roommate got a new boyfriend and we would have the place all to ourselves."

Skyler ignored his gut and put on the charm. "Really, that sounds like so much fun. I'll see you there after class then?"

She moved in and kissed him. "You bet. I can't wait to see you."

She left, but the weird sick feeling was still there. He tried to get rid of it, but his body was not letting him. He couldn't get Kax out of his mind. But she told him before they were friends. What was the problem if he continued to sleep with Roxanne?

Did Kax not want him? He tried to put both girls out of his mind and continued to class.

Commodore Bates was out sick today, so Captain O'Brien was teaching hand to hand combat class this morning. Skyler had little faith in how well O'Brien could teach hand to hand considering his figure. He might know how to fight with a fleet of starships but not much else, it looked like. Skyler changed into his combat uniform, left his cadet one in the locker and went to class.

O'Brien blew his whistle and the whole class stood in a line-up. In his hoarse strong Irish accent, he said, "Ok class time to get ready, I might not be as fit as Commodore Bates, but I tell you'll this I have seen my share of wars I fought in the last Cassiopaean war on the front lines and survived."

The class was silent and listened to his words. One of the Cadets raised a hand and asked, "I don't get it. Why do you have to learn to fight Cassiopaeans? Aren't they the same as fighting humans? We know how to do that."

O'Brien smirked. "Good question. They are nothing like us. Their skin is rough and tough like bark. They have spores; they can project poison. You have to make sure you never get cut by one of them, because when you're in combat there aren't many doctors around."

Skyler examined the scar on his knuckle he got his first day of the academy. That Cass gave him a nasty cut when he punched him.

O'Brien called out to Skyler. "Something the matter, Cadet?"

Skyler extended his hand. "I was cut by a Cassiopaean last year."

O'Brien made his way over and examined Skyler's hand, "Class, come here and see this." He pointed to the scar. "See how it is still red even though it happened over a year ago. That proves it's from a Cassy. This one was treated right away, so he's lucky, but leaving a wound like that too long could kill you."

They all inspected the cut for a bit longer. Then O'Brien backed off and announced, "Okay, class. Back in formation and we will start some training drills. Therris, up here with me. I want you as my sparring partner for this exercise."

Skyler went and stood next to O'Brien. O'Brien faced Skyler and the class and explained, "Now I want all of you to partner with the person to your right and you're going to pretend they're a Cassy and I want you to give them your best shot, but you have to do it the way I do it."

He held up his fists and signaled for all to do it and then moved his hand slowly to the side of Skyler's fist and pushed it away. "I know that's not the way to throw a punch to a human but to a Cassy you want to avoid the knuckles they are rough and will cut you just need to knock them out of the way till you have a better advantage. We won't practice this next one with our partners, but I will explain when you punch them in the face aim for the stupid tattoo on their cheek it marks the softest spot on their face. Now practice the punching about twenty times then change partners and keep doing that."

O'Brien practiced with Skyler a few times then went and checked on the other students. Once they finished that exercise, Captain O'Brien showed them spots to kick a Cassiopaean on his belly and side. He explained that kicking a Cassiopaean was more effective since your boots and pants would protect you from their bark-like skin. They practiced hard with each other during class. Afterwards, as the students were heading for lunch, O'Brien called out, "Hey Therris, come here. How did things go at the funeral, if ye don't mind me asking?"

Skyler sighed. "Things went well, sir; the parents were really nice and understanding. It was hard staying the whole time."

O'Brien nodded. "Yeah, it is hard. I remember my first and I tell you, sonny, they rarely get easier. Worry if they get too easy."

Skyler sighed again. "I guess I got something to look forward to. Cane didn't seem to be that distraught."

The Captain smirked. "Cane has been to more funerals than anyone should ever go to, and when you go to your best friend's funeral everything changes. You just got to do your part, but you can't save everyone. Some missions lots will die and others none; those are the missions you celebrate. When the day comes, and you go into the battle lines and you can bring back every one of your crewmen then that is a good day."

Skyler took a deep breath. “You're talking about my father’s funeral.”

“Everyone was at your father’s funeral, even me. He was a man who touched so many lives, and very well known. Cane fell to pieces after. I remember seeing you so little sitting next to your mother in the front row next to Cane.”

Tears filled Skyler’s eyes. That was a moment that haunted his mind. “Thanks for your words of advice, Captain.”

O’Brien wrapped his sweaty arm around Skyler and ruffled his hair. “Hey, call me Sean. You’re a good kid that’s all in the past, happier memories are coming.”

Skyler smiled, feeling awkward with a sweaty, hairy man arm on him. “Ok Sean, um, there’s one more thing I have to ask.”

O’Brien let go of Skyler. “What is it?”

“There’s a girl I like, and she has no interest in dating me. I have been seeing other girls and there is one who I’ve been going out with for a while, nothing serious, her name’s Roxanne. I like her, and I have a date with her tonight and some stuff happened with me and the other girl and now I don’t know if I want to go with Roxanne.”

. “So, you don’t want to go out with her because you like this other girl, but she doesn’t want you, so what’s the problem? What sort of thing happened?”

Skyler rubbed his face. “Ya, Kax doesn’t want me, but this last week we were starting to get close and I don’t want to go out with Roxanne-”

“-If there is a chance,” Sean finished. “Well sonny, you’re in a pickle there, but you know what Kax knows about Roxanne so just continue with her till Kax makes a move it’s her turn.”

Skyler frowned. “Ya I was going to do that, but it doesn’t feel right I feel like a cheater.”

“You're not cheating, you’re in love. Just finish your date with Roxanne and break up with her then, simple.”

Skyler considered “I guess I could do that. Hope she doesn’t take it too hard.”

Sean smiled. “A woman will always take it hard, but just let her down lightly and explain you’re interested in someone else. You know, I used to be a ladies’ man back in my day.”

Skyler looked Captain O'Brien up and down. He saw an aging man with red and gray hair, stubble and who couldn't hurt to lose fifty pounds. Skyler replied with his first thought, "Really?"

O'Brien laughed. "We all end up looking like this, in the end, sonny."

Skyler peered down at his own gut.

O'Brien just laughed again. "Well I can't make you miss lunch. Get going and don't keep your friends waiting."

Skyler waved goodbye to the Captain. When he reached the cafeteria Kax and Michael had their lunches, so he quickly got his. Kax regarded Skyler not able to hide her joy to see him. "So, what took you so long?"

Skyler shrugged. "Oh, um, Captain O'Brien wanted to see me after class is all."

Michael turned his head in the direction he thought Skyler was in. "Who did you punch out this time?"

Skyler chuckled. "No one. I was partnered with the teacher."

Michael cast a confused look the wrong way. "What do you have to do to get paired up with the teacher in combat class?"

"I don't know, O'Brien just likes me is all, I guess. And what are you doing out of the room, how are your eyes?"

Michael smiled. "My eyes are better. I know my way around, so I thought I would get out for some lunch with Kax. I just can't read or see more than ten feet in front of me, and some things close are blurry."

Kax raised an eyebrow. "O'Brien teaches battle strategy, Bates teaches combat."

Skyler shook his head and took a bite out of his sandwich. "Not today. Bates is sick so, it's O'Brien today. He's really good he taught us how to fight a Cassie."

Michael's eyes widened. "What did you say!"

Skyler put his food down for a second thought then. "Oops I meant to say Cassiopaean or Cass."

Michael frowned. "That's much better they might be our enemy but calling a race of people derogatory names is not right."

Skyler nodded. “I'm sorry, it's the term Captain O'Brien was using so guess I picked it up.”

Kax smiled. “It's okay. You said it once don't say it again. Now you know. But O'Brien shouldn't be using it either.”

Skyler shrugged. “I didn't think of it that way. He just thought of it as they’re the bad guys, so you say insulting things to them. Not arguing about being politically correct.” He continued to eat his food; he wasn't going to let this replicated meatloaf sandwich go to waste.

Kax stared at her fruit salad. She didn't seem in the mood to eat and was slowly picking at it.

Michael then spoke up. “Kax if you’re not going to eat your real fruit don't waste it.”

Kax looked up at Michael and slid the bowl over to him. “Oh, sorry, Michael. You can have it all. I'm not really hungry.” She slid the fruit cup over to Michael and got up out of her seat and trudged away.

Skyler thought this was odd and went to get up and pushed his tray over to Michael. “Here, you can have the rest of my meatloaf. I'm going to go talk to Kax.”

Michael frowned. “I'll throw your meatloaf out then, it's replicated. I'm not touching it, and good for you leaving the blind friend all alone.”

Skyler ignored Michael and followed Kax out of the cafeteria and down the hall.

She was walking faster, like she was trying to get away from something that wasn't Skyler. He picked up the pace and when they were in a deserted part of the hall, he grabbed her shoulder. “Hey Kax, what’s wrong?”

Kax’s eyes were filling with tears and she whirled to Skyler. “Oh, Skyler. I don't know what I am going to do.”

“What do you mean, Kax?”

“I hate Rantra, he is so mean, and I just can't stand him anymore.”

Skyler frowned. “You mean that Squallite guy? If you don't like him break up with him.”

“It's not like that, Skyler. We’re really not together, but he thinks we are. Nothing is going on, I thought he was a nice guy, now it turns out he’s just a jerk who won’t leave me alone.”

He gave Kax a hug holding her close. "Hey there, it will be okay. We'll figure out something."

She hugged back. "Ya, I don't care for him the way I thought I would. It's just one big mess."

Skyler took a deep breath. "It will be okay, Kax. I'll protect you now come on sit down we'll talk all about it."

Kax smiled and let go of Skyler. "Thank you. You are a great friend."

He sighed, *I guess friend is better than nothing.*

They sat on the cold cement floor next to each other talking about Rantra and what they were going to do.

Chapter 14

Working his way through his course books, Michael was glad his tablet could read his work aloud. "Blip," the machine went again and restarted, reading the same page over. Michael groaned and got up and hit the button on the screen to get it back on track. *Ugh, well at least it is better than nothing. I have to get at least some of my work done.* He picked up the bottle of pills on the desk and swallowed one. *At least the pills are working.* He tried to go back to work at the desk. He typed a few formulas into the tablet before he pounded his fist. *Dammit this wasn't going to work. None of this was going to work. What was the point? Even if he did invent something breakthrough, no one would take me seriously. I'm a Squallite. Even if I underwent surgery to change my appearance, it wouldn't help.* He placed his head in hands. *I feel like such a traitor, I love who I am but damn Humans, and so many other races have so many other things I want. I might know engineering, but I am not an engineer.* He pounded his fist one more time on the desk.

A ping sound came from Skyler's tablet. It was flashing under his pillow. "Stupid Skyler forgot his tablet again, now he is getting a call. I should answer it, in case it is important." Michael pressed the button and a little hologram of Skyler's summer roommate, Perry, popped out.

"Hey where's Skyler?"

"In class, Perry. Get confused with the time change again?" This wasn't the first time that Perry had called Skyler.

Perry checked his watch. “I guess I did. Anyway, how are you doing? That is if you have time to chat?”

“I have time, probably a good idea. I have too much on my brain to get any work done.”

“And I don’t have enough. I’m just watching grass grow.”

Michael got an idea. “Hey Perry, you work with plants. What specifically?”

Perry’s eyes lit up, “I’m studying to be a botanist, so I can work with terraforming and making sure once we terraform a place it survives. Why do you ask?”

“They’re plant engineers, right? Are there any Squallites in that division?”

“You mean Chemical engineers who work in botany. Yup there are a few Squallites, they’re not usually on Earth, but they exist. Why do you ask?”

“I’m reconsidering my career and looking into options.” Michael rubbed his temples, “I always wanted to be a captain but even if I alter my appearance that is never going to happen, so maybe there is another job out there than basic engineering.”

Perry frowned. “Dude, there are lots of other careers out there. You just might have to leave Earth and go to other bases. You’re a 3rd year, right? It’s not too late to change. But why would you want to alter your appearance? That seems dumb.”

Michael moved his hair back. “Because I’m a Squallite there are tons of restrictions and racism here for us, I wish we could just be treated equally.”

“This summer was the first time I had ever been to Earth in my life and it is resistant, even if they try to say they are not. I would be looking into transferring to another location.”

Michael let out a long sigh. “But my father is here all I have ever known is on Earth or Squall. I don’t know if I could just pack up and leave.”

Perry gave him a smile. “That’s why we're still cadets we have a chance to see the world and study in different places and then decide where you want a posting. I grew up on Colony G outside of Neptune, and I had to leave to get my education but when I graduate I’m going back there. You could go and try out a few places.”

“Thanks, I will take your words into consideration.”

"No problem. Anytime you want to talk, just let me know buddy."

Michael ended his conversation with lots to think about. He laid down on his bed and started to drift into a meditative trance. He was almost there when Skyler and Kax came into the room.

"Hey Michael," greeted Skyler, "we have an idea and we need you."

Michael slowly got up. "What is it this time?"

Skyler smiled and sat on his bed. "Oh, don't be like that, you'll like this one." He nudged Kax. "Go on tell him."

Kax smiled. "Michael, you and I are going on a date."

What? A date with Kax. Why? I don't know anything about dates. Are they just decided for you? Michael's eyes widened in shock.

Skyler chuckled. "Ya, this is going to be great. Kax went on a date with this Squallite from the academy. She doesn't like him and wants to break up with him, but he won't listen. Maybe if you're dating her, he would get the message. I did think of me but you're a Squallite and he's one too, so it will look like she has a type."

Michael was skeptical. "So, you think I would be a good date? I don't know anything about dating."

Kax smiled. "Yes, it would, and it would just be a one time thing get rid of him. No problem. Come on, you need to get out, so we can go to the bar, I'll help you on your way and have a fun time. I know he will be there, I told him to meet me there for seven and it's six so if we got there by 6:45 then we wouldn't have to worry."

Michael thought about it for a second then shrugged. "Sure, why not? Sounds like fun can't hurt?"

Skyler smirked and was trying to to laugh at Michael's uneasiness. "That's great. You guys have fun and I will be seeing you."

Michael frowned. "Hey, what about you?"

"I have a date too. I saw Roxanne this morning on the way to class." Skyler went over to the closet. He started getting changed out of his uniform and into civilian clothes.

***

Skyler laughed at this arrangement. He could never imagine Kax and Michael as a couple. He hoped in his heart this would help him to survive his date with Roxanne. It sure gave him peace knowing Kax was with someone. He went over to the desk and brushed out his curls, straightening them. Then he slipped his comb back in the drawer and noticed the box with the papers Roxanne had given him. What would he do if they broke up? He needed the formation she was sharing. He shook his head and ignored the nagging concern. He could do fine without them. It didn't matter; how he could sleep with a girl he didn't love? *Love? What girl do I love? Kax is the only one I love, but I have slept with lots of girls I don't love, what do I do? I'm so confused.* He turned to Michael. "Hey, would you sleep with a girl if you didn't love her?"

Michael raised a brow at the odd question. "Of course not, that's the point of sex. To sleep with someone, you love."

Skyler became more confused. "Ya but come on, there has got to be girls out there that you see and are like damn I would like to hit that."

Michael shook his head. "No, there aren't, there are girls that I think are nice, but really I think sex is a sacred thing between two people and sex isn't always the answer."

Skyler frowned. "Really? I guess that's why you're still a virgin, dude you really do need to get laid."

Michael sighed. "Skyler, there are lots of men out there like you, there is nothing wrong with it. You need to know the difference between love and sex before you desensitize yourself."

Michael does have a point. I had been with many women, some better than others, and some I learned from and others were just for fun, but nothing long-term. Kax was the longest I've ever stayed fixed on one girl and Roxanne is the one I have slept with the most. It's just better to brush it off for now and continue with the plan.' With a head full of conflicting thoughts, he said, "Come on, Michael. You don't want to be late for our dates."

Chapter 15

Michael made his way up to Kax's dorm room with no problem. His hands were shaking for some reason. He wasn't familiar with these feelings. This was his first date he had ever been on, and his stomach was starting to flip. He was on time, but his palms were sweaty, and he couldn't get the strength to lift his arm and knock on the door. He stood there paralyzed.

Kax opened the door. She was wearing dark jeans and a loose lavender sleeveless top. "There you are! I couldn't remember if I was supposed to meet you or you meet me. But I'm glad you came. Come on, let's go have some fun."

Wow she looks so stunning. Michael's nervousness was fading and turning into excitement. He was now ready to have fun with Kax.

Once at the bar. Michael pulled the chair out for Kax at a table and said, "I'll be back with our drinks."

Kax blushed. "Thank you, honey," she said, getting into character even though Rantra hadn't arrived yet. Michael blew a kiss to Kax. This was going to be easy. He went to the bar and ordered a Squallite soda and a midnight sunrise for Kax, returned to the table and handed her the drink.

She smiled. "You are so sweet."

Michael blushed. "I'm sweet because you're the woman I love, cutie." All this acting was fun. Leave it to Skyler and Kax to coerce him out of his comfort zone.

She took a sip of her drink. Michael watched her. "How do you think they named a drink Midnight Sunrise? Don't think it works that way."

Kax smiled. "It's a Catillion drink. It's named after the color, it's dark and blue with a yellow ice cube in it. On my home world we have a ring of space rocks around the planet. They heat up and reflect the sun's light and shine even when it is night. It's such a unique experience. I love seeing it. It looks like Earth's dawn."

"Wow, your world sounds great. Mine's not, we have way too many storms to enjoy the environment."

"Is that where it gets its name? There's so many squalls they call your planet Squall?"

He nodded. "They come all after each other. We have learned to build shelters and control the weather in some places, but it is really neat to see a Squall coming."

Kax was about to reply when an eight-foot orange-eyed Squallite with a black crew cut entered the restaurant. She quickly squeezed Michael's hand and whispered, "play along."

Rantra came to the table and saw Michael and frowned at Kax. "Hey, what we are you doing? We had a date tonight."

Kax played dumb. "No, we didn't. We broke up and now I'm on a date with Michael."

Rantra glared at Michael. "She's dating you, the Squallite with a human name. What do you have that I don't?"

"I have a Squallite name! But for one thing, I have a lot more manners than you have. Women like manners."

Rantra yanked Michael by his shirt and pulled him up.

Michael taking a lesson out of Skyler's book responded with, "Oh, ya is that so mature. You can't get the girl so you're going to beat me up. You think she is going to run back to you? Well, buddy, that's not how it works." Michael was not the guy to throw the first punch, but his eyes were still not the greatest and he had a clear shot and if he didn't take it this guy would. He took his fist and punched the guy. "Leave Kax alone, now!"

The guy released Michael and fumbled. He attempted to take a swing. Michael expected it and dodged out of the way. Glowering, the guy lifted a chair and hurled it at Michael. The chair hit him, the impact stinging him. He tried to get a focus on the guy who was coming at him with another punch.

Kax pushed Rantra into the arms of a security guard who dragged him out. Kax rushed over to Michael. "Oh, Michael, are you alright?"

He got up and rubbed his shoulder. "I will be fine. My shoulder is sore, but I'll live."

Kax turned to face the bartender and said, "I'm really sorry about this, is there a way you can maybe put this all on Skyler Therris's tab?"

The Bartender smiled. "I can do that his credit is good, but you gotta know I'm getting quite sick of you kids busting up my bar."

"I'm sorry. We never plan to cause damage."

"As long at Skyler is paying for it, I can't complain too much. That boy has a deep wallet."

"Thank you for understanding." Kax circled her arms around Michael. "Come on, let's get you back to the dorm and check out your wound."

Michael smiled. "You are too kind."

***

Skyler went to Roxanne's room, wearing his boring blue jeans and a navy long-sleeved blue shirt. He knocked on her door. He played with the condom in his pocket nervously, but he brought it just to be safe. She opened the door in her tight blue jeans and a black tank top. She returned to packing a small bag. "There you are, come on in! We've got to get ready to go."

Skyler frowned. "What do you mean? I thought we were staying in?"

"We are sweetie, it's just going to be somewhere else overnight. Come on, we'll take my car."

Skyler scratched his head in confusion. He felt like he should say something to her but shrugged and just followed her out to the garage.

Her car was an older wheeled, electric blue sedan.

Skyler eyed the car. "It's a bit small isn't it, and old?"

She rolled her eyes, as she unlocked the car doors. "It gets me to where I need to go. Sorry it has wheels, it's second hand. I couldn't afford one that hovers."

Skyler climbed into the passenger side. "Doesn't matter to me as long as you like it." Skyler enjoyed the ride except for the bumps on the road. It had been a while since he had been in a vehicle with wheels. He and Roxanne didn't talk, but every so often they glanced at each other. He noticed that she drove past one of the exits. "Hey, don't we need that exit to go to makeout point?"

She giggled, "We're not going there we're going somewhere else."

He smirked. "Nice, so you know a better place to park?"

She let out a louder laugh. "You're always thinking with your dick. You're so cute."

An uneasy feeling came over him. “Well, if we're not parking where are we heading?”

Her tone became serious. “To meet my parents, I told them about you and now they want to meet you.”

Skyler’s heart stopped. *Great. I was going to break up with her, and now she’s taking me to meet the parents. Crap, what have I gotten himself into?* He nervously smiled back at her. “Wow really, that’s a shock. Some notice would have been good. I could have worn some better clothes.” He tugged at his pants. *Breathe, relax, you can do this. You have met parents before.*

“You look fine, it’s just dinner and then we will head back in the morning.”

His palms were sweaty, and his face was flushed, *First it’s meet them, then dinner, now staying the night. I should have broken up with her sooner.*

“That sounds great.” He couldn’t wait for this to be over.

Soon they arrived at a condo block. Roxanne pulled into the underground lot. She parked the car and turned to Skyler. “You know we're early, if you really want to park we can have some fun, you know, relax before we go in?” He saw her leaning towards him in a seductive manner.

Great, now she wants sex. Can I even perform? I’m so damn nervous. He weighed the options in his mind. On one hand, sex, but on the other hand then she might think he was using her. He just shook his head. “Not right now, I really want to meet your parents and if we're staying the night, we can always do it when they’re asleep.”

She smiled leaned over kissing him and began to rub his crotch. “If that’s what you truly want?”

Skyler kissed back and placing his hand on her soft supple breasts. He wanted it to go on. He wanted to continue. He wanted to go all the way. He continued to make out with her, rubbing his hands up and down her body. She leaned down and kissed his chest. He moaned, *Damn, she’s got me. I can’t say no now.* He kissed her. *I hope I don’t regret this.*

She continued to kiss his chest working her way down.

He moved the seat back chair for more room. His troubles and stress soon faded, and he was no longer nervous. He also felt dirty, but he felt so at peace in his mind it all seemed to make sense now. Slowly the negative thoughts started to return, but no matter what he couldn't wipe the smile off his face.

When she was done, she moved back up and laid on him.

He kissed her, holding her in his arms. "That was great. You're a very talented girl."

"Glad you think so, because I think I am falling in love with you."

The stress came pouring back, all he wanted was a fling and now she wanted to get more serious. There was no way out. The only option was to finish the night and break up with her in the morning. His hand began to shake. He felt trapped.

When they were dressed, they headed to the elevator. He looked at the keys. "What's up with the negative numbers on the keypad?"

She laughed. "Don't you know? This isn't just an above ground condo, it's underground too. So, the negative ones are underground, and my parents are on floor -6."

Skyler nervously laughed. "I see, I've never been in a condo before so how I would know?"

She raised an eyebrow in confusion not saying anything.

Skyler was really getting worried. He never wanted to be 6ft under with a girl let alone 60 ft under.

He tried to control his hand trembling. *You can do this. It won't be much longer. It's only right to meet the parents of the girl you have been sleeping with. He took his hand and covered his face, what am I thinking? It's the girl I'm going to break up with, I love Kax and I haven't even met her dad. This is all just, ugh. What am I doing?*

Roxanne looked over at him. "We're on the floor. Are you ok?"

Skyler anxiously nodded. "Oh, ya I just forgot to tell Michael I was going on a date. I hope he isn't too worried about me."

"Don't you worry, I'm sure he is used to you not being at the dorm at night."

"Ya, I guess you're right." He rubbed his neck nervously.

They got off the elevator and walked down the hall to her parents' underground condo. She knocked on the door.

Her parents welcomed them in. Her mother resembled an older white-haired version of Roxanne and her father was a well built older man with salt and pepper hair.

Skyler turned on his charming smile. “Nice to meet you, I’m Skyler Therris, and I must say you have a lovely daughter. I see she gets her looks from her mother.”

Her mother beamed. “You sound like a very nice boy,”

Her father showed them inyo the condo. The condo was a fair size with a small kitchen to the right and the dining room to the left. There was a small sitting room with a chair and couch on very cozy in design. The style was something from the 19th century but with modern touches like the holographic TV. The kitchen was stocked with all the modern gadgets. It was clear they were well off, with a place decorated with antiques.

“So how long have you two been together? Roxanne has told us all about you. She is quite fond of you.”

Skyler kept smiling. “Is that true, I didn't know?”

“We were shocked when she asked to bring you over,” Her mother told him. “You’re the first boy she has brought home.”

He choked on some air. “Well, I have to say this is a first for me too.”

Her father went over to the table. “Dinner is ready. If you want to sit down, we can talk more.”

Skyler sat down at the table. He wasn't claustrophobic, but he felt like the walls were closing in on him. He gulped some deep breaths and tried to relax.

Her father presented two bottles of wine. “What do you drink red or white?”

Finally, some booze. “Red, that would be great.”

He poured Skyler a glass and the rest of them all some wine.

Skyler drank, hoping it would calm his nerves.

The mother watched the wall clock. “He's late again, are you sure we should eat before he gets here?”

The father grunted sternly. “He is always late, and knows when dinner is.”

The mother twisted a napkin in her hands.

Skyler shifted his eyes around the cozy dining room. A hard wood table that could have been an heirloom, pastel painted walls. There was a china cabinet holding the full set of fancy china locked away. They were using modern no stick silver colored plates. "Who are we waiting for?"

The father let out a sigh. "Roxanne's brother. He never makes it on time for anything. He has been late since the day he was born so it's no surprise."

Skyler sympathized with her brother. They passed the food around. There were real mashed potatoes and carrots and a juicy roast. Skyler usually didn't care for roast, but it was a real meal not replicated so it was a nice treat. He didn't want to be rude, but he couldn't stop eating. He hadn't had good food like this in a long time.

Her mother laughed. "I guess my cooking is better than the replicated stuff they have at the Academy?"

Skyler swallowed his mouthful. "Oh, ya that stuff is awful compared to this and I don't normally like a roast, but I like this roast."

"Thank you! You are so kind, I'll be sure to send you home with leftovers."

Her father spoke up. "You know I made the carrots and potatoes. That's one way my wife and I keep a happy marriage all these years: we share the responsibility."

"Well I guess that's one way to do it, congratulations." Skyler went back to stuffing his face.

"How long have your parents been married?" Her father asked.

Skyler lowered his fork. "My father's dead. He died when I was five, they were married just short of ten years. My mother remarried when I was ten, so I guess she has been married for nine years now, I don't keep track, I haven't lived at home since I was sixteen. I moved in with my uncle because me and my step-dad don't get along."

Her father spoke sympathetically. "I'm sorry, I didn't know."

Roxanne butted in. "His father was Captain Therris."

Her mother glanced up. "Ooh really? I remember him! He was a great man. I used to be in The United Galactic Forces in my younger years. I quit when the war started. I had two little ones at home and I wasn't going to risk dying in the war. But oh my, Captain Therris he was a hunk back then all the women wanted him. He was one of the smartest captains too. He really did leave a good legacy behind."

Skyler blushed, drinking more wine. His glass was almost empty. "Ya, so I hear. He didn't live long enough for me to see him in action. Also, my mother kept me on Earth."

The father frowned. "Correct me if I'm wrong. Since Therris is your father then your mother is a Munroe, and she's the one married to Governor Roux. He has a good chance of being president one day. You also mention your uncle, is that your moms or dads brother?"

Skyler wished he had more wine. It was shocked how much this family knew about his. "Mother's, my dad was an only child."

"Justin Munroe is a very rich and powerful man. He is a governor too, am I right?"

"He used to be, but now he is married to a duchess, and is very influential." Skyler drank from an empty glass. His chest tightened, *Do they like me or my family?* "How do you know so much about my family?"

The mother smiled. "Well everyone in United Galactic Forces knows your father. But your step-father and Uncle have been in the news quite a lot recently with the upcoming war."

Roxanne reached over the table and filled Skyler's drink.

Skyler exhaled, *Why do they have to talk about my family? Any other topic, please. If they like them so much they can have them.* Before he could say anything, there was a bang at the door. A breath of relief came over him It was Roxanne's brother.

Her mother got up and gave him a hug as he entered the dining room. "You're late, but we saved you some food. Come in and meet your sister's boyfriend, he's Captain Therris's son."

Skyler turned to look at him; their eyes met. He saw the man's dark hair his tall muscular build and his black uniform with yellow stripes. Skyler's heart sank as he recognized the newcomer as the leader of the group of security cadets who got him and his friends in trouble last year. *Uh oh. Shit. Of all the Smiths in the forces Roxanne had to be related to this one.*

The guy sat down right next to Skyler. They shook hands real tight. “Nice to meet you again, Cadet Therris.”

Skyler slumped in his chair really wishing he had more wine. “Yes, it is Cadet Smith.”

The father smiled. “Ah, you two know each other, do you have the same class together or something?”

Cadet Smith gave a devilish grin. “No that’s not it, he and his friends got me suspended last year.”

Skyler kept his calm. “If I remember that story correctly, you threw the first punch.”

The parents frowned at Skyler. In less than a minute he had gone from hero to zero. He really felt awkward and wanted to leave. Roxanne grabbed Skyler’s arm. “Father, Skyler didn't cause the fight. Look at his scrawny arms, do you think he has the strength to attack Mitchell?”

The father then looked at the mother. “Well sweets, you know that this isn't his first fight Mitchell has gotten into.”

“Thanks, I drive all the way out here, after working a long day to have you take his side. I'm out of here, thanks for nothing.” Mitchell got up and stalked toward the door.

His parents hurriedly followed him outside. Roxanne clasped Skyler’s hand. “Come on, let’s go to my room.”

He finished his drink then accompanied her down the hall to the first door on the right. She sat with him on the bed. “I'm sorry about that. My brother is the black sheep of the family. He doesn't get along with anyone when he doesn't get his way I'm really surprised he showed up tonight.”

“I see, I didn’t know sorry about all of this. I didn't mean to cause a fight. I didn’t realize you had a brother, let alone it was that Smith. It’s such a common name.”

“Sorry me and Mitchell aren’t that close. I know you didn't mean to start the fight, it's not your fault.” She leaned over and kissed him, “No matter what happens I still like you.”

He took a deep breath, “Why did you bring me here tonight I mean we haven't really been dating, and now I'm meeting your parents?”

"I wanted to get to know you better. I know you don't have a family and I thought even if you don't have much in common with me you would like to have a family for a bit."

He rubbed his neck. "You are very sweet. I thank you for all you have done for me, you are so nice, but I'm not sure if this is the right thing."

Her face dropped. "You want to break up? We're getting too close?"

Skyler shook his head. "No, I mean yes. It's odd, I like you, I think you're a great girl, but my heart belongs to another."

Her look turned sour. "What do you mean? Are you cheating on me?"

"No, I'm not cheating on you, the other girl and I would have to be in a relationship to cheat on you and we're not." He noticed the anger in her face, so in fear he blurted out. "Wait, it's Kax. I love her. I liked her before and now I just feel wrong being with anyone else."

She raised her eyebrows seductively. "Is there anything I can do to take your mind off her, for the night?" She stroked his leg and leaned over to kiss him.

He kissed her back. He laid back on the bed and caressed her breasts.

She undid his pants and slowly lowered them. He took off his shirt. This felt wrong, but at the same time, who could say no to a girl like Roxanne, with her Long black hair, dark green eyes, large round firm breasts and an ass you could bounce a quarter off of? He loved her body, and he loved.... Kax. The sex was great, but he could get sex from anyone. He didn't want to go all the way, it didn't feel right. He was feeling dirty. His pants were down, his shirt was off. She stripped off her top.

He shook his head. "Roxanne, keep your shirt on I think you're great, but I can't do this, it's wrong." He got up and grabbed his shirt.

She glared. "You're really serious about Kax aren't you? That's just terrible I mean, how can you? It's not right, I'm your girlfriend."

"Listen you're a great girl, I like you, but I can't do this."

Still on top on him, she leaned down and kissed his chest. "I'm not taking no for an answer."

He forcefully rolled them over. “No is the only answer I’m giving.”

She frowned and grabbed his shoulder and dug her long nails into his back. “Where you going to go? You’re sixty feet underground.”

Skyler winced at her nails seeping into his back. He pulled them out of his shoulder and pushed her off and put his pants back on. “I'm sorry, I do like you, but this isn't going to work out.”

The rage built in her eyes, as he got dressed.

He made his way towards the door.

Roxanne snapped. “You walk out that door and I tell my parents you tried to rape me.”

It's seems like he had no way out. There were no windows to jump out and what if her parents believed her and not him? Skyler remembered he had his communicator in his pocket, along with a condom. He smiled and fiddled with his hand in his pocket. Dialing Michael’s emergency code. He looked at her and smiled. “Come on you really going to do that? Do I mean that much to you?”

She stared at him. “Yes, I like you and I want you.”

“Well then tell me you really love me, and I will stay.” He was trying to stall time until Michael got closer. *Damn I hope this plan works.*

She took a breath and stared into Skyler’s eyes bright green eyes. “I....I.... can't say it.”

He went over to her and put his hand on her shoulder. “See? We don't love each other. What we had was fun, but it's not going anywhere. What we had is over.”

He kissed her on the forehead.

A tear formed in on of her eyes. “I will miss you.”

“Ya, and I will never forget you.” He walked out her door. *Phew. That didn’t need to get out of hand. I’m glad she is letting me go calmly.* He went back into the main room and saw her parents on the couch playing with their tablets.

Her father looked up from his tablet. “You're leaving already. Is everything alright?”

“Ya, all is well,” Skyler answered. “I just got a call from headquarters. I’m needed back tonight. A friend is picking me up, so it was nice meeting both of you." *Roxanne can tell them the truth,* he thought.

"You are a good kid. I hope to see you again sometime."

Skyler smiled. "We will see about that."

The mother went and fetched a container of food. "Here is some food. Take it, since you loved it so much."

"Thanks, I'll make sure you get your container back I'll pass it on to Roxanne."

She shook her head. "This is a replicated container, so you don't have to return it."

He laughed "Thank you, you're sweet it was nice meeting both of you and hope you have a good night."

He headed to the parking garage, where he had told Michael to meet him.

Skyler waited inside the parking garage, watching for a sign of Michael and his bike. He double checked his texts to make sure that he had written the right directions when he was in the elevator. He tried to think of something else, but all he could think of was Roxanne and how he knew he had hurt her.

Eventually, Michael showed up on his bike. "So how did you get all the way out here?"

Skyler rolled his eyes. "Long story, but me and Roxanne are over."

Michael nodded. "Figured that is what happened. So, there's a bottle of booze in the sidecar for you thought you might need it."

Skyler patted Michael on the back and got into the side car. "Thanks, buddy you are a good friend."

"I thought we agreed that you were a pain in the ass and not my friend?"

"Ya, well sometimes friends are pains in the ass." Skyler took a drink. "Wait, a moment aren't you blind, how can you drive?"

Michael tapped his helmet. "It has a navigation sensor in the view screen. I can read that because it's close it shows me the road, should be safe I got, here didn't I?"

"I guess, either way driving down the road with a blind guy doesn't seem so bad with the night I had."

Michael laughed. “You’re not far off the highway, so it's mostly a straight path.”

Skyler downed a few more sips and then said. “Come on Jones, take us home.”

“Aye, Captain.”

Skyler enjoyed the ride. It gave him lots of time to think about Kax and how he wished she wanted him the way Roxanne did.

Chapter 16

Monday came. Skyler didn't feel like leaving the room to go see Kax. He couldn’t face her. If she learned about the break-up, she would think it was about her. Which was the truth, but Kax didn’t need to know that.

Michael returned to the room after his shower. “Okay, lazy bones. I know you slept most of the weekend away. Now it is time to get off your ass and head to class.”

Skyler got out of bed, examined his fluffy lifeless hair and scruffy beard. “I know, I just don't want Kax to find out.”

Michael rolled his eyes. “That’s why I told Kax you needed time. But it is Monday and they don't excuse you for missing class, because you had a bad break-up.”

Skyler frowned. “That’s not it. I don't want Kax to think I broke up with Roxanne, Because of her. Our relationship wasn’t going anywhere.”

“Well don't miss these classes, it's late fall and exams are soon, these are the classes we need now.”

Skyler’s eyes widened. “This close to exams already!” He looked at the calendar on his tablet and saw that it was close to the middle of November. It shocked him how much time had gone by. He stared at his box of papers Roxanne gave him. He was beginning to worry. He brushed the life back into his hair and got dressed.

“Wow, I never thought I would see you this excited to go to class,” Michael marveled. “What’s the rush?”

Skyler looked at the mirror and ignored Michael. “Do you think I should keep the beard?”

"Maybe for today, but it's not you. It makes you look old and doesn't suit you."

"Dude, girls like guys with beards, I'll just try it out."

"So, we're just going ignore all I say today?"

Skyler checked the clock. "Dude, we gotta get ready! We're going to be late."

"Skyler, classes start at nine. You're too early, it's only seven a.m."

But of course, Skyler wasn't listening to anything Michael said and took off.

Skyler got to the door of his first class. He wanted to be early, but he didn't realize how early he really was. He sat on the floor waiting for Captain O'Brien to show up. O'Brien arrived minutes later and unlocked the door. "You trying to suck up or something lad? I never seen you this early."

Skyler stood up, brushed himself off and answered. "Good morning sir, I was wondering since exams are coming up, could I schedule some extra time with the battle simulation program?"

O'Brien, shocked, turned the lights on in his classroom. "Exams are a month away and you have one of the top scores in the class. Why would you need extra time?"

"I just think now that I have real command experience, I want to try to use that to my advantage in the simulations, just to be the best I can be."

He made his way over to his desk. "Lad, you're only the best you can be, and you are up there at the top of the class. I wouldn't want you to use up all your free time, but I will schedule you in for a few extra classes. If a student needs the time I will have to bump you, though."

Skyler followed him to the front of the class. "Thanks, Captain. I can live with that."

"So, lad, did you break up with Roxanne?"

Skyler leaned on the desk. "Ya, she tricked me into meeting her parents and then when we were alone she came on to me, I had to tell her no. Michael came and picked me up."

O'Brien placed his bag on the desk setting things up for class. "Good friend you got there, I wouldn't expect any less from a Squirrel."

Skyler frowned. "Squirrel? Really, I know I let you be when you called the Cassiopaeans, Cassies, but who calls Squallites squirrels nowadays?"

"So sorry. I didn't mean to be negative, I'm just not used to the fact that all the slang we used to use is now derogatory. When I was a wee lad like yourself, everyone said it. But my point stands. Squallites are loyal to their friends, even if they won't admit it. I know they are good people, I used to work with a bunch of them when I was Chief Lieutenant of an engineering vessel. They were so loyal, it was so boring working back there, they just knew what to do no questions asked."

"I hope you didn't call them Squirrels to their face?"

O'Brien chuckled and sat down at his desk. "We all did, because when you looked in the back watching them work they looked like a bunch of little squirrels running around. They understood the nickname. We never meant it to be negative, but that was about thirty years ago now." He counted on his fingers. "Ya, that would be right, because it was a couple years before Emily was born. Damn, way to make me feel old."

"Wow, your past sounds interesting."

O'Brien switched on the desk controls. "I have lived a long life and been on many ships, some boring as hell but others you have the time of your life."

Skyler stepped back when the clear-topped desk lit up. "How long did it take you to make Captain?"

"I would say about fifteen years. Now I know it sounds like a long time, but I wasn't looking for a promotion. Not until I was posted to a freighter ship. Which all we did was drop cargo off and nothing else. It was boring as anything. So, I took the first promotion I was offered. I was a Captain of a small ship, nothing big. I had to leave my wife and daughter on a nearby space station. I ran that ship for 10 years until the war was over and now, I'm a teacher and I love it."

Skyler smiled. "It took you that long to figure out what you wanted to do with your life?"

O'Brien laughed as he typed a few things into his desk with a built-in computer. "I know you want to be a Captain of a fancy starship, but really until you have years of experience they will get you commanding small garbage ships. You will probably get it faster than anyone else. You're top of the class if you keep your grades up. I mean you're a smart kid, but they don't give ships to boys, they want experience."

It was hard to hear the truth, but Skyler couldn't argue with the facts. "Ya I know, I'll just have to do better I guess."

O'Brien stood up and put his bag under his desk. "If you really want to know what it is like to be a Captain, more than you do already, I could run some advanced simulations with you. Warning, they will be some of the hardest decisions a Captain has to make."

Skyler brushed his hair back. "Thank you, you're so good to me."

O'Brien peered up at him. "You remind me of me when I was a lad. Oh, and shave that beard for tomorrow, you got a baby face. Don't want to ruin it with all that hair. Well, not just yet."

Skyler laughed rubbing his stubble. "I thought women liked beards?"

"They do, but you're in school with girls, not women. You got a few more years to go, speaking of women have you talked to Kax yet?"

Skyler shook his head. "How? I don't want to, I know she is going to say no and I'd rather just study."

"Well now that's not the Skyler Therris I know. Go on and talk to her. Tell her how you feel. She needs to know, and if she turns you down go to the bar and have a drink. You can tell them put it on Potatoes O'Brien's tab they'll know."

Skyler laughed. "Potatoes O'Brien, that's your nickname?"

O'Brien puffed out his chest with pride. "Yes, I got it years ago when I was the only Irishman on another freighter. They thought I was funny I ate potatoes with every meal."

Skyler was still laughing. "Well, that's one way to get a nickname."

The first bell rang, and the students started to show up for class.

Skyler made his way to his desk. O'Brien smiled. "Wednesdays after classes, simulation room five."

***

Michael was getting dressed when the eye doctor's office texted with a cancellation and invited him to come in that morning. He called Kax and asked her to accompany him. A little while later she was holding his hand, helping him into the medical building.

"How is Skyler doing?" She asked.

What's the point in hiding it? she deserves to know. Michael shrugged. "He's a bit off. He's madly in love with you, just doesn't know how to tell you. He also just broke up with Roxanne."

Kax rubbed her forehead. "Well he can take his time. He's just a friend to me. I'm not interested in him at all. He's a nice guy, just not my type."

Sure, that's the reason. Kax I know you care about him but your secret's safe with me. He planned his next words out carefully. "I personally think he needs to grow up before he gets a real girlfriend." He heard Kax sigh and saw her clench her fist. "Give him time, when he grows up he'll be worth it."

Kax scrunched her lips giving and uncertain expression.

Only if I was good enough for you. He gave Kax a reassuring smile.

When they arrived, Michael had a short wait. They were told to go right into the exam room where the eye doctor was waiting. Kax sat down in the corner.

The doctor put his visor on and checked out Michael's eyes. "Well you have some major nerve damage, but nothing that isn't fixable. But may I ask, why are you wearing contacts none of your records indicate you are prescribed to have them?"

Michael sighed, feeling ashamed for his lack of pride. "They're fake ones and I bought them a long time ago. They are just to change my eye color."

The doctor looked at his eyes. "Yes, well there is lots of damage from over the years. They aren't the right size, I wouldn't recommend you wear them again."

Michael's chest became tight. "Well doctor, what are my options?"

The doctor checked Michael's eyes one more time. "I can repair the damage, but you will have to start coming to see an optometrist once a year, to make sure you are still fine, nothing major. But sometimes the repair of these nerves can degrade over the years. The sooner they get fixed the better. As for your eye color if you really want I can perform the changing of the color permanently, when I fix your eyes?"

What would my dad think? What would the other Squallites think? I want blue eyes, but I can't betray my people. He let out a long sigh. "I don't know if I want that. See, I wear them when I am on Earth, it is fine. But with my people, I take them out. If I change them, they will see me as an oddball and a traitor."

The doctor moved away preparing one of his tools. "Well none of us choose what we look like. But the contacts you are wearing will do more damage you may not be able to come back from."

Michael looked to Kax for guidance. "You got an opinion?"

She pursed her lips. "Your choice, but I don't care what your eye color is, you're still my friend."

Michael nodded he knew what he needed to do. "Not today doctor. I won't wear the contacts, but I will try to see how this goes with the orange eyes."

The doctor smiled. "It's best to accept who you are, and anytime you change your mind come see me."

"Thanks, doctor."

The doctor leaned the chair back some more. "You may feel a few pinches, but it will be ok. I'll fix your eyes and in a few hours, you will see perfectly." The doctor hit a button on his visor and turned it into an x-ray. He took his tool held Michael's eyelid up and used another tool with a micro-laser and slowly reattached the nerves. Once he was done the left eye, he moved over to the right eye. When he was finished, he took another tool and sprayed something in both eyes.

Michael jerked up and blinked uncontrollably. "What was that for, doctor?"

"It's just a finishing spray to make sure it all holds. The spray is kind of like an eye glue. It's safe, it just encourages the nerves to grow and heal."

Wow, it is so nice to have my vision back. Michael looked around the room; it was quite clear to him he faced the doctor, "You have gray hair, I didn't notice before."

The doctor brushed his hair back. "Oh, I see I fixed your eyes too well."

They all laughed. The doctor then brought down the big eye tester. "Okay Michael, tell me if this looks fuzzy to you."

Michael peered through the lenses. "Looks clear to me, doc."

"Your eyes are fine Mr. Jones, I hope you take care of them. Next step is time, I don't want to see you doing any more damage to them."

Michael smiled. "Thanks doc, I'll do my best."

He got up out of the chair and went to leave the room. "Wait a second. I want to give you this."

The doctor handed Michael a pamphlet. "It's info on if you ever want to change your eye color."

"Thank you, doctor, I will read it."

He and Kax left the office.

Kax turned to Michael. "What do you want to do? You're supposed to rest so you don't have to go to class. I missed the morning, want to just hang out?"

Michael paused for a second, "Sure, let's stop by the dorm first, then go visit my dad."

Chapter 17

Michael entered the room and saw Skyler standing in front of the full-length mirror next to the closet admiring his beard. "Shave it!"

Skyler scoffed. "You know everyone keeps saying that, but maybe I should grow it out a bit more, might look better."

Kax came in behind Michael. "Get rid of that thing, it's so gross." She gave Skyler a flirtatious wink.

Skyler pulled an electric razor out of his pocket. "You know, I think Kax is right." Before he could turn it on, a knock sounded at the door. "Come in!"

Fleet Admiral Cane strode in and his is eye searched around the room. “Okay, well, you guys need to clean this place up before inspection.” He pointed to the pile of clothes circling Skyler’s bed. “But first, why I’m here. I need you three for another mission.”

Skyler turned around to face Cane. “So, you can emotionally damage us before exams, I don't think so.”

Cane’s face went white when he saw Skyler’s beard. “Wow, you look so much like your father with that beard...” He sat on Skyler’s bed.

Kax went to Cane’s side. “Ok, so what we're going to say?”

Cane regained his train of thought. “Emotional scars are never my intention, but I need you to go on this mission because you are the top of your class.”

Michael gave Cane a look of suspicion. “What does his mission entail?”

Cane took a deep breath. “I need you to go to planet Squall and pick up a package. They will only release it to a Squallite. We are short on pilots who have adept level training. The Cassiopaeans gave this item to the Squallites years ago and now they are willing to trade this box if we keep them out of the war.”

Michael’s eyes widened. “You want us to take the worm orb from the Squallites and bring it to Earth?”

“Yes, with its power it will create a one-way wormhole to the Cassiopaeans’ home world. Hopefully end this war before it starts.”

Michael frowned. “I will not do that. That item is sacred on my home world, it was given as a sign of peace. To take it so the Earth can commit genocide, I will not allow. I don’t even think the Squallites are even truly willing to give it up, if they have put these conditions down.”

Cane sighed. “I understand, you’re not the first Squallite who we have asked, but this could save millions of lives.”

Michael glared, holding firm in his decision. “No one will agree to this. That item is a sacred thing in our world and genocide is just wrong!”

The Fleet Admiral groaned. “It's not genocide. We just want to get our troops around their planet and prevent them from leaving. Giving them no choice but to surrender. Please, Michael, I don't know who else I can ask.”

Skyler leaned over and whispered to Kax, “You ever seen Michael like this?”

Kax just shook her head.

Michael spoke in a booming voice. “You know why the high council asked for a Squallite? Because they know no self-respecting Squallite would do it. This is an item of great importance, if anyone were to remove it, he would be labeled an enemy of the Squallites. No one will agree to this.”

The Fleet Admiral let a long sigh. “Michael, I know this must be hard for you, but you have to understand. I don’t know if there is any other option. I also know for a fact you don’t possess Squallite citizenship. You were born on Earth and have UGF citizenship. Please think about where your loyalty lies.”

Michael sat on his bed glaring at Cane for a long moment. “I’ll do it. I will go on the mission and talk to the council, but I will not guarantee I will return with the orb.”

Cane gave a serious nod. “Do what you can, but I'm not sure what else we can do. We want to stop this war, before more people are killed. By the way, the government is making this war official next week.”

Skyler eyes popped in shock. “If the war is next week, doesn't that mean all fourth year and higher Cadets instantly graduate?”

“Not instantly, but some of them. That’s another reason I want you kids doing the mission. I will be able to keep you off the front lines. There is a potential too of not coming back from this mission. Please make sure your family recordings are up to date. There is still some bureaucracy to go through first, so this mission won’t happen till this spring.”

“What do we do if something does happen to us?” Skyler asked with a glimmer of worry in his eyes.

“You die heroes.” Cane responded, “I’m sorry.” He examined Skyler’s face. “I’m not sure if a full beard is the right look for you? If you’re serious, I recommend a van Dyke or something along those lines. Your father took lots of time grooming his beard. He didn't look good with one when he was younger. It might suit you when you're older, but you got your mother's nose, so we'll see."

Skyler covered his nose. "What about my mom's nose?"

Cane laughed. "You're a great kid, Skyler. See you around." He stood up. "I believe in all of you." He left the room.

Michael put on his coat and headed for the door looking worried.

"Where are you going?" Kax asked.

Michael turned and answered. "I'm continuing with the plan going to see my dad, I have to go talk to him now."

Skyler grabbed his coat. "I'm coming with you, I got to hear what he has to say about all of this."

They soon arrived at the hospital. Sam Jones was lying in his bed when Michael came in. "Hey, Dad, any change?"

His father lifted his head from the pillow. "Hey son, what's with the visit?"

"Can't I visit my dad?" Michael took the seat next to the bed. "We have been given the opportunity for another mission and I need your input about whether I should do it."

His father bit his lip. "The worm orb. Cane came in and talked to me about it. I told him you would do it."

Michael's jaw dropped. Gasps could be heard from all of them.

Michael shot back. "What? Dad, how could you? That item is the most sacred item..."

His father's tone went serious. "One of our most sacred. It is also very powerful and useful, that's why it must be put to good use. It's going to be wasted in hands that won't use it. I know it was given as a sign of peace, but the Cassiopaeans are hurting us all. Their war is with humans and they are hurting the people of Earth and some are Squallites. They might say they're not, but when they attack the base, they attack all who are in it. So, in my eyes they have broken their bond of peace and I will not stand for it. They wanted to be our friends and they now hurt us. I know it is tragic, but the humans are our friends now."

Michael snapped. "Humans are our friends? You realize they have enslaved us?"

His father shook his head. "No, they have not, we chose to come to Earth. We knew what we were doing. Humans didn't come to Squall and enslave us, we are free. It could always be worse."

Michael clenched his fist. He made his way toward the door.

His father said one more thing, "Blue eyes are from Earth. No one will judge you."

Michael left the room furious. He rushed out of the hospital. Once outside in the fresh air he went to a corner at the side of the brick building and panted. His heart was racing, head pounding, and he was fighting back tears. He found a corner and slumped down sitting on the ground. These past few weeks had been an emotional roller coaster he wasn't sure what he was going to do. Everything he knew in his life was falling apart. Nothing made sense to him anymore. He was a Squallite, but he was a citizen of Earth. He had two homes, and he walked in two worlds. Even if it was okay to change his eye color, taking this orb was another thing entirely Squallites didn't support wars. If he got the orb that meant he would be encouraging war. He gripped at his hair in frustration. *I don't have a choice. I have to do it.* "Dammit!" He cried. "I want to make my own choices."

***

Skyler went over to Michael's father's bed. Sam looked very much like an older Michael but with a few slight differences. His hair was a shade darker, his features were sharper, and he had a good twenty years on Michael.

Skyler went to say something, but Sam spoke first. "You're a good friend to Michael. You are what he needs."

Skyler laughed and made a joke. "He doesn't need me, he needs to get laid."

His father laughed and shook his head. "Do you realize he didn't have many friends growing up? He's always been a little uptight and having you around is a breath of fresh air. You know, I had the chance to raise him on Squall, but I didn't want to. I wanted him to embrace human traditions along with his Squallite ones."

Kax came closer. "That explains your religious beliefs."

He shook his head. "No, that is my own. I believe in one God and I think you humans found him and if not, I would follow anyone with those teachings."

Skyler gave a puzzled look. "So, what should we do with Michael and is this mission? Is it really that important?"

Sam sighed. "Yes, this must be done, but I worry that it will not stop the war."

Kax put her hand to her mouth. "Why did the Cassiopeians give an orb so powerful to the Squallites in the first place?"

Sam shook his head and answered. "I can't tell you that. Squallite secret. What I can tell you is that it was given as a thank you gift. The Squallites did a huge favor for the Cassiopeians and the only way they could repay them, was to give them their most valuable item."

"So, why don't the Squallites use it?" Skyler asked.

Sam shook his head. "I don't know, that's the council's choice."

Kax smiled. "I think I understand, thank you, Mr. Jones."

None of this was making sense to Skyler. He just nodded and agreed. "Ya, it's late. We should be heading out. Thank you for everything."

Mr. Jones smiled. "Thank you, kids, it was nice to hear from you. Please take care of Michael and save him from himself."

They both nodded and headed out the door back to the dorms where they knew Michael would be waiting.

Chapter 18

Kax's curiosity on Squallite history and the orb was getting to her. The only Squallites she knew well were Michael and Rantra. She wasn't going to ask Rantra, who might lie to her. She was going to have to look in the archives and see if there was anything she could find. There had to be something.

She went to the library and combed through all the public Squallite history books. All she found was the basic knowledge of how the Squallites came into possession of the orb, nothing else. It almost seemed that she had more info on the subjects than the books. She was running out of ideas.

So many dead ends. I'm getting nowhere. I've got to find a Squallite willing to share. She scanned the room checking out all the people. Then she saw sitting at one of the tables a tall slim man with human ears but orange eyes. *Bingo. He was clearly a Squallite who didn't like to be regarded as one.* She made her way over to his table and sat next to him. "Your ears look good, mind if I ask you a few questions?"

He glared at her with his dark orange eyes. "The library is not a pickup place, please leave me alone. I need to study."

She laughed, brushed off the comment and put on a cute pouty face. "You should tell that to my friend. How about I help you study and you do me a favor?"

He rolled his eyes in annoyance. Then noticed her charm. "Well, it couldn't hurt to take a little break."

Kax smiled and signaled the guy to follow her to the back of the library.

He put his books down and trailed her. "Why are we going here? There are still people who can see us."

She sat on one of the bean bags and answered, "Yes, but it is quieter here. I have some questions to ask you." She tossed her hair flirtatiously.

He plopped into the bean bag next to her grinning. "Anything you want."

She whispered into his ear. "I need you to tell me all you know about the worm orb, its powers and history."

He jerked back. "I can't tell that to an outsider."

"Oh, I'm an outsider and can't know. But you're a Squallite who is trying to be an 'outsider,' come on, what is the story? I'm just curious." She pouted.

He frowned, paused for a moment. "Fine. You want to know, let's go to my quarters and talk about it in private."

Kax got up and waved her finger. "Are there any books here that will help?"

He shook his head. "No there aren't, and if there are, I will bring them."

"What time?"

He went and grabbed a pencil off the nearby table and wrote on a piece of paper. "Here is all you need. Now I suggest we go back to actually studying."

Kax went back to work smiling, feeling very proud of herself.

***

Michael checked on his experimental metal. He had left it alone too long. He was going to finish the experiment today. He hoped it would hold up. He believed this war could be won with defense, not with weapons. If the people of Earth could show that they were strong enough to hold off any attacker, there would be no way you could win. He knew the metal could hold its shape in the vacuum of space and undergo high amounts of radiation.

What about durability? That is what he had to test next. He took the decontaminated metal out of the engineering lab and headed to the firing range. He was going to give it some final tests, before he delivered it to the Commodore to check out. He put the sheet on a target board using the weapons to fire at it. No dents or scratches were appearing. He continued to fire; he wanted to give this thing a beating. Finally satisfied, he wrote down the last details in his notebook, transferred it onto this tablet and copied the file. He left the metal there, put a hold on that range and went to get Commodore Ipinik.

The Commodore was in his office, doing paperwork. Michael knocked on the door. Ipinik looked up. "Come in."

"Sir, I want to show you some new specs I have been working on for a new alloy. It's super durable and I think it could be the new face of the defense."

He put the tablet with the info displayed on his desk. Ipinik brushed his gray hair back. "What gave you the idea it would work?"

Michael took a deep breath. "I know we are already using titanium compound alloys, but they are still not the strongest. This one I have created, you can see here, I mixed that, added some carbon magnesium and a bit of trisqulium, I think this might work on the ships. I have run all the tests, no dents, scratching or melting. I don't know if it has a liquid form. I do know I used heated metals to make it. I cannot seem to revert it back to its original form but what shape you make it, is the way it stays."

The Commodore scrutinized the chart before looking up at Michael. "You are an engineering Cadet. You study repairs and wires. What do you know about ship design?"

Michael felt slightly offended. "I might major in the basic engineering, but if you check my record I have taken plenty of ship design classes. I know my file, sir, even if I don't know that much this metal is unlike anything you or I have ever seen before. I really wish you would look at it."

Commodore Ipinik got up from his desk. He looked down at Michael. Ipinik was almost 2 feet taller than Michael. He grabbed his tablet and followed Michael's lead. "Take me to the metal and I will have a look at this."

Pleased, Michael hoped he had impressed his superior officer, and gladly took him to see his work.

Chapter 19

Skyler rested his eyes outside of O'Brien's class. He sat on the stone floor waiting for O'Brien to show up.

O'Brien came over and gently nudged Skyler with his foot. "Two days in a row, lad. Are you trying to win a prize or something? Because you got it from me for showing effort."

Skyler rubbed his eyes and stood up. He pulled a flash drive out of his pocket and handed it to O'Brien. "I stayed up most of the night working on this program, I really need to work on this kind of mission today."

O'Brien took the stick and unlocked his door. "What is on this program?"

Skyler followed O'Brien into the class. "I got the specification form Cane. It's a simulation of a mission I'm going on this summer and I want to know what I'm getting into."

O'Brien placed his bag on his desk. He examined the flash drive. "Cane, you say? I'll look over it around noon, and we can check this out after school. But for the future, try to get more sleep tonight."

"I will do my best."

That afternoon, Skyler came not a minute too late. "So, I'm here, O'Brien. I'm ready to start when you are."

Captain O'Brien sat at his desk waiting for Skyler. He had on a serious face. "Sit down, Skyler, there is something I need to talk to you about."

Skyler obeyed. "What is it, Captain?"

O'Brien frowned and sat next to Skyler with the file in his hand, "I had a chance to look over this file and I did some tweaking to it, making sure it wasn't too easy for you. What is up with this kind of mission?"

"Fleet Admiral Cane is sending us on a mission just like it this summer, and I need to make sure I'm ready for it."

O'Brien nodded. "I didn't realize Cane had chosen you to go on this mission. I heard rumors about this mission through our grapevine. Thinking of it now, I'm not surprised Cane is sending you. I will help you in the best way I can, but you need to remember, this is just a simulation."

Skyler nodded. "I understand, Captain."

"I told you to call me Sean after classes," O'Brien said. He stood up and patted Skyler on the shoulder. "So, let's get going, this is a long SIM and we need to cover as much as we can of it tonight, so you can get enough sleep."

Skyler followed O'Brien to the simulation room. Skyler was a bit nervous going in, but this was something he had to do, if he was ever going to be a great captain.

***

Classes were over for the day. Kax knew where she was going. She was going to the older Squallite cadet's room, to talk to him about the Orb. She checked the room number on the paper and made her way to the Cadet wing. Dorm number 565, that was where she would meet her new Squallite friend. She was more determined than anything to find out what was going on and what that orb meant. She took a deep breath and knocked on the door.

He answered and let her in. She looked around the room; it was the same layout as the other dorms with the two beds on the right and left, a desk in the middle window in front and the closet facing the bede. She smiled nervously. *This is really happening.* Her eyes widened, when she saw another cosmetically altered Squallite enter the room. *Oh no I'm in a room with two strange men and I don't even know their names.* She looked over at her new friend. "I thought this was just going to be the two of us?"

"It will be. My friend isn't staying long. Don't know if I mentioned it before, my name is Jake and my roommate's name is Ronald, and you were?"

"Kax Tillion, it's nice to meet both of you."

Ronald frowned and grabbed his jacket out of the closet. "Well it's time for me to head out. I will see you later, roomie."

Kax stood in the middle of the room, not sure where to sit. Jake pointed to his roommate's bed. "You can sit there, and we can talk about this."

She smiled and sat down on the bed, across from Jake. "What is the orb and what does it do, why is it so important?"

He laughed shaking his head. "Wow, straight to business. Before we get started, I want to get this out of the way. It's nothing against you, I don't like Catillions. I only like human girls."

She frowned, "Really, you didn't like me even with my charm?"

He laughed. "I notice it and it is nice but the ears, teeth, and eyes they just don't do it for me."

Impressive, yet a little disappointing my charm didn't work. But at least he likes me for just me. She twirled her hair around her finger. "That's so funny, I have never had a man not find me attractive or at least not like Catillions."

"Still haven't, I'm bisexual but I only interested in male Squallites or human women. It's a bit odd with me, sorry to burst your bubble. Ronald is actually my partner."

He's got a boyfriend. Her face went bright red in embarrassment. "I'm sorry, only flirted just to see if it would motivate you. I'm glad you don't expect anything. But back to business, what do you want from me in return for the info then?"

"Don't worry about it," He waved his hand. "Nothing much. Just tell me you will spread the stories, I tell you and don't tell anyone it was me who told you, I wish to forget my past."

She pulled out a box of blue contacts. "My friend can't wear these anymore, when I saw your orange eyes I thought these might interest you."

"Wow, thank you, I have been considering the surgery." Jake examined the box. "But wow, it's so hard to find opaque blue contacts, where did Michael find them?"

She raised an eyebrow. "How do you know my friend's name?"

He flipped the box over and pointed. "He put his name on the box."

She laughed and shook her head. "Oh, I'm so sorry about that, I didn't know."

"It's fine, but ask him where he can get more. I would love them till I can get my surgery, same with Ron."

"I'll ask. He just had eye surgery and was told not to wear the contacts anymore, so he is considering changing his eye color too. So, what makes you want to be more human-like?"

"The fact is I like Humans, I don't like my people. They are annoying boring and lack the fun and the freedom Humans have. I just see Squallites are too passive. I don't even sleep like them, I have been training to not meditate and just sleep when I get tired."

Kax listened close. "Really, you go through all that trouble just to change who you are, I mean what do your parents think of this, do they know?"

Jake sighed. "They still call me Jariak, but they know, and they still don't like it. Ron hasn't told his parents."

Sat in silence for a few seconds. "I guess this is a touchy subject, I don't think my dad would like it if I told him I wanted to be Human or a Squallite. Dating one is fine but not being one."

Jake nodded. "Yeah, it's hard to change, but I know it is the right thing for me. I don't know why, but I have always felt more comfortable being a Human than a Squallite. Even as a child raised on Earth, I have felt being one of the humans was right. I never quite fit in with the Squallites on my home world, it's hard to describe but it just was never right."

"Why are you choosing to join United Galactic Forces then? I mean you had to join as a Squallite and even if you complete your transition, you can't go and say you're fully human and get out of the engineering department."

"You are right but there are humans who are engineers, and my file will still say something like Human/Squallite or altered Squallite and if I choose to have children, they will be Squallites. It is more physical than anything. To my people, I'm a traitor. I'm abandoning their ways for another. This isn't just about wanting to eat Human food. I want to be a Human. I'm not complete till I'm Human."

Kax nodded. "I get it and I don't hold judgment, that is not my place. But can we get on to telling your stories about your culture?"

Jake smiled. "Pull out your tablet record this, it is a Squallite tradition that we pass our stories of our people on to the next generation. I don't plan to be a Squallite when I have children, so I will have no need for these stories. Humans seem to just pass on their knowledge and tell their kids to find out the rest, so I will tell you about the Orb tonight and then once a week. If you don't mind coming to visit me, I will tell you more. Record them so that you don't forget it because, these will be the stories of Jariek Mosklin."

Kax pulled out here tablet and hit record. "I'm ready when you are."

Chapter 20

Michael was on his stomach looking at his tablet when Skyler stumbled into the room too tired to function. "You're back late for a weekday, it's almost 10 p.m. what happened?"

Skyler went to his bed and flopped down. He groaned, trying to stay awake. "Running simulations with O'Brien for our summer mission. I just wanted to be prepared."

Michael's eyes widened. He had been so busy with work that he mostly forgot about the mission. "So how did it go?"

Skyler shrugged. "How would you prefer to die, with us all being thrown into a boiling pot of water or just you?"

"That bad, huh? Well just to let you know my people don't boil people to death."

Skyler started taking off his clothes, getting ready for bed. "Oh no, the Squallites don't kill us, the Cassiopaeans do when they find out we have the orb. They decide to barbecue us."

"You have some imagination there, Therris."

Skyler dropped these clothes on the floor. "I would love to stay and chat but I'm going to go to wonderland now." He closed his eyes and passed out.

Just to be on the safe side, Michael checked online to see if the Cass really did barbeque people. To his relief, he found out they didn't. With Skyler passed out, Michael felt it was the time he got some rest as well.

Kax came into the room. The lights were off. She was about to leave.

Michael opened his eyes and turned on the desk lamp. "I guess Skyler didn't lock the door. You can come in, I was just trying to meditate, nothing else to do."

She perched at the end of the bed, next to Michael. "I'm sorry, I know now about the orb and what it means to your people and how this is tearing you apart. But I also understand your father too."

"Where did you find out this story?"

Kax sighed. "From this guy I met in study hall. He is the one who told me, and he plans to tell me more stories. His name is Jake."

"Jake? You don't mean Jariak?" Michael frowned. "I would say stop, but it seems jake is doing the ritual of On-Mire and I can't interrupt that, so I will tell you this: don't share that info, wherever you have it documented. Don't tell people, save it for now. But it would be a disgrace if you just threw it away. Feel honored that you are one of the few people outside of the Squallites to know this info. You better treat it like a gold necklace your grandmother gave you."

Kax smiled. "I will not tarnish this tradition of your people."

"I guess he picked the right outsider to tell."

She gave Michael a hug.

He hugged her back. “Well I hope it helps you with a mission.”

“Oh, right I forgot to mention I gave him your contacts. He hasn't had the surgery for his eyes yet and didn't know where to get them.”

Michael checked in his drawer. “Why did you take them?”

Kax shrugged. “Well you weren’t going to need them anymore.”

“I guess you're right, that part of my life is over now.”

Kax put her arm around Michael. “It might be over, but that doesn't mean it's the end.”

Michael looked at the clock. “It's getting late. You want to get going? I think it would be best if we get a good night’s rest.”

“I will be in my room and getting some sleep. See you in the morning.” She leaned over kissed Michael on the cheek, got up and left the room.

The night was rough. The only one who seemed to be able to sleep right was Skyler. Michael laid back and tried to go into the meditative trance. It didn't seem to be working then out of nowhere there was a green flash in the sky. He looked around. He was standing on a rock in the middle of space. The green light got bigger and closer to him. He was worried but didn't have anywhere to run.

He stood there and watched the green light intensify. He wondered what the meaning was. It finally got closer, until it looked like it was going to go blind from the light. The wattage turned down and from the center of the light, a woman appeared. “Michael Jones, you walk in both worlds, confused about who you are. Only you can find a balance. Your mission to get the orb, you must complete it. Bring the orb to its rightful place.”

Michael shook his head, all confused. “What are you talking about? Who are you?”

The woman, a human woman with red curled hair, looked at him and answered. “You will know who I am. One day. But today is the first step on your journey, to your destiny. You must get the orb and the rest you will know what to do.”

Puzzled, he scratched his head. “I don't get any of this, but I feel I should trust you. What is going on?”

"All in good time, but get the orb."

The vision faded, and he soon opened his eyes more curious than before. He looked up, and the sun was now up, it was now morning. He shook his head, trying to make sense of all of this. Nothing like that, had ever happened to him before. *It must have been a dream. Was that a dream? No, Squallites didn't dream.* He got up and rubbed his face. He must have been too tired and stressed and fell asleep. It was uncommon, but it could happen. He sat up in this bed, wearing only his blue issued boxers. He sat thinking for a long time. "Maybe it is time for me to be my own man and get the surgery and get that orb."

Chapter 21

Michael was on his way to class with Skyler.

"Hey Captain, long time no see!" Called out a voice. Skyler turned around and smiled.

Michael saw a brown curly haired, tanned skinned, dark-eyed, small built guy coming towards them.

"Perry! You're back! Oh buddy, I missed you!" Skyler cheered.

Perry gave Skyler a tight hug. He stood just a little shorter than Skyler. "Dude, you would not believe how awesome watching grass grow is, come to the bar with me and I will tell you all about it."

Michael cleared his throat. "Skyler, we have to get to class, you can get caught up with Perry tonight."

Skyler gave Michael a set of pouty eyes. "But Michael, he just got back, we want to party now."

Perry held out his hand. "Hey Michael, nice to see you again. You can't still be this uptight after hanging out with Skyler this long?"

Michael shot both a glare. *Why do I put up with this?*

Skyler chuckled. "Prove me wrong, skip class with us and listen to stories about grass growing."

He took a moment to weigh his options, *Maybe this will help me get my mind off a few things. Maybe I should take a page out of Skyler's book.* Seeing no other option Michael continued. "I guess one day of skipping classes won't hurt."

Skyler and Perry high-fived and made their way to the bar, with Michael following behind them.

Skyler grabbed them a booth and sat next to Michael.

Perry smiled, stood at the end of the table, "I'll get the drinks, what do you two want?"

"I'll have a beer and Michael drinks a Squallite soda, with extra rum." Skyler winked at Michael.

Michael groaned his head. "Not right now, it's early make it a virgin."

"You got it!" Perry snapped his fingers and started toward the bar.

Maybe this was a bad idea, I don't want to really do anything. I wish I was back in the room resting. Michael put his head in his arms, on the table and groaned.

Skyler watched Michael. "You could have still gone to class, I didn't stop you."

Michael noted the smile on Skyler's face. *He says that, but I know he wouldn't have stopped until I agreed.* He paused and shook his head "It's not you it's me. I've had a rough week. Maybe this is what I need."

Skyler patted Michael, on the back. "Trust me buddy, we will show you a good time."

Perry came back with the drinks. "So, Skyler, you still dating Roxanne?"

Skyler shook his head. "We weren't dating. But I stopped seeing her shortly into the school year. She got too clingy, tricked me into having dinner with her parents."

Perry chuckled, as he took a sip of his beer. "Dude that's rough. Hey, now that she's single, do you think I have a chance with her?"

He shuddered. "She is not worth the time. I'll find you a better girl, if you need."

Perry swallowed another sip of his beer. "Too bad, she was hot. Oh man, did she have curves."

"That's one thing about her I miss. I also found out her brother is Mitchell Smith."

Perry's eyes widened. "No way! That guy who got you into trouble. I would stay away from her now. He is a bad egg." He turned to Michael, "Hey, did Michael ever sleep with her?"

Not this subject again. Michael sipped his tea and scoffed. "No, I'm asexual." *Why do I keep up this lie? No one listens. I like women, but I don't want people bothering me about my sex life.*

Perry smiled. "That's so interesting, tell me more."

"No big deal, I just don't have an interest in men or women for sex. It's not something I like talking about. Can we just drop it? I thought we came here to hear about you growing grass." Michael was genuinely interested.

"That's right, there were normal grass seeds you get on Earth growing. But then we had some other ones, and we got this new one from Vergon 8. They have tall, vine-like purple grass, which is cool, but we had to use radiation on it, bad mistake. It grew normal for the first week, then when it was full grown it spontaneously combusted. The whole lab caught on fire, we lost most of our work. It was funny watching the security tapes of the grass, because it was like an exploding birthday candle." He demonstrated with his hands.

Michael raised an eyebrow. "That's odd. Did you use too much radiation?"

"No, it has to do with one of the gases, that makes the grass purple. It wasn't my department. I oversaw the ursine grass."

Michael looked at him confused. "What's so great about ursine grass samples?"

Perry finished off his beer. "There isn't much grass in that system, so they were rare. My job was to assist in finding a way for them to survive the elements, it was fun. Well, not watching them grow, but the pranks we would pull on each other. My job was writing down the growth status of each specimen. Once, I came into work early and Officer Frost switched mine, with one of the other similar plants. I didn't know how it could have grown five inches in one day. It was crazy. A lot more fun, than you would think it would be."

Skyler finished his beer and laughed. "I guess, you really did have a good time. So, what is your next adventure going to be?"

Perry shrugged. "I don't know, I know I'm here till the end of the year but summer, no clue yet. I wouldn't mind collecting rock or dirt samples, but nothing is set. Do you know what you're doing yet?"

"Me, Michael and Kax are all going to Squall for the summer. Nothing much, just out of planet training."

"Oh, that sounds like fun. Orange isn't my favorite color, but it would be nice to see how orange grass grows."

Skyler might have fun this summer but I'm still stressing. Michael finished his drink. "We don't have orange grass. National color is orange, but the grass and vegetation are all green."

Perry rubbed his neck. "Oh, oh sorry that's Ariesian grass, didn't mean to offend."

Skyler waved to the bartender, for another round.

"It was a harmless mistake," Michael narrowed his eyes, at Perry. "Zyrix, that's an odd last name. You from Earth?"

Perry shook his head. "One hundred percent human, but I'm from colony G outside of Neptune. Close by, but still not Earth. It's mostly humans there. It's a small station, but I miss it. When I graduate, I want to get posted there. But it will be hard, there is a population of 5000 and I'm not sure if they will take me back. My last name is a colony name. My family has roots on Earth but to when the first member of the family came to the colony they assigned new names to track bloodlines."

Michael frowned. "Isn't there a law that says if you were born a place you can always go back, no matter your job in the forces?"

Perry nodded. "I can move back, I can live there if I wanted to, but there aren't many forces jobs, so I might have to work elsewhere and go back and forth. There aren't many shuttles or ships that go there so computer time would be unpredictable. I think I will just have to find another job elsewhere and visit on my time off."

That intrigued Michael. "What's back on the colony for you?"

Perry pulled a picture out of his wallet and handed it to Michael, "My mom, dad and little sister. But it won't be long before she starts the academy. It's my home. It's where I belong. It might be small, but it's where I was meant to be."

I wish, I had a family like that. Michael examined the image. “You take after your mother, how old is your sister?”

“Three years younger than me. She has always looked the up to me, I love her.”

Skyler rolled his eyes. “You’re showing that old family photo again? Are you ever going to get an update, you’re what, 16 there?”

Perry took back his photo and smiled. “Next time I go home, we’re doing updates, but till then, this is the last one with all of us. I have lots with me and my sister, but not many with my parents.”

Perry has a home but lives away, but his culture and pride follows him. I thought I was like that. Maybe Cane was right, where does my loyalty fall? Michael slumped in his seat, taking larger sips of his drink.

Chapter 22

By noon on Saturday, Kax had not heard anything from the boys. She went to their room and used her key to get in. She froze, in shock at the spectacle before her. Clothes scattered the floor and Michael was passed out, face down on his bed. Skyler sprawled on his bed half-dressed with Perry fully dressed, curled at his side.

She let out a screech. “Ah, what’s going on here?”

Perry picked up his head, rubbing it. “Hey, you’re cute, please tell me you’re single.”

Skyler elbowed Perry, in the ribs. “Paws off, she's mine.”

Perry winced in pain. “Ow dude, sorry. But how come you get all the hot chicks?”

That joke is so old Skyler. Kax rolled her eyes. “I’m not anybody’s, Skyler just likes to pretend he has a chance. But from the looks of it I said no to him one-to-many times, and he’s turned to men.”

Perry and Skyler jerked away, from each other.

Skyler sat up. “What happened was me, Perry and Michael went out drinking last night. Perry was too drunk to make it back to his room. After we carried Michael back and well I'm used to having someone in my bed, more than Michael I said he could share."

Sitting down on the end of Michael's bed rubbing her temples, Kax muttered, "You guys are so immature."

Perry got up and straightened his orange uniform and extended his hand to Kax. "Hi there, I'm Perry Zyrix, and what might your name be?"

She looked him over, thin, medium height, dark wavy hair, tan skin, dark eyes, and a cute smile. *Time to make Skyler jealous.* She took his hand and batted her eyelashes. "I'm Kax Tillion and it's nice to meet you."

Perry's eyes widened, and his head turned behind him to look at Skyler, "This is Kax? The Kax the one who you talk about in your sleep? The women you want to m-"

Faster than lighting Skyler jumped off the bed and covered Perry's mouth.

Well, I had no idea I had that effect on Skyler. It's nice to feel wanted. If only I could trust him not to revert to his lady killer ways. "Yes, I'm that Kax Tillion, the one he won't stop hitting on."

Michael got up and grabbed his clothes off the floor. "Skyler, stop hitting on Kax, she doesn't like you."

Perry jerked away, making Skyler let go. "So, if you don't like him why do you have a key and come visit him? Sounds like you're being a tease."

Kax had never thought of it like that. *Am I, leading Skyler on?* Kax ran her hand through her hair and sighed. "Because we're friends. Me, Michael and Skyler. Michael gave me the key. Skyler just wants to be more than friends."

Her heart rate increased. *Maybe one day we will be, when Skyler grows up and stops acting like a horny rabbit.*

Skyler awkwardly smiled. "Well I'm fine with just being friends, sweetie. Just if you ever change your mind, the doors open."

I'll hold you too that, when you grow up.

"So, what are you doing here?" Perry asked.

Kax shrugged her shoulders. "Well, I didn't see you guys yesterday and I have nothing planned today. I was wondering, if you guys would like to do something. But it looks like Michael, is in no condition to do anything."

Michael put on his jacket, "No, I'm awake and ready for anything."

"It's Saturday, and I was wondering if you would like to go up to the cabin, for the weekend?"

"There's four of you, the bike only holds three?"

Perry smiled. "This cabin sounds cool. If you want, I have a car. I could drive us."

Skyler teased Perry. "Sorry you can't come dude, members only."

Kax could see a disappointed look on Perry's face. "Perry can come, this isn't an exclusive club."

Perry pumped his fists in the air. "Woo, I can go to the cabin."

Skyler groaned. "Thanks, Kax, I was just teasing him."

"And maybe I'm just teasing you." Kax smirked, *With Perry and Michael around, I will be easily distracted from Skyler's charm.*

***

Skyler and Perry made themselves at home on the couch, watching the holo-tv. Michael was in the kitchen, cooking them a late lunch. While Kax worked in the basement, getting the spare room ready. She came up, a bit of time later. "Perry do you want me to show your room now?"

"Yeah, sure I would love to." He got off the couch and followed her down to the basement.

"I'm sorry this room is in the basement, it is my brother's room and he can't walk stairs. Good news is you're right on ground level. The backyard is right through that screen door. If you want to go to the kitchen you can take the indoor stairs, or the ramp on the porch. It does get cold down here at night, so gave you a few extra blankets. There is also another couch and TV down here. You can enjoy it, like a little apartment."

Perry walked around looking at the Seafoam walls and the out-of-date couch facing the smaller holo-tv. He followed her into the bedroom.

"This is your bed, sorry there is medical equipment in here. We keep back up for when he comes up here."

Perry sat on the bed testing its firmness. "This is a nice bed. But might I ask, what's up with your brother?"

Kax sat down on the bed, next to Perry. "He's in a wheelchair. Paralyzed from the waist down, has been from birth. He was the runt of the litter. Catillions don't have one kid at a time they have litters of three to five. My sister and me turned out fine, but my brother got a deformed spine. The doctors have done lots for him, but he is never going to walk."

Perry put his arm around her, to comfort her then peeked behind her. "If you're a Catillion where is your tail?"

Kax pointed, to the fluffy ears on the top of her head. "Not all have tails. My mom, my brother and sister do. My dad and I don't. All Catillions used to have tails, but they have been fading out."

"That's an interesting story. I have a little sister." He pulled out the picture of his family and handed it to Kax.

"Oh, she looks so sweet. It's nice to have a friend who has siblings, Skyler and Michael are only children. But that's common, in our generation. Lots of people were left single parents in the war, so not as many kids were born."

Perry nodded. "One of the benefits of being on a colony, is the wars usually don't come to you. They attack the main planets but not the weak colonies, it's almost like they just want to hurt Earth and not wipe out human life."

"Or they know that the colonies are reliant on Earth and other planets," Skyler said walking into the room. "Sorry to barge in, but foods ready."

Kax had the feeling Skyler had been eavesdropping. She could tell by the look in his eyes that he was jealous.

Perry looked up at Skyler. "You know the colonies can make their own food and supplies, right?"

Skyler shook their head. "Not as much as you would think. You can live but I have some books on how much Earth sends for maintenance to the colonies. If Earth was destroyed or could not send supplies anymore, you would have no more than a year of life support. The Cass don't attack because they know there is no need. The colonies would be nothing without support from Earth."

Perry was doubtful. "You can be a real downer."

Kax looked at Perry and gave him a hug. "Skyler that was mean, that colony is Perry's home. Don't tell him that they're doomed."

"I was not saying they're doomed, just without Earth they are on their own and will need to get help from other planets. Some might make it, but Colony G is too close to Earth. It would be hard."

"Just shut up about it now, Skyler. I will talk to you later." Kax snapped at him.

Michael called down the stairs. "Are you coming up? The food is ready."

Kax and Skyler glared at each other before going up for dinner.

Chapter 23

Kax tossed and turned in her bed. She kicked the sheets off and then peeled them back. No matter what position she was in she could not seem to fall back to sleep. There were too many thoughts going through her head. She got her up and made her way down to the kitchen. The clock read 3 a.m. The thoughts of the upcoming war and mission were weighing on her. She went into the fridge and started making herself a snack.

"Hey, you can't sleep either?"

She spun around, with a butter knife in hand. "Who said that?"

Perry held his hands up in the air. "Whoa, calm down Kax. I'm just here to get a snack."

Kax put the knife down on the counter. "Sorry Perry, I'm just a little on edge."

"Don't worry about it. Who wouldn't be with a war this close." He walked over and grabbed two pieces of bread. He began to make himself a sandwich.

"You're a science officer, you have less to worry about. You're not going to be sent to the front lines."

Perry scoffed, "I might not be dying on the front, but I will be working behind the scenes. Making new weapons that will kill people. To me, that is a fate worse than death. Knowing my work is put people to death."

Kax took her lunch meat sandwich and sat down at the kitchen table. "Wow, I never thought of it that way."

"If I were to work with making weapons, I would try to make ones that could do some good. Find a way to outweigh the negative. Like bombs that had seeds in them to grow plants."

"You and your plants." She took a bite out of her sandwich. "That makes sense. I never really thought of it like that before. I mean, I'm a pilot and I must be the one to shoot the lasers. It didn't occur to me that there are innocent people on the other side…"

"They do a good job at desensitizing us, that's why." Perry finished making his sandwich and sat across from Kax at the table.

"So why not just quit the forces and move back home?"

"Because I will still need a job. I love plants and I want to one day be working in the hydroponic garden, or something to do with terraforming. This is my only way. But I just know they will be sending me to make weapons, one way or another before then. We all do things we don't want to in war."

"You're not helping my insomnia." Kax said looking down at her sandwich.

Perry bit into his food. "Do you think of ever going back to your home world?"

She narrowed her eyes. "Earth is my home world."

He cleared his throat. "Oh, I'm sorry I just assumed with the ears…"

"It's fine. I was born on Catillion, but I have lived most of my life on Earth. I wouldn't mind going back to visit, but it's not my home, Earth is. My Mom moved us to earth when we were about a year old. My brother moved back to Catillion for medical help and my sister moved to to take care for him. My dad is on Earth still. He has a condo in the city." Kax turned her head. She heard the front door open and shut. She put her sandwich down on the plate and called out. "Who's there?"

Skyler's voice called back. "It's just me, no need to worry." He entered the kitchen a moment later and glanced between them. "So, what you two doing up?"

"Kax and me had problems sleeping. What were you doing out? I didn't even notice you left."

Skyler sat down next to Kax and invited himself to half her sandwich. "Ya, I got called into the base and just got back."

Kax narrowed her eyes. "Why would they call you back? They didn't call any of us back in?"

"O'Brien just wanted to go over some stuff with me, is all. No big deal." Skyler got up and went into the fridge and grabbed a beer. "You two want one?"

"Yeah, get me one, buddy," Perry called out.

Skyler came back to the table and slid Perry his beer. "So, both of you had problems sleeping? Were you two together?"

That jealous bastard. Kax's jaw dropped. "No! We were not...I'm not that kind of girl."

"Dude, do you have a problem with us being friends?" Perry asked. "You seem to move right in whenever me and Kax get a moment."

Skyler slammed his beer down and glared at Perry. "I just want to know where we all stand."

"Friends, that's where we all stand." Kax stated, "We are all just friends. I know you like me, Skyler, but until you grow up, we're just friends." She finished her sandwich.

Skyler took a long sip of his beer. "Well then, if there is nothing to worry about I'm going to get some sleep."

Chapter 24

At lunch Skyler was sitting at the table next to Perry, Michael on the other side sitting next to Kax. Skyler was drinking a beer, with his lunch of fish and chips.

Michael narrowed his eyes at Skyler. "So, where did you go last night?"

Skyler picked his head up from his plate. "Like I told Kax and Perry I got called in and had to just pick up some paperwork."

"I don't buy it. Especially since the paperwork you have been doing is on your tablet. So, what is it?"

"You told us it was O'Brien who wanted to see you, not paperwork." Perry pointed out. "Where were you really?"

Skyler went back to his food, not saying a word. A moment later his eyes widened. He lifted his head from his plate with a large grin. "Kax is that your foot I'm feeling under the table?"

She batted her eyelashes. "It is, and I will keep doing it, only if you tell me what happened last night. I'm now curious."

Damn Kax is a tease, she doesn't like me but then she does this. Oh man, I wish she would do more. Skyler put down his fork. "You guys really want to know?" He paused trying not to moan, "Last night, I went to see O'Brien for some afterhours simulation tests. We do have time booked for after classes, but he had just gotten in a new program and wanted to do a test run with me before classes."

Michael raised an eyebrow. "That was it? I mean, why so secretive?"

Skyler took a bite of his food. "Because these simulations are not for school credit, they're practice for the upcoming war and our summer mission."

"And you spilled the beans, because a hot girl played footsies with your?" Perry spoke up. "That's not really good if you become a captain."

"This isn't just any hot girl, that was Kax. I would tell and do anything for her."

"Dude, you really have to watch that. Kax is your weakness. Never let the enemy find out." Perry added.

Skyler paused and glanced over at Kax. *I don't trust her with Perry. What if she likes him more? I know she said we're all friends, but I'm not so sure.*

Kax looked back at him, with sad eyes. She stood up. "Find someone else to be your weakness." She grabbed her plate, and walked away.

Skyler was dumbstruck. "Um, what did I say?"

"Too much," Michael said.

Perry left his plate and went after Kax.

***

She went to her bedroom, to think and have time to herself.

Perry followed her. He knocked on her open door-frame. "Kax, do you want talk about this?"

"Come in." She turned to face him. Her face covered in tears. "Perry, even if I explained it to you I don't think you will understand."

Perry entered the room and sat at the end of the bed. "I think I will."

She let out a deep breath. "Ok but you have to promise not to tell anyone."

Perry nodded. "I promise."

"I do like Skyler. I'm just not sure I'm ready to like him. Oh, dear I sound like I'm in high school. I want us to stay friends. At least for now and I'm not sure if I'm ready to date a guy like that. There is a war coming, I should be worried about my work, not boys. Skyler is so immature. Also, he says he likes me. He is sleeping with all those women; how do I know he is not lying and just wants to make me a notch on his bedpost."

"I totally get it. But I want you to know Skyler, He sees you as more than just a girl." Perry face went red, "I'm not good at putting this into words. But he is serious about you. I have seen him with other women. They mean nothing those are just because I think he needs someone. There is more to him than he lets people know. I don't know if any of this is making sense."

She stretched and gave him a kiss on the cheek. "I think I get it."

Perry's body shook. "Um, what was that for?" His face went bright red, "Kax, I think you're cute. I will admit, I did like you when I first saw you. You're an amazing girl and I want you to stay. Just put up with Skyler a bit more. But um..."

"You are like a brother to me Perry. I don't know you that well, but you should meet my brother Tom you two are very much alike." She brushed the curls out of Perry's face.

"You're a nice girl and I'm glad Skyler introduced us, I wish I had a girlfriend as nice as you."

She gave him a hug. "You will make a wonderful boyfriend to a very lucky girl one day."

Chapter 25

"Okay class, time for battle simulator. This mission I'm not going to tell you what you need to watch out for. Your mission is to go to the neutral zone, deliver food supplies, receive their cargo of clothes and other goods. This is a peaceful mission of trade. I will tell you that this planet has begun to side more towards the Harcargs's. Their support is moving away from the federation. Remember to treat these simulations as if you were on a real mission." O'Brien looked at his class, "Okay, class, get in your positions."

Skyler listened with the rest of the class. When O'Brien was done explaining he saw Kax go up and talk to O'Brien. He listened in on their conversation.

"Sir, I would like to be on Therris' crew this mission."

He narrowed his eyes. "I don't think that is a good idea, remember the other times. That's why I switched you with Warner."

"Sir, I'm confident that me and Skyler will not have any issues. Please let me be Skyler's pilot."

What about the other times? I just wanted to protect Kax, so I sent her in an escape pod. He paused and replayed that thought in his mind. "Oh, I see, I have to take the risk." He whispered to himself.

O'Brien typed in a few things on his tablet and called out. "Warner, you're in crew B now. Tillion is taking your place."

Skyler went and took his seat at the center of the bridge. *Yes, I get to be captain again! Missions suck when I get a different assignment. These chairs are so fun to spin.* He stopped spinning in his captain's chair when Kax stepped onto the bridge.

"Good day, Captain Therris." She sat down on at the helm.

The lights went down, and the door closed. O'Brien's voice came over the intercom.

"Okay, class simulation starts now."

A view of the nearby planet came on the screen ahead of them.

Skyler pressed the intercom to engineering button, on his controls. “Prepare the cargo for transport to the planet.”

The first officer looked at Skyler. “Sir, are you planning an away party to go down to the planet?”

Skyler shook his head. “No need, I will call the planet and do the negotiations here.” He turned in his seat towards the communications booth. “Pull up the communications to the planet.”

“Aye sir,” The four-armed green alien said.

A blue-haired, pig-nosed alien appeared on the screen. “Your delivery is on time I see. Thank you, we will be sending up our half of the bargain.”

“The federation will always keep up their end of the bargain and we will deliver these supplies to the people of Earth. You will always have a friend in the federation.”

The Harcarg read the screen down at the screen. “The transportation of the cargo has been completed.”

“Thank you. And I will send you a message when the cargo has been delivered.”

“I wouldn’t expect anything less.” The communications were cut.

Skyler turned in his seat towards the helm. “Officer Tillion, take us on the path through the neutral zone for as long as we can. Take the jump gate at Sagitarion.”

Tillion turned around in her seat. “Captain, we are on a time limit.”

“That’s why I said take the Sagitarion gate. We pay a small fee but can go 3 times as far, we will make up for time.”

The first officer turned to Skyler. “Captain, explain to me why you want to stay in the neutral zone?”

“To stop a war, officer, do you think an unfriendly planet like that is going to let us leave without being followed? Once we leave the neutral zone, there will be a ship of Cass waiting for us. We won’t make the delivery on time. So, we stay here and throw them off.”

“But in the neutral zone we could be attacked by pirates easier.”

"True, but we can handle pirates. They can be bought, and we will have the chance to save the cargo. There are other ships in transporter range, that could take the cargo."

"Captain, if they are as untrustworthy as you say, why don't we search their cargo they might have hidden something or sabotaged it?"

"Then run an x-ray on the cargo, but I trust that they would not harm their own cargo and people. They are losing trust in us, why would they sabotage us?"

The first officer nodded "You're right Captain, sorry for questioning your judgment."

They flew further into the neutral zone. Skyler turned in his seat. "Navigation officer, keep those scans on high we are having to keep watch for anything that may show up. Anything at this point will be a threat."

Kax looked at her screen. "Captain there is a Cassiopeian ship approaching us."

"Open channels, I want to talk to them."

The communications officer hit a few buttons. "They are not responding."

There was a loud thunk.

Skyler stood up, and he hit the intercom. "We are being boarded, battle stations everybody now! Code RED!"

He got up and ran off the bridge, to the armory. Kax and a few bridge crew followed. They grabbed their weapons.

Skyler whirled around to face Kax. He grabbed her hand and pulled her towards the escape pods.

She pushed him away from her. "No Skyler, I will not abandon this ship. I'm a crew member, just like anyone else, and I will fight!"

"You are not like everyone else, I care about you and you are my friend, I never want to see you get hurt! Now get in the pod, that is an order!"

"I will not get in the pod. You as a captain are supposed to care about everyone on this ship equally, and right now you are putting my safety above others. We have no time to waste and if you care about me so much you say, you will respect me as a person and let me fight."

Skyler paused, his confidence failing. "Ok Kax, you're right. Go fight and help win this."

She smiled and sprinted with Skyler to the center of the action.

The Cass boarded the ship, through a hole that they made in the hull. Skyler inspected the damage. *Shit, how are we going to fix that when this is done?* He held his weapon tight, when he saw the Cass captain. Their captain was wearing a brown and gold uniform, with red and brown tattoos on his face. His horns were long. He hissed, when he saw Skyler. "Sso yous ares the Captain of thiss sship?"

"Yes, I am Captain Therris, and you are?"

"I ams Lord Jexloss and I demands yous hands over thiss ships and the Harcargss cargos." He gave Skyler a death stare.

"And if I don't?" Skyler stood his ground.

Lord Jexloss held his gun towards Skyler's head. "Then alls yours crews will dies."

Skyler stared into his cold dead brown eyes. He took a deep breath. "If that is the way it has to be." He pushed Kax against the wall away from him and ducked. He rolled on the floor and aimed his gun at Jexloss's stomach and fired away.

Jexloss fell to the ground. The Cass crew started firing everywhere, and the crew shot back. Skyler got back on his knees and went to see Jexloss. His eyes were still open, and he snapped his fingers. Two of his men dropped fire and grabbed Skyler's arms, restraining him. Jexloss struggled to get up. He walked away from the battle, with Skyler and the two guards who ushered him to their ship.

Skyler tried his best to struggle and break away from them. But their grip just got harder.

They dragged him to what looked like their med bay. They began strapping him into a dental like chair.

Jexloss grinned like the devil himself. "Sso Captain yous thoughts you weres sso tough. Your crews iss going to bes deads ssoon and yous ares on my sship. Thiss coulds have alls beens avoided ifs yous just ssurendered."

"I will never surrender, this is my ship, and this is my crew. I made a promise to the Harcargs that I would get their cargo to them on time and I never break a promise!"

Jexloss clutched kyler by the throat. “Yous a sstuborn little brats. Yous thinks yous gots balls ssaying those thingss to mes? Wells nots for longs.”

The two guards held up sharp and odd shaped tools.

“I’s won’t kills yous but I wants infos froms yous abouts the United Galactic Forcess and brings yours sship back tos the palaces. Yous wills makes a nice pets.”

The guards got dangerously close to Skyler’s man parts.

He tried to struggle away, but the straps were too tight.

“Yous will makes a fines Eunuch.” Jexloss teeth showed in his grin.

Then before Skyler could scream they all turned to dust in front of him.

Kax appeared behind the burning ash cloud. She smiled. “Page 41 of our textbooks, Cassiopeians’ weakness is fire?” She went over to his chair and started to unstrap him.

He sat up rubbed his wrist. He leaned up and kissed Kax on the lips. “Thanks, you just saved my balls.”

Her jaw dropped in shock. “It’s just a simulation.”

“Ya, but it’s still not something you want to happen.”

She helped him up out of the chair. “Come on, the crew has taken care of the rest of them. Only a few casualties but we can still make it on time.”

Skyler walked with Kax back to his ship. “How are we going to do that? We have another ship attached to us and it has a big hole in the main hallway?”

She smiled at him. “You’re the Captain, you're supposed to know. But a Captain asking for help is not weakness.” They jumped down back onto their ship. “Well, you have two options. We have enough crew to drive the ships together and get there on time or we disconnect them and close the main hall till we get back to Earth?”

Skyler grinned. “Take the two ships together, we have a schedule to keep.” They made their way to the bridge. “Did you burn up all the Cass?”

She shook her head. “Nope, the ones who surrendered we took to the brig.”

With the attack over, there was nothing stopping them from completing the mission on time and as planned.

Captain O'Brien called out. "End simulation." He walked over to Skyler first, "5 casualties but you defeated the Cass and kept the trust with the Harcarg. Very impressive, Captain Therris. You have a few things to learn but that's expected for your age."

Chapter 26

Kax went up to and knocked on Jake and Ron's door. Ron answered, in his underwear. "Kax? Is it Tuesday already? I forgot what day it was."

Jake walked behind Kax, wearing his blue robe. He must have been down the hall in the bathroom. "Hey Kax, it's Tuesday already?"

She turned around, to look at Jake. "Class just got out less than an hour ago and you're already naked, did you two have plans?"

Jake walked into the room. "I just had a shower and me and Ron were going to spend some time together alone, but we forgot it's Tuesday, and we have 6 other days to spend with each other."

"I can leave, if you two want to be alone?"

"Stay, there will be plenty of time later tonight. Ron is taking medical leave off from school tomorrow. We both have surgeries."

She stepped into the room, and closed the door, "Wait, you both have surgeries, but Ron is taking medical leave?"

"I'm just getting my ears done a couple of hours and I will be fine. Finally going to have human ears and won't have to wear these elf ears no more. Ron is going for his bone shortening surgery."

Ron put his clothes on, "Yup I'm going to be 5'9 tomorrow now. Goodbye 7'7 I will be able to finally shop at human clothing stores." He went to the closet and pulled out a pair of blue jeans and a black t-shirt that read HUMAN, "I bought this to wear home from my surgery."

"I'm so happy for you, I hope it goes well and I wish you the best."

Jake sat down on his bed and pulled out a notebook from the desk drawer. "Ok so where did we leave off?"

She sank onto the end of the bed next to him. "Something to do with Palmov."

Jake smiled. "You mean Palmot it was the table manners when you are with a group of Squallite's."

"Ya, about that I have been eating food with Michael for a long time. And I have never seen him eat the way you do, why is that?"

Jake shared a look with Ron. "I'm not trying to put your friend down in any way, but Michael doesn't really act like a Squallite. Sam his father, likes humans too much. He has passed their customs onto his son. Michael doesn't realize how human he acts."

I wonder if Michael realizes this? She looked down at her feet, "Oh I see. Is that a bad thing?"

Ron laughed, "For us it's not, but when he tries to act like he is this super orthodox Squallite, he is very far off. Don't tell him we said that, he will get all preacher on our asses."

"You would like that wouldn't you Ron?" Jake winked.

"Not in front of the girl," Ron snapped back.

Jake leaned in and whispered into Kax's ear. "He has a thing for Michael."

Kax blushed and covered her face. *Oh my, only if Michael were here. I should probably tell him he doesn't act much like a Squallite as he thinks.*

Ron rolled his eyes, "Great you told her. Can we just get on with tonight's lesson?"

Jake nodded and flipped through his book. "Ok let's go with a short lesson tonight. Here is one it's called Yakitoc, it is part of spring. Well Squallites celebrate it the same time of year humans celebrate the first day of spring. It's more of a small feast. We take what food survived the winter, and share it amongst the people in the village or city. We put on our orange robes again and bring all our remaining food to the town center where there will be people cooking and setting up tables. Everyone helps. It's helps bring us out of our homes for the winter and allow us to catch up."

"Interesting. Is there a certain day when this happens? Because the first day of spring isn't always that nice of weather?"

"This isn't Earth spring. Traditionally it didn't have a set date because we would just wait till we could leave our homes. In the time before that when we lived in trees, it was the day the ground wasn't covered in snow and the vegetation came back. But now we do it at a set time. Nowadays we have better food storage, so we just plan for the last Sunday of your June. Our seasons are different than Earth ones"

"So, anything else special about this?"

Ron spoke up, "Not much, but it is a good way to gain 20lbs in one sitting."

Jake turned his head to Ron, "You are so vain." He looked back at Kax, "He is right though you do eat a lot."

"That's ok Catillions have a high metabolism. We love to eat."

"Squallites do too, we need the vitamins to fuel our tall bodies. But our bodies store vitamins differently so we need less and less as we get older."

"Ok so what else happens besides this feast?"

Jake and Ron exchanged glances.

Ron spoke up. "Not much. I haven't been back there in a few years but besides food there is a nice festival, but it is required of all Squallites to participate."

Kax smiled. "Sounds very lovely."

Jake checked the time on his watch. "Kax as much as we love your company, we both need some rest before the big day tomorrow."

Kax packed up her things. "No problem, and I wish you both all the best."

Chapter 27

Michael looked up from his desk and saw Perry struggling to carry a tray of plants into engineering. He got up from his desk and went over to help with the tray. "Perry what are you doing, in engineering with a tray of plants? Water is banned here."

Perry handed Michael the tray. "Commodore Ipinik ordered a tray of these plants. They don't need water to survive."

"Well, if Ipinik approved them, where do you want them?"

Perry pulled out his pocket tablet and read the screen. "Engineering room 3T."

Michael raised an eyebrow, "3T? That's my experiment office, why would Ipinik send you there?"

"Because I want you to expand your ideas and use these plants." Ipinik's booming voice came from behind them.

Michael jerked around, "Sir, I didn't see you there."

"No worries Jones, let's just get to the room and I will explain your assignment."

They all made their way into engineering room 3T.

Michael placed the tray of plants on the desk, and Ipinik locked them inside the room.

"The higher-ups are impressed with your work on the alloy and would like you to do more work. I told them you had an interest in plants, so I called in one of the top budding Botany Cadets to assist you." Ipinik stated.

Michael turned his gaze to Perry. "Perry, you're one of the top Botany cadets?"

Perry modestly scratched his head, "It's not something I brag about, but yes I am."

You learn something new every day. Michael thought.

"Good you two know each other, that will make things easier. The assignment is to develop a plant that can benefit the war and the soldiers. It could be a weapon or a new set of rations. Put your minds together and create something."

Perry smiled with glee. "Oooo it is a genetic engineering assignment, these are my favorite."

. "Have fun you two, I have faith in you." Ipinik unlocked the door and then left the two alone.

Michael turned to Perry, "So plants?"

"Plants," Perry smiled excitedly.

Chapter 28

Skyler awoke to the drone of his communicator buzzing. He reached over and answered it. "Hello, Captain Therris, speaking."

"Cadet Therris, how many times have I told you not to answer your phone like that?"

Skyler rubbed his eyes. "Sorry, Cane, it is a habit."

"Habit or not, stop it. I want to see you in my office ASAP."

"Got it, I will be right there." He hung up and got out of bed. He shook the arm of the girl next to him. "Hey time to wake up, I got to go."

She sat up and rubbed her face. "Will I see you again?"

"If you want to call me, you have my number." He finished getting dressed and headed towards Cane's office. Skyler walked in and sat in his usual chair. "Good morning sir, what did you want to see me about?"

"I have been looking over your reports from Captain O'Brien of the last year, and I must say they're very impressive. You have the highest scores in the simulator I have seen in years. What is your secret?"

Skyler grinned. "I was born to be a captain is all, nothing more. And I am certain O'Brien told you that I have been taking extra lessons with him to prepare for this summer."

"I am impressed, but I just wanted to check." Cane paused. "Skyler, be honest with me. Are you cheating?"

Cheating? How dare he. I have wanted to, but I have worked hard. What makes him think that? I do something right for once in my life and I'm accused of breaking rules. Skyler shot Cane a sharp glare. "No, sir!"

"Then how do you have all those officer's security codes on your tablet?"

Skyler brushed his hair back. "Oh that. My ex gave it to me. Roxanne Smith, she is a security cadet and gave me a few of the higher officer's security clearances. That has nothing to do with O'Brien's class though. I have never used those codes, just collected them. With O'Brien's class, it comes easy. Because I have read all the books." Skyler narrowed his eyes. "How did you know about the codes?"

Cane took a deep breath. "When a cadet is accused of cheating, we have no choice but to hack his personal cadet data and scan first. That is where a few of the codes popped up. I'm going to have to ask you to destroy all your records of those security codes."

Skyler's face went red, he shifted his face to the side. "You looked at everything, sir? Isn't that an invasion of privacy?"

"When you are a cadet, everything you own or that has been issued to you belongs to us, it is just on rental to you. So, we can search it at any time. We did find no evidence you were cheating. If you willingly destroy the codes, you will not be penalized for it, since there is no evidence you used them. But they're not your codes and you are not authorized to use them. No matter who gave them to you. If you type in a code and it says anything besides a Skyler Logan Therris then it is not yours to use. So, delete any record of that or anyone else's codes."

Skyler nodded. "Yes, sir, I will do that."

Cane shuffled some papers around on his desk. "There is one more reason I wish to talk to you Skyler."

"Yes sir?"

"Since there is no evidence to support you are cheating. That means you will be advancing in your studies a little faster than other cadets. You are already doing this as a 2nd year advanced. 3rd year advanced are usually ready for graduation or do mostly field work for their 4th year. But when you joined, you signed on for the full 7 years with only one division. So, my question is, how do you want to continue your career? You could choose to pick up a second division,"

If he graduated at 4 years, he would be given some low ranking job. Skyler didn't want to take orders from anyone. He would rather stick to the plan and get his experience as a cadet. Skyler took a long pause. "Sir, I want to just want to be a captain. I will take whatever classes you throw at me."

Cane laughed. "I wish I was that ambitious when I was younger. I wanted to be a captain, but I thought doing all my work and showing up on time would get me that promotion. All command Cadets want to be a captain when they join, but few get to be. You have the brains for it but are just missing the experience."

"Did you ever get to be a captain?"

Cane shook his head. "Technically, but I think it was only for about three months before they gave me the promotion to commodore. After your father died, they needed someone to do all the paperwork and fill out the logs. The ship was in the condition it is now. But technically for three months, I held the rank. I was so jealous of your father."

Skyler leaned closer in his chair. "You were jealous?"

Cane sighed, reached into his filing desk and pulled out a bottle of sherry. "Your father had everything I ever wanted and was younger. The job, the wife, kid, good looks, charisma." He poured two glasses, "He realized this usually when it was too late, but he did the best to share or give me everything I wanted."

Skyler took his glass. "That's why you are looking out for me?"

Cane sipped his drink. "No, I would do that for anybody who made such a big impact on my life. But I did promise your father, I would watch over you. I personally want you to succeed, so I will look at what can be done to best further your career and go from there. I'm not going to let you fail."

Skyler finished his glass. "Sir, before I go...if getting this orb is so important and necessary, why are you waiting for this summer for us to go and collect it?"

"There are lots of background politics going on. This orb will start working as soon as we get it. So, we can wait until the last moment to get it. Also, by being 100 percent ready it will give us a more convincing argument in obtaining it. That answer your question?"

"Yes, it does sir." Skyler placed his glass the desk and stood up. "I will see you later."

"See you later."

Chapter 29

Kax walked by O'Brien's classroom. She was wandering down the halls later than normal, returning from one of her piloting exercises that ran long. She saw a light on in O'Brien's class. Curious, she leaned in to peek through the window on the door. She saw Skyler walking towards the simulator with O'Brien.

Is this is the night he did his extra training? She knew she shouldn't but decided to check up. She placed her hand on the doorknob and walked in. She went to the back room, where Skyler was sitting in the captain's chair of the simulator.

Skyler spun in the chair. He stopped and stared right into Kax's eyes. "Kax, what are you doing here?"

O'Brien called out. "Simulation will begin in five, four, three, two-"

Skyler pressed the button on the chair, to communicate with O'Brien. "Wait, stop!"

It was too late, the simulation began, and now she was in the middle of it.

Kax watched the view screen and saw there was a group of Cass ships surrounding the ship. "What's going on?"

"I'll explain it later. No time, just follow my lead." He turned in his chair and faced the view screen.

The Cass leader spoke. "Captain Therris wes have yours sship ssurrounded. Handss over thes worms orb or wes wills have nos choice buts to destroys yous."

Skyler grinned. "You're not going to destroy this ship, because if you did that the orb would be destroyed. I think you are best to just step aside and allow us to pass. If you board, my crew will be more than happy to blow you away."

"Iss Thats a challenge sss?"

"What do you think?"

Kax's jaw dropped. *I know this is a simulation, but he is sure acting cocky and overconfident.* She took the first officer's seat, next to Skyler. She shifted in her chair and whispered into Skyler's ear. "What are you doing?"

Skyler narrowed his eyes. "I'll explain it later. Just play along."

"Ares yous havings issues withs yours first officer, Captains?" The Cass Gul put on an evil grin.

Skyler shot a nasty glare at the Gul. "No issues here. Now I think you were about to concede and move your ships."

"Wells wes have moved ours sshipss. Ands haves attached thems to yours hulls. The orbs wills ssoons be ourss and sso wills yous." The Cass bared his teeth.

Skyler stood up, and went over the navigation desk. He took off his sidearm and tossed it to Kax. "You're going to need this, follow me to deck C."

Kax ran after Skyler. "What is going on?"

Skyler stayed focused ahead. "I can't pause the simulation, but this is what I have been doing every week in extra training with O'Brien. Testing out every possible outcome for this summer's mission. It's normally the same, but he changes something each time. This time O'Brien had them attack Deck C, that's the engineers' living quarters and close to the vault. They are very close to the orb."

Kax tried to keep up with Skyler. "You gave me your gun, do you have a way to defend yourself?"

Skyler stopped to pull up his pant leg. He withdrew a smaller gun. "This will just have to do."

Kax froze when they got to deck C. Dead holographic bodies littered the floor, of both forces officers and Cass.

Kax watched, Skyler lean down and retrieve one the fallen soldiers' guns. He placed it in his side holsters. There was a large hole blasted in the wall, to the room where the orb was being held. Skyler readied his gun and approached the opening in the wall. He halted, when he stood in front of the opening.

Kax stood behind him and her heart dropped. "No, Michael!"

They both saw the Gul Cass, clutch the hologram of Michael in a chokehold in one hand and worm orb in the other.

"Wells Captains. I wills gives yous a choice." He tightened the grip on Michael's neck. "I will give you the orb and your friend dies. Or I can give you your friend and keep the orb. What will it be?"

Skyler stood frozen. Kax could see, the confidence drain out of him.

Skyler took a deep breath and lowered his guns to the ground. "I'll give you a better deal. I surrender. You can have the ship, the orb, my crew and me." He put his hands behind his head. He made a gun symbol, with his one hand.

Kax understood the message.

The Cass Gul released his grip, of the holographic Michael and placed the orb down. He whipped out his blade and pressed it to Skyler's throat. "I'ms goings tos enjoys thiss."

Kax readied her gun and took two shots at the Cass, pushing him back.

Skyler grabbed the gun off the floor and got up and shot the Cass in the knee. "I will be taking your ship, your crew, and the orb now."

The simulation ended. Kax flew forward and gave Skyler a big hug. "Oh, Skyler, I was so worried."

He hugged her back. "I wasn't. But I'm glad you were there."

Without thinking and full of relief Skyler was alive and safe she planted a kiss on his lips. "Don't ever worry me like that again."

"I can't make a promise like that, in this line of work."

O'Brien entered the room. "Well Skyler, you did quite well this time. But next time, tell me that Kax or anyone else is going to be joining you and I will adjust the simulation. She might be the only reason you survived this time."

"It was my fault, sir," Kax stated, "I saw the light on and Skyler. I was just checking on him when I ended up getting involved with the simulation."

"It's fine Kax, you are welcome to join in anytime you want." He turned to Skyler. "So, do you want to run another, or is one near-death experience good enough for you tonight?"

"One is good sir. I'm certain Kax, is a little too shaken up to run another."

Kax nodded. "It was fun sir, but I would like to just get some rest now."

"Alright, see you next week."

***

Skyler walked with Kax down the hall. "So, that's what I have been up to."

Kax smiled. "There is nothing to be embarrassed about, I'm impressed you are taking this so seriously."

"I always take being a captain serious. I just know when I have a moment to have fun I'm going to grab it and not waste it." He looked into her worried eyes. "It's actually kind of fun, having these extra sessions with O'Brien. He is a good guy. It's weird. I didn't really have a father. But since joining the academy Cane and O'Brien, have been taking me under their wing and treated me like their own son."

They got to Kax's dorm, and she opened the door. "That is so good to hear. Do you want a father?"

He shook his head. "I had a father, I don't want a replacement. But it's a nice feeling, having someone watch out for me."

She checked around, and saw that there was no roommate. "Hey Skyler, I guess my roommate is out for the night. Want to come in?"

Skyler tried to hide his grin and managed to say in a serious tone. "You're asking in a friendship way, right?"

She blushed. "I'm not sure, but after that scare I just know I don't want to be alone. Just pretend Michael is watching."

Skyler couldn't help but laugh as he entered the room. He sat down on her roommate's bed. "This is a nice room."

She unzipped her uniform. "Look away, I'm getting changed. And the room is the same as yours."

Skyler laid down and put his face in a pillow. "I know it is, I was just trying to make conversation."

"Well then tell me more about O'Brien being your father figure." She took off her tunic. She went into the drawer and pulled out her night pants and top.

"O'Brien isn't really a father figure. He already has two sons and a daughter. He admits he wasn't there for them. His second son is from his second wife, he was there for a bit more. But he was too busy with work. He says I'm like the son he never had."

She got the rest of her uniform off and started putting on her pajamas, a set with a purple tank top and purple short shorts. "I'm very happy for you. I hope all things work out." She finished getting dressed. "You can look now."

Skyler rolled over on the bed. "Purple and flannel, that's cute."

She took her uniform and placed it on a coat hanger. While hanging it up she gave her butt a little shake. "They're not flannel, they're soft but it's a material that regulates to your body temperature. So, you can sleep better in any climate. It's the same sleepwear the men get."

Damn she is such a tease. Skyler raised an eyebrow. "You can't do that, if you want me to stay in this bed. We got issued sleepwear? I don't remember that."

"Sorry," She batted her eyelashes. She pulled back the covers of her bed and got into bed. "Um, might I ask then what do you sleep in?"

He rolled onto his side and bent his legs up trying to cover his crotch. "Nude, I sleep in the nude. Always have."

She covered her face. "Oh, my why did I even ask. Well, Michael must wear them?"

Damn, I'm so tired even if Kax wanted me I couldn't. Skyler shook his head. "He doesn't sleep, just meditates, so he is in his briefs or sometimes he wears pants. And don't go asking about Perry either, he is a shorts guy too."

"You guys are so odd." She looked over at Skyler, who let out a loud yawn. "So, what is the real reason you're taking extra classes with O'Brien?"

I can't hide anything from Kax, at least not for long. He brushed his hair back. "Because I'm worried about this summer. We are going to be committing treason, and I'm not sure if I can stand for that. I do know this war has to end."

"And you think this orb will do that?" Kax burrowed under the covers.

Skyler's eyes started to close. "It will at least throw off the balance and give us an advantage." He laid his head back on the pillow.

Chapter 30

A loud screech woke Skyler up. He rubbed his head and saw a dark-haired girl in an orange uniform, standing next to the bed. "You know, women don't usually screech when they find me in their bed."

The roommate glared at him. “What are you doing in my bed?”

He sat up in the bed. “I came here to talk to Kax after classes, and I must have fallen asleep here Sorry. What’s wrong with that? I think the real question is, why weren’t you in your own bed?”

Kax started to wake up.

“It doesn’t matter. All that matters is, you’re not my boyfriend, so get out of my bed!” Her eyes flashed.

Skyler rubbed his face and stood up. “I’m sorry, okay, you can have your bed back. Lucky for you, I fell asleep in my uniform.”

Kax opened her eyes. “What is going on?”

The roommate turned around. “I know, I said it was okay if you brought a guy back to the room, but he is supposed to be in your bed, not mine!”

Skyler frowned. “Hey, I said I was sorry. I’m leaving now, and just so you know I didn't touch anything.”

Skyler went over to Kax, who was now sitting up. He gave her a kiss on the cheek. “See you later, sweetie.”

Kax just sat there shocked and confused.

He winked before he walked out the door. Skyler made his way down the hall, heading to the cafeteria for breakfast.

“Hey Skyler, wait up!” called a familiar voice behind him.

Skyler stopped, turned around and smiled when he saw Perry. “Hey buddy, what’s up?”

“I was about to ask you that. When was the last time you were awake for breakfast?” They continued their way to the cafeteria.

“This is typically my bedtime.” Skyler laughed.

Perry sighed. “I wish I could stay up late. I’ve been working on projects with Michael. He makes you stick to a sleeping schedule. I did pop by the room last night, where were you?”

“I was with Kax last night.” Skyler raised an eyebrow, “You and Michael are working on a project together?”

Perry's eyes popped. “You finally slept with Kax? How in the world did that happen? You have to tell me everything!”

They got to the cafeteria, and both grabbed trays as they entered the line.

"I didn't sleep with her. We had a late night with class and I went to her room just to chat. I slept on her roommate's bed, who was out. That was all. Her roommate returned in the morning and kicked me out. Nothing happened between me and Kax." He grabbed a replicated fried egg sandwich off the counter. "It would have been nice if me and Kax did something, but nope I just passed out."

"I see," Perry picked up a fresh Cobb salad. "So, have you picked your summer assignment yet?"

Skyler froze. *Shit, I didn't tell Perry. Well, I mean, it is top secret, but what do I tell him?* "Um, well, not really sure about it yet. I haven't really applied too much."

They advanced further down the line to the checkout. "Well we don't have much time left, all the good ones will be taken soon. I'm trying to get something to do with plants, but they're all filling up. Is it wrong for me to just want to work in a greenhouse?"

Skyler laughed. He swiped his cadet card. "Follow me, I want to talk to you about something important."

Skyler motioned Perry to the back of the cafeteria, where there was a small hall that lead to the janitor's closet. No one could see them; there were no security cameras. It was a common spot for cadets to make out.

Perry followed Skyler. "Dude, this is an awkward time for you to tell me you like guys."

Skyler shot Perry a glare. "I'm not into men. I have to tell you a secret." They got to the spot and Skyler sat down on the cold stone floor.

Perry sat down next to him.

"Perry, I do have my summer plans all set up. -"

"You're not going back home to your mom's, are you?"

Skyler shuddered and snapped back. "No! I wouldn't dare go back there. What would make you think that?"

"Just you're being so secretive and uneasy about it. I thought maybe there was a reason you had to go."

"No, me, Michael and Kax have to go to Squall this summer. To go and get the worm orb. No one is to know right now, it's just a training mission on Squall. Only a few of us know why we are going. If you want I could talk to Cane and you could come with us?"

Perry put down his fork. "Wow, that's a serious mission. But I don't want to go to Squall. I'm trying to stay away from the war as much as possible. Thanks for the offer, but I just want to watch the grass grow."

Skyler put down his sandwich. "I totally understand."

"I would like to hang out with you guys more, but I'm trying to keep myself separate from this war. All I want to do with my career is get a job with the habitat systems on my home colony. I'm not a hero. I'm just a regular guy who dreams of working with plants and raising a family." Perry went back to finish his salad.

Skyler ate the rest of his sandwich. "Well then, Perry, before you go and live your vanilla lifestyle, I hope you continue to let me corrupt you."

Perry laughed. "There is nothing wrong with a little fun from time to time, but dude, what do you mean I'm vanilla? There is nothing wrong with wanting to have a regular family."

"Dude, that is the definition of vanilla. But you're right, there is nothing wrong with it." Skyler finished his sandwich and stood up. "Come on, let's get out of here before people start to talk."

"Or we could stay here longer and make them think you're giving me the full treatment." Perry joked.

Skyler grabbed Perry's tray, then pushed him out of the hall. "Don't make that joke, or I will say you tried to jump me."

"Well, you were the one who took me to the makeout corner of the cafeteria."

"Because I had to tell you a secret, and we needed breakfast. We can't take our lunch trays out of the cafeteria."

Perry shrugged. "I guess you had the right idea. I hope you have a good summer."

Skyler stood up and walked out, carrying a tray. "You know I will."

Perry's communicator buzzed. He pulled it out of his pocket and answered it. "Hello, Cadet Zyrix, speaking." He paused. "Okay, see you in 5 minutes, admiral." He hung up his communicator. And handed his tray to Skyler, "Got to go see Admiral Fir, she has called me to her office to talk about my summer. Wish me luck."

Before Skyler could say good luck, Perry dashed off.

Skyler took the two trays over to the return station. There was a tap on his shoulder. He turned his head and saw Kax.

"Skyler, I'm sorry my roommate kicked you out." Kax said.

"It's not the first-time roommates have kicked me out. Don't worry about it, are you okay?"

"Of course, I'm alright. I never realized how peacefully you slept on your own before. it was a surprise seeing you so relaxed. Also, you talk in your sleep." She stopped herself form saying more. "I'm sorry, I wanted to talk about your training sessions with O'Brien."

Skyler narrowed his eyes. "I'm aware of my sleep patterns, please don't make them public. But what do you want to know about me and O'Brien?"

She rubbed her arm. "I wanted to say, I think you are smart for doing those extra training sessions. And I think we work good as a team. I was wondering—"

"—If you could join me?" He smiled, *Kax you are such an amazing woman, I wish you were mine.* "Sure, I guess. Me and O'Brien do usually hang out after, but I don't see why he would have any objection to you." He paused. "You drink scotch, right?"

Before Kax could answer, Roxanne wrapped her arm around Skyler. "Hey captain." She kissed Skyler on the cheek.

Kax walked away with a disappointed look on her face.

Skyler jerked away, *Damn it, Roxanne, you ruin everything.* He snarled at Roxanne. "What are you doing here?"

Roxanne pressed another kiss on his lips. "I haven't heard from you in a while. Want to go to my room and have some fun?"

Skyler shoved her away, rage building in his eyes. "No, Roxanne. We broke up months ago, don't you remember? You tricked me into meeting your parents."

She gave him a pouty face. "I thought you would like to meet them, and that we were just taking some time off?"

He narrowed his eyes. “No, we broke off whatever we had, and it’s over.”

She leaned in closer to his ear and rubbed his leg. “I thought you couldn’t say no?”

Damn that feels good. Skyler held back his urges. He remembered how she hurt him and how they both wanted different things from each other. “No, Roxanne.” He pushed her away again. “I don’t know what is going on in your mind, but it is over, and I can say no to you.”

She gave him a nasty frown. “You know, I thought you were different. I thought maybe you just needed some time apart, but nope, you’re just a jerk.” She turned around and stormed off.

He felt the urge to fight back and correct her, and tell her that it was she who was delusional. He just shook his head. “She’s not my problem anymore.” He put his head down letting out a sigh of relief. “I got bigger things to worry about.”

Chapter 31

Michael placed his folded dress uniform into his suitcase. A look of remorse fell over his face. He signed and stared into his suitcase. There was a knock at the door. He didn’t take his eyes off his packed suitcase. “Come in.”

Kax entered the room. “Hey Michael, what’s going on?”

Michael stood there silent just staring at the suitcase. *Do I tell her?*

Kax placed her hand on Michael’s shoulder. “What’s gotten you this time?”

“I don’t know if I can do it, Kax. I don’t know if I can go through with this summer’s mission.”

Kax sat down on the bed next to the suitcase and patted the side of the bed. “Michael, sit down let’s talk this out.”

He took the spot next the Kax. He stared blankly at the wall. “I know, I have to be the one to get this orb, but I don’t know if I can betray my people.”

Kax put her arm around him. “Michael, you can do it. You will save so many lives. You need to be the one to do this. How is your father doing?”

I wish I could face my father. Michael buried his face in his hands. "My dad's doing well. I arranged for a health care nurse to watch him over this summer. I just wish I didn't have to be the one to get this orb. There are other Squallites in the forces that were born and raised on Earth."

Kax sighed. "You're different, even my friends Jake and Ron say you are different. They can't explain it, but even they see it."

Michael shot her a dirty look. "I don't mind you being friends with them, but I do not need them making decisions for me. You know my personal feelings about what they are doing-"

"Stop it. They weren't telling you what to do. They were just pointing out the obvious. I'm certain if they can see it, other Squallites can too. You're not like them." Tears came to her eyes. "Michael, I care about you."

Michael covered his face with his hand. "I can't do this, I can't betray my people."

"What people are those? You're an Earthborn Squallite who has federation citizenship. So what people are you betraying?"

He hit his fist on his leg and let out a scream. "Damn it, I'm a Squallite, that is my DNA, I'm not a human. This choice should be easy to make!"

Kax placed her hand on Michael's back. "Life isn't easy. I'm not going to tell you what choice to make, but what I will say is: I know whatever choice you make is the right one. Sometimes the Squallite way, isn't the right thing. Think about what side will benefit more."

Michael held back tears. "I wish things could go back to the way they were before. When my dad was healthy, and I was just going to be a boring engineer."

Kax picked up Michael's head and gazed into his eyes. "That's not how life works, but now you have me and Skyler by your side. We will give you strength."

He gave her a subtle smile. "I hope you're right."

KAY HAWKINS
PART 2
CHASING
THE STARS

Part 2

Michael sat up all called over to Skyler and said. “Hey Skyler, time to wake up!”

Skyler rolled over and went back into a deeper sleep. Michael got out of his bed, went over and shook Skyler’s shoulder and said. “Time to get up, now!”

Skyler rolled over and said. “Do we have to?”

Michael frowned. “You don't have to, but if not, you can watch your dreams of being a Captain wash away.”

Skyler yawned and sat up, in his bed and said. “It so doesn’t feel like morning, yet.”

Michael smiled sarcastically. “Ya, I know, a few more hours would be nice.”

Kax entered the room, dressed and ready to go. She laughed and pointed to Skyler and Michael who were next to each other in their underwear. “Good morning guys, I hope that’s not what you're wearing today,”

Skyler smirked. “Oh no, I only wear these for sleeping sometimes, I don't have a pair for daytime.”

Kax shook her head. “EW! That’s gross, thanks for the image you just put in my head.”

Skyler grinned and stood up. He put his thumbs in his waistband and said. “You want to see what’s underneath, to help that memory?”

Michael stood in front of him, blocking Kax from seeing anything else.

Kax covered her eyes and looked away. “I don't want to see your man bits, okay? Please, just get dressed.”

Skyler smiled and picked his uniform off the floor and said. “Do you want to watch me get dressed?”

Kax turned away. “You know what, I’m going to just wait in the hall. Michael, tell me when both of you are fully dressed.”

Skyler couldn’t stop laughing as he put his top on.

Michael gave him a disgusted look. “What is the matter with you? You say you like Kax and then, you do something like that, to turn her off.”

Skyler put his pants on and said, “Come on, women love my 'manly bits,' well, they’re more like large manly parts, but she hasn't seen them, how would she know?”

Michael turned away from Skyler, and got dressed. “I really don't need a better description than that.”

Michael and Skyler finish getting dressed. Michael then went to the door. He waved to Kax. “We are dressed, but I don't think Skyler’s attitude has changed.”

A look of worry cast over her face. “It's fine, I know he is just too full of himself is all, and I know he is not a bad guy.”

Kax and Michael went back into the room. Michael looked at Skyler and said. “So, are we to go somewhere, or do we just wait for Cane?”

Skyler checked his tablet, and said, “I didn't get a message, I’ll call him and find out.”

He picked up his communicator and called Cane to find out what was going on.

Cane picked up his phone and said. “Fleet Admiral Cane speaking, how may I help you?”

“Hey Cane, it's Skyler, we are in the dorm and all ready to go, but we’re not sure where or what we do next.”

Skyler could hear Cane type in a few things.

“Just go to hangar two, there will be a ship ready for you to board.” Cane said.

Skyler nodded. “Thanks for letting me know, we're on our way now.”

Cane calmly replied. “I wish you all the best.”

He hung up the phone. He looked at everyone and said. “Hanger two, that’s where we are to go, they’re already waiting for us.”

Michael nodded. “Then let’s get going.”

***

Anxiously, Skyler and the gang arrived at the ship and ready to go. His heart was heavy and palms sweaty, but knew he was doing the right thing. Skyler went over to the computer and checked them in. He checked Michael's file. "Hey, looks like you're not an engineer this time, they put you down as 'cargo carrier'."

Michael moved Skyler aside and checked the screen. "What, really? That sucks, I know why but still, all I am doing is getting the Orb."

Kax giggled. "Well you could have worse jobs, you know."

Michael lowered his brow, "With my qualifications, delivery boy is an insult, not a promotion."

Skyler laughed and patted Michael on the back and said. "Come on, it will be fun."

He headed into the ship; the others followed him. Skyler went to the bridge of the ship and saw the red velvet chair. The first thing he did was sit down, rubbing the arms of the chair and said. "This is nice, I like this ship."

He looked over at Michael and said. "Hey, do all the ships come with these chairs?"

Michael looked at the bridge of the ship. "Just galaxy class ships, they are more luxury models, since they're made for long journeys. But they do have some of the best security lock-ups, I guess that's why we are using it."

Skyler smiled still rubbing his soft comfy Captain's chair.

Kax rolled her eyes as she sat in her navy-blue leather seat and said, "Quit rubbing off on your chair, we have work to do."

Skyler gave her a seductive smile. "Hey, you can't talk to me that way, I'm your Captain. But if you want we can share the chair?"

Michael rolled his eyes. "You might be a Captain, but that doesn't mean your ego has to grow three sizes."

Kax let out a laugh of relief. Another Officer came on to the bridge and stopped when she saw Michael. Skyler turned his chair and looked at the Officer and said. "Hello?"

The women stood at attention, “Officer Faith, navigator reporting to duty, sir.”

Skyler causally greeted her. “Welcome aboard Officer Faith, you may take your post.”

She didn’t move and looked worried. “Sir, are you aware there is a Squallite on the bridge?”

Skyler looked Michael over, and then back at Faith and said. “I guess there is do you have a problem with that?”

She nodded quickly. “Yes Captain, Squallites are not allowed on the bridge of any ship, Rule 56.”

Skyler smirked. “Is that true now?” He winked at Michael. “Did you know that Squallites aren’t allowed on the bridge?”

Michael played along, “Really, well someone should have told me that sooner, oh well, what can you do?”

Officer Faith looked at them all huffy. “Sir, I will not be mocked, and I will not stand for this ridicule.”

Skyler took a deep breath. “Do you know what this mission is for? Do you know who this 'Squallite' is?”

She shook her head. “I was told that this is a mission to the planet Squall and to retrieve an item for peace.”

Skyler nodded softly. “Yes, that is correct, and this 'Squallite' is the one we need to complete this mission. Without him, we are just wasting our time. So, I don't care if it is illegal, without him we have nothing. I'm the Captain, you will follow my orders, and I say he goes where he wants to go. If you have a problem with that, I will accept your resignation.”

She took a deep breath. “I wish to stay on, but when I write in my report I’m not responsible for any of your rules, or the company you keep.”

Skyler felt smug. “That’s all I ever asked.”

She went to her post, ignoring the Captain. Soon, one by one, the ships personnel arrived at their posts on other places on the ship.

Michael went to science station on the bridge, and the monitored the progress of the ship’s capacity. A few other crew showed up at the same time, to take their position on the bridge. There was four of them: two female Science Officers, a male Command Officer, and the other, a male Modorlean doctor. They waited at the door. The highest ranking of them all the male First Officer said, "Captain, I'm Lieutenant John Pike, and I wish to come aboard with my fellow crew mates, may I ask why there is a Squallite on the bridge?"

Skyler looked at them seriously and said. "Because he wishes to be."

Lieutenant Pike went to comment, Skyler cut him off. "I'm very aware of the rules. Are you aware of the rule, that it doesn't matter what the regulations say? What the Captain says is law. So, I say this Squallite is allowed to be on the bridge, do you understand?"

Lieutenant Pike nodded his went to his post next to the Captain.

Skyler turned in his chair to look at the Modorlean doctor and said. "Your race is modest; how can you be a doctor?"

The doctor looked at Skyler and replied with a question. "If we were all that modest, how would we heal our own people? Besides you're a human who is friends with a Squallite, how does that work?"

Skyler grinned. "Touché, doctor, I think I'm going to like you, more than I thought, um, Lt...?"

"Saliks, Captain, Lieutenant Saliks."

Skyler smiled and said. "Thank you, Lieutenant Saliks, I look forward to working with you and not being your patient."

He paused and corrected himself and said, "I mean, I do not wish to be sick or injured during this mission."

The doctor nodded. "Of course, that is what you meant, Captain."

Skyler rotated his chair to the other side and said. "Jones, what is our status for takeoff?"

Michael looked at the computer, with the operations officer and said. "Captain, we have all 239 crew members on board, we are ready to leave on your command."

Skyler smiled and turned his chair, back to the front and looked at Kax. "Set course for planet Squall, quickest and safest route possible."

Kax smiled, looking at the controls, typing in the coordinates and turned on the ship.

Skyler hit the intercom button and said. “Crew of the HMSS Seeker, this is Captain Therris speaking, I want you all to know we are about to take off and leave atmosphere. Please get to a secure area, this may be a bumpy ride. We’re heading to the planet Squall for a mission I’m sure you are all aware of. I hope this is a clean and quick mission, any questions, feel free to contact me at any time. Captain out.”

Skyler looked at Kax. “Are we ready to go, Tillion?”

She nodded still looking at the controls. “Yes, Captain, and with any luck, we will be there in about six hours.”

Skyler nodded smiled and said. “Sounds good to me, let’s take her out.”

Kax released the break and started to fly the ship out of orbit. The ride was a bit bumpy, but once they got into space it was smooth sailing.

Skyler got up and looked at Lieutenant Pike and said. “I'm going to stretch my legs, you have command while I’m gone, don't worry, I'll be right back.”

Skyler walked to the door of the bridge. Before he left he turned toward to Michael and said. “Jones, could you come with me?”

Michael nodded and followed Skyler off the bridge. While walking down the hall, Skyler looked at Michael, “I'm sorry about everything back there. I forgot for a second the rule and I just....”

Michael smiled. “You a good friend. Thank you for everything.”

Skyler headed to the second room on the left and said, “join me in my quarters, we need to talk.”

Michael followed Skyler into the room.

Skyler sat on his bed and felt the bed was quite soft, “Hey, I like this bed, it’s softer than our bed in the barracks.”

Michael frowned. “You didn't just bring me here to try out your new bed, because I don't think I am your type.”

Skyler laughed. “No, I wanted to talk to you about the Orb. What are your plans to do with it when you get it?”

Michael sighed and sat down, on one of the chairs and said. “I'm not sure, I plan to go talk to them and get the Orb. If they will release the orb to me, I will take it back to the ship and decide from there. I'm not sure what else I can do, I have tried to come up with something. I think that's all I can do, until different circumstances occur."

Skyler nodded. "Ya, I don't know what I was thinking, go do what you may. I'm going to catch a few z's, let me know when we get there."

Michael looked at Skyler and said. "Sleep already? You only woke up about three hours ago, really?"

Skyler laid on the bed. "What? This is comfy, and I have to wait six hours to get to your home world. I'm not going to get there when I'm tired."

Michael laughed. "Okay, I will see you later, till then I am going to walk around the ship and check out the aspects. I always wanted to see a ship like this."

Skyler smiled, took his tablet and sent Michael's tablet a message of clearance. "There you go, buddy, that's in case you want to go to the bridge again. I want to make sure you are well taken care of, friend."

Michael looked at his tablet and said. "Thanks, buddy, see you in five hours."

Skyler smiled and closed his eyes, getting some sleep.

***

Michael looked around the ship. He followed the corridor to engineering. He loved the layout; it was clear and well laid out, with all the latest in engineering technology.

Michael examined the controls in columns on the wall, going all the way up to the ceiling. He loved the design, but didn't like that the important controls were at the top. He could not reach them, meaning he would have to reroute the systems to the lower panels. That was one thing he didn't like about himself, was his height. He was only six foot five, not as tall as most of the other Squallites. He loved this ship design. He was sad that it was only a loaner for the mission, but he would love to spend months on ships like this every year.

He saw all the Squallites working, running around trying to make sure the engines working and operational. This was the first time he didn't have to work as an engineer. For once in his life he felt equal. He felt like one of the crew and not a slave in the back. He stood there just watching the engineers working all by themselves. He smiled; he knew the ship was in good hands. He left and went down the hall to check out the eating quarters. He wasn't sure what the ship had for dining. Really, they all had something different. It just said "dining room" on the map.

Michael headed down the long corridor. He was not too fond of the long corridors that seemed to go on forever. He headed down the hall and then turned right down another long hall till finally he saw a room with a sign that said, 'Dining Hall.' He walked in and it was nothing like he had expected. It was built with a 1980s pub style, and all the food came from the android bartender in the center. Michael was confused. Why would a ship this modern want a dining hall of something that was from 200 years ago? The floor was hard laminate flooring. The lights were soft and there seemed to be a fog in the air. The booths were cheap plastic leather. He went to the center bar and sat on an old stool said, "Since when are there androids working for the United Galactic Forces?"

The Android looked at him and corrected him, "I am not an android. I am merely a hologram made to look like an android."

Michael frowned, "Hologram? Why would someone program an android hologram? couldn't they just program a Human or another Alien life form? I don't anyone has built a fully functional android."

The bar stool was starting to bug Michael's backside. The hologram android said, "I do not know what you are talking about. I do not have the answers you seek."

Michael frowned and looked at the crowded room and wondered if this was all just a hologram. A red-haired man came out and hit a button on the remote and said, "Sorry for the confusion. This is all a hologram I programmed. Trying to add an antique look with a modern flare. Android not believable?"

Michael frowned and turned in his chair. "This is all a hologram? Why? What is the purpose?"

The guy smiled and answered, "It's a new system they're trying out. Instead of having to eat in the same boring room, there will be room selections and you can choose what setting you prefer to eat in. I like androids. I hope to make one, one day, but till then I'm just adding them all over my programs."

Michael shook his head and got off the bar stool, "I see, well, that's kind of clever. Good for long trips."

The guy smiled and held out his hand. "Exactly this way you can bring home a little closer to you when you're 5000 light years away, oh, by the way, the name is Dr. Franklin Haas. I'm a doctor in robotics, science and holograms are my hobby."

Michael looked at the short man and shook his hand and said, "Really, you are human and love science that much?"

He grinned and nodded, "Yes I know I'm a big nerd in science, Mr. Squallite. Surprised I'm not like you?"

Michael shook his head and said, "Well you're in kind of a mixed subject. On the one hand you're an engineer, and on the other you're a scientist."

The guy nodded, "Ya, I'm in engineering right now but I have training for both. This ship I was assigned to program the rooms to whatever specifications they need so when you use your automated locks in your quarters tonight, thank me."

Michael laughed, "I will keep that in mind, but may I ask then, where am I supposed to get some food around here if you're programming the dining hall?"

Dr. Haas raised and shook his finger, "Just one second."

Haas turned around and went to a panel on the wall, typed in a few codes, and then the back wall rotated and a mini kitchen and bar showed up. He looked at Michael and said, "That's a real kitchen and real food now. I can use the holograms to work as your servers, never have to worry about finding a finger in your food with these workers."

Michael was a bit shocked by all of this and went to comment when Haas asked, "So who do you want to be your chef? I have a few thousand people in the program. Do you want the King to make you a sandwich, or would you prefer a pope?"

Michael laughed, rubbed his face, and said, "You really have too much fun on the job. Doesn't matter to me. Who do you want to make us food?"

Haas smiled and typed in a few more codes and picnic tables appeared and three servers: Abe Lincoln, Mary, Queen of Scots, and Henry Ford on the grill.

Michael frowned. “Really, isn’t this kind of degrading?”

Haas smiled. “No, it’s just the images. They only know the job assigned. They can’t talk about who their image was or anything.”

Michael was a bit confused. “So they are the image but not the person, like a new skin for your cell phone?”

Haas smiled. “Yup, you know it. That’s as simple as it gets, and when you design these programs you got to have a little fun.”

Michael laughed, “Ya, I can see how you would find this entertaining.”

They went and sat down at the table, and Abe Lincoln came over and asked what they wanted to order.

Chapter 32

The Navigator looked at Kax and said, “We’re about to leave the portal.”

Kax smiled and said, “I know that, and this is our last jump, so I would say we are going to be in planet’s reach in about forty minutes, so how about someone wake up the Captain?”

The Communications Officer paged Skyler’s quarters and sent him the message, “Captain Therris, please come to the bridge. We are about to come into contact range with the planet.”

Skyler took his time getting out of bed, then headed to the bridge once he was dressed.

Once on the bridge, he went to his Captain’s chair and said, “Lt. Pike, you are relieved from duty. Thank you for your work.”

The Lieutenant got out of the chair and then Skyler took his place.

Skyler looked out the bridge crew and then looked at Kax, “Tillion, what’s our ETA?”

Kax looked at her navigations chart and said, “Fifteen minutes, Captain.”

Skyler smiled, "Send a message to the diplomats and tell them we will be there soon. We will be taking a shuttle down to the planet."

The Navigator turned in her chair and said, "Captain wouldn't it be faster to just transport down?"

Skyler shook his head. "No, because we are not certain how their transporter pads will work with the storm you can see in the view, so why to risk it?"

The Navigator nodded, understanding. Skyler looked at Kax and said, "Would you let the navigator take over and meet me in the shuttle bay?"

Kax nodded and got up from her post.

Skyler looked at the communications officer and said, "Send a message to Jones and get him to meet us in the shuttle bay ASAP."

"Aye Captain." She proceeded to send the message.

In the shuttle bay, Michael was there waiting when Kax and Skyler arrived. They all loaded into the shuttle and headed for the planet. Once in the planet's atmosphere, the storm on the planet was quite harsh. Kax tried to pilot through it and head to the ground. Michael tweaked the controls for Kax so it piloted a lot easier onto the surface.

Kax looked at Michael and said, "How did you know what to do?"

Michael smiled, "My home world. I know my winds better than most, is all."

Kax shrugged it off and smiled. "I guess you're right then."

They all got off the shuttle and there they saw a group of three very tall Squallites waiting to greet them.

Skyler walked out first and did a peace with his hands and said, "Peace we come and peace we come from a faraway planet known as Earth and bring messages of peace."

Kax covered her face.

The Squallites looked annoyed at Skyler. Before they could say anything Michael butted in and said, "Sorry about that my Captain's first contact with another planet, we're here about the Orb."

They nodded and the tallest one said, "Come this way."

They followed behind the Squallites. Michael hit Skyler on the back of the head and said, "Hey, don't do that again. These people are a higher power on this planet, and need to be treated with respect. Don't pull a stunt like that again. If you're not sure what to do, then just copy what I do."

Skyler rolled his eyes, "Great, I'm stuck on a planet with all these boring aliens with no sense of humor."

Michael rolled his eyes. "If we have time I will take you to a comedy club. Till then, joke's on you."

Skyler grumbled under his breath.

They headed into a giant tall cyclone-shaped building. The inside of the building was glass reinforced with cement pillars. It ceilings were twelve feet high. The whole office was decorated orange and blue. They went going ahead to the glass elevator. Going up, the fifty story building. Skyler was amazed at the architecture. Michael noticed Skyler and Kax's amazement. It had been years since he was last in this place, and even then he never got to go to the top level.

"This building is not made from glass. It is made from a clear titanium alloy and in the sunlight it shines orange. That is how it can stand winds over 200 km/h," Michael said, showing off his knowledge.

Kax looked and said, "Isn't that what they use on Earth for glasses and other tall buildings? How would yours shine orange then?"

Michael shrugged, "Yes, it is the same stuff on Earth. Our sun is orange all day and it makes most things orange, but this building in the day is very gorgeous."

The female elder admired Michael's enthusiasm. They finally reached the fiftieth floor. Michael was just as awestruck as the others. He had never been here. He heard stories about the place and never knew how amazing it really was. The orange carpet rolled right out to the large set of three chairs: one was for the leader and the other two were for the elders. They saw the leader was already sitting on his chair. The two elders went forward to take their places next to the leader, one male and one female. The other male went to a desk that was just off to the side. The three of them went forward. Michael tried to hold back his excitement. As they got closer to the front, Michael looked at the view from the top. You could see all of the city; it was gorgeous. He began to feel homesick and wanted to stay there forever.

They approached the leader and Skyler spoke. "I am Captain Therris of the Earth. We seek your help, and only you can help me."

The leader, a tall long dark haired Squallite with aged face and dark orange eyes, spoke next. "Yes, we know of your situation, Captain. Please step aside. We wish to talk to your Squallite crewman."

Skyler nodded and stepped aside.

Michael came forward, "I am Michael Majerik..."

The leader cut him off and said, "We know who you are. But we want to know why you feel Earth should have the orb and not us?"

Michael's heart sank, he knew this was a hard thing to say. He thought the Orb should stay with his people and didn't think this mission was right for any side. His duty as an Officer was to bring the Orb to Earth. But these were people his duty was to keep the Orb safe.

Michael looked at Skyler, his elders, and the view of the city, and said, "I don't think the Orb should be moved. The Orb has held as a symbol of peace and protection to our people over the years. I do not believe this is how the war can be won, and I would prefer to discuss another way to help in the war."

The leader of the Squallites leaned forward and said, "You came all this way to tell us not to give Earth the Orb. You do realize by doing this you are defying orders?"

Michael nodded, "Yes, I know, but I do know if we come up with a better way to stop this war, then there will be no orders broken."

The leader sat back and thought. "I like your suggestion. Come back here at noon tomorrow and we will have a meeting about this."

Skyler frowned. "Tomorrow? You know how long it took to get here?"

The leader frowned. "We can just cancel your request and let you go, but I suggest it is better for you to stay."

Skyler nodded, "I will inform my superiors about this and we will see you at noon tomorrow."

Michael bowed and they headed out of the building. Once they had left, Skyler looked at Michael and said, "Are you sure you are doing the right thing?"

Michael shook his head. "I don't know if there is a right thing, in this case, but as a Squallite, it is my duty to protect that Orb."

Skyler shook his head, pulled out his phone and called the ship. "Hey, we're going to be stuck here for another day. If anyone wants to come down and see the place you can."

Skyler headed back to the shuttle. "I have to call Cane. Won't be long—but what do you think we should do after this? Go back to the ship or look around?"

Michael smiled. "I wouldn't mind showing you guys around if you don't mind. It's been years since I have been home."

Skyler nodded, "Sounds like a plan. Let me just talk to Cane and we can go and have some fun."

Skyler went into the shuttle alone and used the video phone to call Cane. "Admiral, were going to be stuck here a few days."

Cane frowned. "How hard is it to pick up the Orb?"

Skyler shook his head. "They need to talk a few things out and the only time they have is tomorrow at noon, so I told the crew to enjoy themselves because we're stuck here for the night."

Cane nodded. "The Cassiopaeans warned us they plan to attack soon. We don't want this but we're getting ready if you take longer than tomorrow, tell me and I will find out when you can come back."

Skyler frowned, "What do you mean? Is this attack that bad? I will come back right now."

Cane shook his head and shouted, "No! Only come back if you have the Orb beside that. I don't know how safe it will be to be here. Do you understand?"

Skyler nodded and thought, "That's why you gave me the ship and mission? You don't know how long we would be put here if we fail?"

Cane shook his head, "Not really. But if you don't return the orb or something better, then don't return for now. If you would continue your education, there is a small United Galactic Forces training base there, if you can't make it back by summer's end. But you will be back with the Orb. I know you won't let me down."

Skyler nodded, "Ya, we will be back sooner than you think."

He closed the transmission and went to Michael and said, "I talked to Cane and just want you to contact your dad. We might be stuck here for a while. The Cassiopaeans are going to attack Earth; that's why Cane wanted us away."

Kax was shocked and said, "What? this is horrible! How can this be?"

Skyler sighed, "Don't tell anyone about this till we have the orders to stay. Tomorrow we will get the orb and save the day and but, for now, let's go out and have some fun ok?"

They all wanted to say more but what could they say? They knew what was going on and hoped they would make it home safely.

Chapter 33

Michael was nervous. He knew what this meant. If he was here and not on Earth, this wasn't a simple attack. This was big. He knew in his mind that it would be all right, but he still wasn't sure in his heart. He thought about his father he wasn't there to be at his side and how his dad told him to go on this mission. What if something happened to him when he was gone? What if his dad died? If he was not there his father would die alone and Michael would be left alone in the world. He told himself he couldn't let it weigh him down. It was time to enjoy his home world once again; he never knew how much he missed it. Michael looked at his friends and said, "Come on, I told Skyler I would take him to a comedy club, so let's get going."

Skyler managed to find the strength to follow Michael. He groaned while walking next to Michael, "Are you sure it's walking distance from here? What if we get another storm?"

Kax was excited, but she didn't let on to the others.

Michael laughed, "Naw, no storm for a bit more, and come on. A good walk never hurt anybody."

Skyler shrugged and they walked for a bit to downtown. Michael went to go to the place he remembered: 'The Orange Ball.'

Kax looked at the sign and asked, "Why is it called The Orange Ball?"

Michael laughed, "Because our national color is orange and you're going to have a ball of laughs, get it? It's funny."

Any excitement Kax and Skyler had had was now gone. Inside the club, they saw a stage and the guy at the front, an oddly dressed Squallite with yellow suspenders and pink shirt, said, "You know people from Earth are like—" he stood up straight with a pipe—"Hmm hmm. While us Squallites are like 'mmm mm mmm'." And did a more relaxed learning on the wall gesture.

Skyler looked at Michael. "You call that funny?"

Michael tried not to laugh and said, "There is much more. Come on, sit down and watch."

Skyler shrugged it off, thought maybe it was just a bad joke. Throughout the night, there were many comedians that told a variety of jokes from, "The universe is dizzy because it just keeps spinning," "It's not easy being orange," and "Why did the cow jump over the moon?"

All were just plain and boring. The Squallites in the club found them funny. Kax and Skyler were just confused how the jokes could be that funny.

Michael was having a good time and looked over at Skyler and Kax and said, "What's the matter? You two don't look like you're having a good time."

Kax sighed and said, "I don't mean to insult you or your culture, but we're not finding any of these jokes funny."

Michael took a deep breath, "I'm sorry you aren't having fun we can go if your world like?"

Skyler's voice jumped and he said, "Sounds like a good idea. Let's get out of here."

Kax whacked Skyler in the arm and said, "Don't be so rude!"

Michael nodded, "Don't worry it is about time to go, I don't mind."

They all got up and walked out of the club together. When a huge gust of wind picked up and there was a storm clearly an in front of them. Skyler and Kax headed back inside.

Michael frowned, "What's wrong? it's only a little wind."

Skyler and Kax stared at Michael. Skyler said, "That's not a little wind that is a huge storm coming! We can't walk in that!"

Michael looked about and said, "It's a little squall. It won't hurt us, I am used to them."

Kax glared, "You might be used to them but we're not! And I don't like getting wet."

Michael stepped outside for a second.

Skyler noticed the power of the wind against Michael's limber body helped him stand and hold his balance in the wind.

Michael looked around and then stepped back in, "Okay, it is a little too strong out there. I will call us a cable cab and we can go back to the ship."

Skyler frowned, "The storm is strong too bad to fly out of and there is only one bed in the shuttle. I have the expense card Cane gave me and we can just book a hotel."

Michael shook his head, "Naw, I will call my dad's cousins and see if they have room."

Michael called up and they answered. He talked and explained the situation, smiled, and hung up the phone.

Kax looked at the clock on the wall and said, "Isn't a bit late to call them?"

Michael looked at the clock and was shocked. "I guess it was, but they said it was fine for us so I guess they were still awake." Michael then called up a cab and they headed to his cousin's house. They got to a tall slender milk carton shaped house. They knocked on the door and a tall dark haired women answered. Dhe smiled and said. "Oh, Michael, there you are. Haven't seen you since you were a child. Come in and introduce me to your friends."

Kax whispered to Michael, "This is your cousin?"

Michael smiled and nodded. A light brown haired Squallite came down the stairs and said, "Hey Michael nice to see again an interesting bunch of friends you brought with you."

Michael smiled, "Hey Danrik. Nice to see you, these are my friends. Kax is a Catillion and Skyler is Human."

Danrik and his wife shook their hands.

Michael smiled and introduced Kax and Skyler, "This is Kanrick, my dad's cousin and Danrik is her husband."

Skyler smiled, "Nice to meet you, and what a what a lovely house you have here! It's very tall."

Kanrick smiled. "I guess compared to your human houses it is, but ya we need the height. There are some who are taller than us and some shorter."

Michael sighed, "I am sorry, I am the short Squallite, I know."

Danrik laughed, "Michael, your height is fine. Your dad's not that tall and there are shorter ones out there, so don't worry."

Kax yawned uncontrollably.

Kanrick smiled and said, "It is late. How about I show you to your rooms and we can all talk to you in the morning?"

They all nodded and Skyler said, "sounds great."

They took them up the really tall stairs up to their bedrooms. The hallway was narrow and the so were the doors. Skyler was trying not to lean the wrong way and fall over the railing.

The first room was theirs; the next few were the guest rooms. They were small and the beds were long. Skyler looked at Danrik and said, "Why have a house with so many rooms if it is just the two of you?"

Danrik smiled and said, "This is Michael's dad's old house and I bought it from him. We plan on having kids one day, but it hasn't happened yet. Till then it is a great house."

Kanrick smiled and said, "You kids can figure out the rooms. If you're hungry, help yourself to the kitchen, and washroom is at the end of the hall. See you all in the morning."

The couple went to their room they all picked a room Michael went and laid down in his bed.

Skyler was laying in his when Kax came in, "Hey Skyler, can I talk to you?"

Skyler looked up from his pillow and said, "You can do more than talk."

Kax shook her head, “No this is serious, I want to know what your thoughts are about us stuck here all summer?”

Skyler sighed, “I don’t think it looks good. This is not an easy thing but if we don’t get back, I will make sure you are safe.”

Kax smiled and sat on the bed and said, “I’m worried about what might happen if we stay too long. How long will it be before we see the green hills of the Earth again?”

Skyler smiled, “One day off the planet and you’re homesick. How long has it been since you saw the purple mountains of Catillion?”

She frowned, “It’s Katalian, and we don’t have purple mountains. That's Lyria Four! And too long since I have visited it but I would hate to make a home in a third place.”

Skyler sat up and gave Kax a hug, “We have a galaxy class ship. If we can’t return to Earth you pick a planet and I will take you there.”

Kax smiled and gave Skyler a hug back, “You always know what to say, don't you?”

Skyler joked, “Naw I just bought a book, 1001 right things to say to women.”

Kax shook her head, “You never stop, do you?”

Chapter 34

Morning came. Skyler woke up to the smell of food.

Michael and Kax had already woken up and were getting ready for the day.

Skyler put his jacket on, but didn’t zip it up and headed downstairs. Skyler sat down at the table half awake and said,. “Food smells great Kanrick.”

She smiled and put the plates in front of them and said, “Thank you, Skyler, I hope you like stir fry. This is a traditional Squallite breakfast, stir fry. It has cashews, Almonds, other veggies and meat with a side of toast.”

Skyler looked at the food and poked at it, with his fork and said. “Why is the toast orange?”

Michael laughed. “It comes from gumtate flour, it makes it orange. Don't worry, tastes just like real bread, just the color is different.”

Kax started eating her food and said, “Try it, Skyler, it is really good.”

Skyler was nervous, he never had stir fry for breakfast and the orange bread, it was just turning him off.

Danrik smiled and pulled out a chocolate bar, out of the cupboard. “Listen, you don't have to eat the toast. I'll have it, but if you eat the stir fry and I will let you have this chocolate bar.”

Skyler smiled and said. “I’m not trying to be rude, it smells great, it’s just...”

Danrik smiled and said. “Don’t worry, I know what it is like to eat Alien food. For me it’s Earth food, I like some, like chocolate, but not Pop Tarts, they just bug me.”

Skyler smiled and ate at his stir fry. It tasted a bit odd but not as bad as the food he got sometimes from the replicator.

Michael smiled and said. “My cousins grew all the veggies, in their garden outside, it is great. You always know you are getting fresh food.”

Kax smiled she was enjoying her food and asked. “Is that why you love whole food so much?”

Kanrick smiled and said. “No, Michael’s love for whole food is a cultural thing, most Squallites grow and make their food. Some buy from the stores but we have more markets. We believe in living off the land for the most part. From what I have been told, humans don't care to.”

Skyler ate some food and replied, “No, we care a lot, just we get others to make the food for us. We use the replicators for groups and when food supplies could run low. Lots are health conscious nowadays. How else do you think we live so long?”

She laughed. “Humans live to be 130 if they are lucky Squallites live to be 200 on average.”

Kax smiled and said, “Catillions live for about the same time as humans we just age differently.”

Skyler shrugged and finished his food, “Well I live as long as I do, and die living on the edge.”

Danrik smiled. “You know, Skyler, you remind me of a younger version of myself.”

Skyler smiled. “I hope that’s a good thing.”

They all laughed. They finished their food and Michael looked at the clock. “Thanks for everything, cousins, but we must be going. We have got to get to the city hall and talk, we will see you again, hope it won’t be too long.”

Kanrick gave Michael a hug and said, “We always have a place for you here, Michael. I wish you well on your mission.”

They headed out the door and went on their way to city hall.

***

They arrived just before noon and waited for the meeting to start. They sat at a long table that was put out for them.

Michael was nervous; he was more nervous than he thought he would be. He didn’t know what he was going to do, but he did know that he wanted to go home.

The meeting began and his heart sank. He didn’t know what he was going to say to them. He really couldn’t think of a better plan than give Earth the Orb to win the war. The second elder looked at Michael and said, “We have called this meeting because you wanted to talk about other ways to help the Earth in this war without the orb. What are your ideas?”

Michael had a choice and answered with the craziest thing he thought of, “We join the war and use the Orb on our side, but we fight as Squallites we don’t have to fight with the Humans. But we need to tell the Cassiopaeans who’s boss, we know why they are hateful and we are the only ones who they trust. So what I propose is we gather our ships and use the Orb to surround the planet making them surrender. And knowing that Earth is our friend and if the Cass want to be our friend they have to agree or we have the ability to destroy them.”

The Elders looked at each other and then leader said, “So you want us to do what the Earthlings want to do, but we do it and we have fewer resources?”

Michael nodded, “Yes but we have the Orb. We can use it, the Cassiopaeans listen to us, no one else. We might just be able to scare them into peace.”

The Elder shook his head, “No, it’s their time to suffer. We have nothing else to do with this fight, just give them the Orb because we are peaceful and as a statement that we take no side. The Cassiopaeans will know we are backing out and understand to leave us out of this war with the Humans.”

Michael and Skyler frowned. Michael stood up, slammed his fist on the table and said, “Dammit, these people are warlords, they don’t care if we give the Orb to the Humans. They will think we betrayed them and turn against us no matter what they say. They want to punish the humans for some reason and they will hurt all who side with them. Giving the most powerful weapon in his war to the Humans is the sign we are betraying them. We have to fight, or both my homes will be destroyed!”

The Younger Elder snarled and said, “Calm yourself, Majerik! Or you will be asked to leave. You are a Squallite of the planet Squall you are not a human!”

Michael frowned at the use of his name, never had he heard his name used with so much negativity. “I might be a Squallite but I was born on Earth, planet Squall is only my second home and I will not stand for either of them to be destroyed. If we don’t stop this attack on Earth my home and the home of my fellow crewmates will be destroyed!”

The High Elder looked at Skyler and asked, “Is there really an attack planned for Earth?”

Skyler nodded, “Yes there is, and we either come up with a plan to help or bring back the Orb by tonight, or we are not allowed to leave till I get word from the Admiral.”

The High Elder nodded and looked at Michael and Skyler and said, “Calm your Officer, Captain Therris, or we are cancelling this meeting for the day.”

Skyler jumped out of his seat and said, “Damn you! By you cancelling this meeting you are sentencing millions of people to death. I will not allow that. Give us the orb then, dammit, if you will not help in any other way!”

Michael was shocked at Skyler’s reaction. The high elder got up out of his chair and pushed it in and said, “It doesn’t matter. We never had any intention in giving up the orb. We just wanted to see what condition you humans were in. Please leave now.”

Skyler knew they were acting out of line with their anger, but he was sent on this mission, no one else. It was his job to get the mission done by whatever means necessary. He was hurt that theses Squallites just wanted to know their battle plans. Skyler shouted, "We just gave you our battle plans, very dangerous information. Almost as dangerous as that Orb. We gave you something and I suggest you give us something or we take the ship we came there with and blow your headquarters up!"

Michael turned his head and was mortified at what Skyler said. The High Elder looked at Skyler and said, "You would go to war with one world to stop another?"

Skyler stayed serious and said, "You don't have the power to defend yourself, you said before. Means you're vulnerable. I wouldn't see it as a war, I would see it as more of an occupation."

Michael smiled. He knew that Skyler was doing now, but was still horrified that Skyler would say these things to his people, but he knew Skyler only had good intentions.

The High Elder looked and Skyler and said, "The Orb is ours, but we will help in your war. You seem to need it."

Chapter 35

The three of them were back on the ship waiting for their final orders to return the home.

Skyler sat in his comfy captain's chair. He was waiting to hear back from Cane.

Cane showed up on the view screen soon and said, "Well congratulations, Captain Therris, on bringing the Squallites into the war and on our side, but that wasn't the plan."

Skyler nodded, "I'm aware of that, Fleet Admiral Cane, but they never had the intention of giving us the orb. They just wanted to use us and turn us away. Sir, it was the best option I had."

Cane nodded, "I understand your situation. I just wish it could have gone better. You still have your summer of classes there. If you can try and get the Orb one more time, that would be great."

Skyler nodded, “We will do the best we can.” He was about to turn the view screen off when Kax came running onto the bridge.

Out of breath she panted, “Sir the portals are gone, and it looks like it has been destroyed!” She went over and typed in a few things and pulled up the screen and showed the video coverage of the debris of the portals.

Skyler quickly hit a button on his chair and brought up the view screen of the portal. He looked closely at the view screen and was petrified by what he saw. “Tillion, is there another way home? Do you have to take this route?”

She rushed to her desk on her panel for optional routes, “I’m sorry sir, but it looks like all portals leaving planet Squall are destroyed. We are stuck here.”

Cane typed in a few things on his computer. “This isn’t good. We need to get that orb now, or you kids might be stuck there longer than this summer.”

“Why would the Cass do this?” Skyler asked.

Cane cut him off and said, “My guess is instead of attacking Earth they decided to attack the gates so the Squallites can’t join the fight. There is only one portal that can take you home, and you have to go into Cassiopaean space; their portals are functioning. We will be sending repair crews out to fix the portal, that should be done by the end of summer..”

“How do I tell the rest of the crew?”

“The United Galactic Forces will be sending everyone messages on their tablets soon enough. You won’t have to worry.”

***

Michael was in the holo-cafe with Dr. Haas. He had been there when he got the message to the crew. He was having a drink of Squallite run and he looked at the Doctor who was working on his laptop tweaking some of the programs. “Haas, what do you think is going to happen if we’re stuck here?” Michael asked while drinking his drink.

Haas looked up from his computer at Michael and answered, “Not sure, really, but if we are stuck there for a long time it would give me a good chance to get some three-dimensional images of the place, there are still so many things this data bank doesn't have to offer. They might be in the archive footage but so many things have changed, and this stuff is only on loan and for business use, but if I take the photos myself I can do whatever I want."

Michael laughed, "Is this all you talk about holograms?"

Haas Smiled, "Holograms and robotics are my life, that's my job, of course, I want to improve my work at any chance I get. Working in a room like this all the time, I don't get out much."

Michael nodded, "I know what you mean, engineering is a hard life. No sunlight." Michael thought to himself then he looked at Haas again and said, "One reason I don't want to be an engineer for the rest of my life is, you might control everything, but no one ever sees you or gives you the credit you deserve. Captains get all the credit."

Hass looked up from his computer again and said, "Captains do more. we keep the roads a rolling, captains pave the way. They are always going to get the credit, but they don't make our work any less important."

Michael sighed, "Maybe you are right but this is not my life."

Haas smiled, "I know what you mean. My parents wanted me to the be a ballet dancer. I know it sounds odd, but there are quite a few men who are in it, and coming from a long line of dancers and performers it would be the logical choice. But that's not what I wanted. The only other scientist in the family was my great uncle Wilhelm. He mostly spent his life trying to make an artificial potato clocks, that doesn't explode."

Michael laughed, "My family is not that serious, really it's just me, my dad and a few distant relatives around but if were stuck on Squall I will staying with them for a while."

Haas's eyes picked up. "Oh, can I join? I would love to get some images of a lived in Squallite home and what they look like when they're eating in said home."

Michael laughed and shook his head, "It would be up to them, but I would be glad to show you around."

Chapter 36

The crew of the HMSS Seeker was not happy about the possible extended stay on Squall, but there was no choice and knew there were risks in their job. Hoping for the best and knowing things could be much worse.

Kax went to visit Michael in his quarters. She noticed that he was packing. She smiled and said, “So you’re going to stay with your cousins, then?”

Michael zipped up his bag and replied, “Yes I just feel it would the best time to get to know them, if you and Skyler want to come you are welcome to join me.”

Kax smiled, “Well it would be nice to see more of them. They seemed so nice. I guess I could stay a night and then figure out where I really wanted to stay. Might find something at the local Academy.”

Michael put his matching uniform bag over his shoulder and looked at Kax, “Sounds good to me. I’ll meet you outside when you are done the packing.”

They both laughed and headed to the door.

Kax went down one hall with Michael, headed over to Skyler’s quarters and knocked on the door. The sliding door opened. Skyler was laying on his bed, and looked at Michael and said, “I guess you’re going back to your cousin’s house then?”

He nodded and replied, “You could come too, Kax is going to.”

Skyler rubbed his soft bed and said, “I would love to, but I was just getting to like this room. I kind of don’t want to give it up. Your cousin’s place is great, don’t get me wrong. It’s just here I have my own place.”

Michael understood. “If my quarters were half as nice as yours, I would be staying too, don’t you worry.”

Kax came in and looked at Skyler’s room. “Damn did they spend all the budget on your room and on nothing else?”

“They always give the Captains all the luxuries.” Michael answered.

Skyler rubbed his bed. “If you like my room so much Kax, I’m willing to share it.”

She rolled her eyes and said, “No thank you. I prefer Michael’s. Will you ever give it a rest?”

Skyler shook his head, "Not until the day you become my wife."

Kax laughed in shock, "Wife? Really you want me to be your wife? Is that what you tell all the girls?"

Skyler stood up and looked into Kax's eyes. "I might joke, but when it comes to you I am always serious."

They stared into each other's eyes and he put his hand under her chin and they lean in to share a kiss when there was a knock at the door. Skyler was shocked quickly gave Kax a peck on the check and went to the door. He frowned at the red haired man in a lab coat.

"Hello, Captain, sir. I am Dr. Haas. I'm here to set up the replicators."

Skyler aggrievedly smiled back at the doctor and said, "what are you talking about?"

"Since you and some of the other crew will be living on the ship, I need get them to run while the ship is docked." Dr. Hass walked further into the room.

Kax waved goodbye, leaving Skyler with the Doctor.

Skyler glared at Hass. "If your fixing all the replicators why do you need to be in my room? Isn't this in engineering."

Dr. Hass made his way over the the bed, "Captain, sir, your room holds the master replicator. Along with all the others are controlled from yours. It's very fitting for a captain to have so much control."

Skyler was confused, "Why would the Captain have all the controls for the replicators?"

Dr. Haas frowned then laughed, "Your kidding right third-year academy lesson the Captain's cabin has most of the controls for the ship."

Skyler smiled and nodded, "Yes I know I was making sure you knew, but what do we do when it breaks down?"

He watched Haas go over to a panel by the back wall of his bed, "Are we supposed to just let strangers into our rooms?"

Dr. Haas opened the panel and looks inside fixing a few wires, "I didn't realize the rumors were true that we have a student captaining this ship."

Skyler was shocked and said, "What where did you get that idea?"

Haas looked at Skyler and said, "You reek of inexperience and you didn't realize you had such power, my boy. I won't tell the crew but before you explain why you're on this mission, I need to finish this job. Maybe you should read some older class material so you bluff a bit better."

Skyler wasn't sure how offended he should be. He knew Haas was giving him good advice, but he hated to be told what to do. He frowned and watched Haas fix the replicators on his bed. He wanted, on some level, to throw the doctor into the brig for questioning his authority, but with a second thought, he knew this guy was okay and was only doing his best to help.

Haas finished the repairs. He closed the door and went to the replicator. He hit a few buttons, swiped a card and before their eyes a new pair of running shoes appeared. The doctor took off his old tatty ones and placed them in the replicator. They dissolved. He put the new shoes on and wiggles his toes. He reached up and pulled his card out, a receipt printed out. He smiled. "Sweet, I got a few more credits back then I thought I worn out of those awful shoes, these ones are much comfier and look cooler there all black with orange stripes."

Skyler frowned, "What do shoes have to do with this? Is the replicator fixed or not?"

Haas smiled. "Yes, that was just part of my test, you can inform the crew the replicators are back online."

Chapter 37

Skyler didn't really want to go back to the Academy, especially a Squallite branch. He wanted to be a Captain and nothing else, not learn how to be an engineer. He got dressed and headed out. He checked his tablet if there were any messages from Kax or Michael, he was still not sure where they were going to meet up. He checked his GPS and looked to make sure he had the address for the academy. For such a small area it was hard to find what he was looking for. He headed down the streets on the narrow paths and extended tall buildings. It was very Alien to Skyler. The architecture might be like that on Earth but when he walked down the street he felt like his vision was stretched vertically. The place just didn't feel right. It wasn't home.

As he walked down heading on the long narrow road to a place he wasn't sure he wanted to go to now, he heard a familiar voice call from behind him. He turned around quickly and saw Kax running up the road calling out his name. Skyler stopped and smiled. "Hey, there you are Kax I was wondering when you would show up I didn't get a message."

Kax checked her tablet and said, "Oh I forgot to send the message, I woke up early and invited you to try this breakfast place Michael recommended."

Skyler searched around, "You went with Michael? Where is he?"

Kax put her tablet down and answered, "Michael headed to the academy extra early he said he had things to do."

Skyler nodded his head, "Ya that sounds like Michael alright, I just wonder what he is doing."

Kax shrugged, "Who knows with that guy, let's just head down there and see what we're going to be doing for the rest of the summer."

Skyler sighed, "Is it just me or does it feel odd going to this branch of the Academy?"

Kax looked down at her feet and said, "It's a bit odd probably because we're not use to this city, but this is normal for Cadets to finish or take part of their training on other planets it's a learning experience."

Skyler sighed, "Ya I guess you're right I just would have wished to do it on a cool planet like Venus or Sagittarius."

Kax shook her head, "Sagittarius is not that great from what I here I figured you would have taken Orion prime?"

Skyler shook his head, "Orion prime what do you take me for sure the brochures make it look fun, but I tried to see about taking my fifth year there, but you're on outpost and not allowed to leave the base because the place was almost 3rd world. Sagittarius you have longer nights and shorter school days, of course, that means you just go to school all year, but it's a real party planet."

Kax rolled her eyes, "Is that all you care going to parties, I thought for a second you would pick Sagittarius because it has some of the best light shows and LED art in the galaxy."

Skyler smiled, "I care about you does that count?"

Kax clenched her fist and answered, “No it doesn’t.”

“In that case holier than holy where were you going to choose to go on you out of planet training?”

Kax laughed, “I was thinking of either home to Catillion where my family is, or Star base sixty-two or Capricorn prime.”

Skyler laughed, “Star base sixty-two? Wow, that’s secluded and Capricorn prime you want to hang out with all them horny heads?”

Kax looked at Skyler and said, “I’m hanging out with one right now.”

Skyler frowned, he was about to reply when he saw ahead of them was the academy, “Hey we made it, now quit talking.”

Kax rolled her eyes, “Yes my Captain.”

They both laugh and walk into the building. They head to the registration desk. An older male Squallite in working the computer and said, “How can I help you two?”

Skyler pulled out of his pocket his ID card and said, “I’m Cadet Therris of Earth and I believe Fleet Admiral Cane has Transferred my files for summer classes.”

The man took the card and looked at Kax who was holding out hers and asked, “Same thing?”

Kax nodded and handed in her card.

The man swiped the card and looked over their files, “All checks out we have room in our command classes, but this isn’t the best place to be taking command training you know? You can get the rest of the lectures on your tablet.”

He handed Skyler a piece of paper to sign and looked at Kax. “You are the hard one were only offering ship design classes right now, no piloting is you ok with that change?”

Kax thought, “Don’t you need test pilots for the new designs?”

The man nodded, “Yes we would they why is it on the recommended list for classes we offer if not I would say your best option is to just switch to full command.”

Kax nodded, “I’ll go into ship design it’s only the summer, does my uniform change?”

The man looked and said, “On duty you will get a blue uniform but when you are in class you will wear your purple and you get a special pin.”

The guy reached into the drawer and grabbed a small silver circular maze-like pin and handed it to Kax, "Wear it at all time."

Kax smiled and took off her pilot pin and put on the ship design pin.

Skyler examined Kax's pin., "Not fair you get all the fancy pins what do I get?"

Kax smiled and signed a piece of paper, "One day you'll get the fancy ship. But for us special divisions we only get pins."

Skyler shrugged.

The man looked over both their paperwork and then hit a button on the computer, "Check your e-mails and you should have your schedule and locations of the classes please enjoy the Academy and welcome to the United Galactic Forces."

***

Michael was in the engineering room waiting by the transporters.

Dr. Haas came over and looked at the transporters, then at Michael. "Is the transporters going to explode or something?" He asked.

Michael who was really looking worried. He stopped looked at Haas and answered, "No I'm having my father beam me something from the Earth and it is taking forever."

Haas was, even more, puzzled, "So it's that important you can't just replicate another you have to transport the physical item?"

Michael nodded, "It's a new alloy I am testing and I need to make sure it works I had a meeting booked but since I'm not going to be on Earth I asked to have part of it sent to me for testing and the other is being researched on Earth them. The admirals want me to send it here so we can continue my work with it."

Haas grinned, "New alloy for the ships and it's taking this long it must be one heavy metal."

Michael nodded in reply still concentrating on the transporters status.

Dr. Haas checked the transporters computer and checked the status. He typed in a code. Michael's eyes widen and he grabbed Dr. Haas' hand and said, "What do you think you're doing?"

Dr. Haas looked up at Michael and said, "They gave you a transporter with Cadet securities with that it really limits what you can send, because they were charging it to your replicator card. I'm just going to enter in my information I have an unlimited card and that's way more data can be transferred."

Michael relaxed, letting go of the doctor and frowned, "Why would they do such a thing?"

Dr. Haas finished typing in the code and looked over the diagnostics, "It appears they do this to all Cadets by the look of it so the cadets don't waste the energy matter is all but that's fine I'm more interested in seeing this new alloy."

Michael looked at Dr. Haas, "How is it that you have such a clearance for things?"

Haas smirked, "Because I told you I'm a doctor working on the holograms I have access to most things that involve engineering."

Michael shook his head, "Right I forgot, hey since you're doing that hologram project want to go hiking with me this weekend on the red mountain?"

Dr. Haas perked up, "Oh that sounds like fun will your friends be attending or is it just us?"

Michael thought, "Well I have to ask them but I plan to do it doesn't matter who shows up it's one of my favorite things to do when I come back home."

As they were talking the transporters was finishing up the materialization of the alloy. The transporters made a Bing when it was done. Michael rushed over and picked up the alloy and hugged the square foot tile of metal and said, "Oh I'm so glad to have this, you know what this means right doctor?"

Haas nodded, "I am guessing from what you have told me that it could be the future in starship technology?"

Michael smiled, "That's what I am hoping."

Chapter 38

Kax and Skyler were sitting in the small cafeteria eating some alien fruit and veggies. Kax put her food down when she saw Michael walking in the distance. She waved and called him over.

Michael noticed her and went over to the table.

Kax gave Michael a hug and said, "There you are stranger, I was wondering when we were going to see you."

Michael hugged back and said, "Sorry I had to get a little bit of work done."

Kax smiled, "It's fine, we understand. Are you going to sit down?"

Michael shook his head. "I'm just going to get some lunch and be right back, then I will sit with you guys."

Michael headed off to the cafeteria line.

Skyler looked back at Kax and said, "He's in a good mood."

Kax laughed and responded with, "Why wouldn't he be? at least, we found him and we don't have to worry that he'll ditch us."

They both laughed and waited for Michael to return. Michael got back quickly with a tray full of fresh fruit and veggies. Skyler looked at it and said, "You sure you're going to eat all that?"

Michael laughed, "Yes I am, I love this stuff. You never get good fresh fruit on Earth anymore."

Kax smiled and asked, "So are you still in the same division as you were on Earth, or did you get the transfer?"

Michael looked up from his plate and answered, "Well they didn't transfer me, they promoted me, I'm currently not a Cadet I'm a second petty officer and I'm helping them design a new ship, what about you guys?"

She put her hand on her pin and showed Michael, "They switched me to ship design as well, but they want me more as a test pilot. Maybe I'll be flying the new ship you are designing."

Michael looked a bit worried and was about to say something when Skyler jumped in and said, "I'm still in command they were actually happy to have me, they said they didn't have too many command Cadets and they always need more."

Kax looked over at Skyler and frowned. “That’s not exactly what they said, but he is right. He is the only one who got to keep his division.”

Michael ate some fruit, laughed a bit and replied with, “That’s good that you're still in command, but there quite a few reasons there it is a high demand.”

He looked around, “So besides that, how are you enjoying the place? I’m referring to the city, not the academy.”

Skyler groaned, “The doorways are too tall, and everything is narrow.”

Kax laughed at Skyler’s whining, “It’s not that bad and I like it here with everything being narrow. I do feel a bit short, but I also enjoy the architecture it is a really nice city.”

Michael nodded, “Yes and if you notice we cramp our cities close together so that we can persevere the wildlife more.”

Skyler shook his head out of confusion. “Wouldn’t cramping buildings make it worse for when a storm hits?”

“No, the strength of the structures and the close grouping it gives us a higher chance that the storm will just pass by and not actually hit anything.”

Skyler still a bit confused continued to eat his food.

Kax smiled at Michael and asked, “So if there are so many storms here why are there still forests? wouldn’t the trees be ripped out of the ground by now?”

Michael nodded, “There is lots of that but when you go outside and see how many trees we have now it isn’t a lot. Our ancestors lived in the trees and this whole planet was filled with them it was just as they started to thin out we built homes to have more protection.” He looked around and smiled, “You know what if you guys really want to see more of the landscape here, how about this weekend we all go for a hike up the red mountain it's a really nice place, great view of the city.”

Kax smiled and finished her food and replied with, “Sure that sounds so great.”

Skyler shrugged, “I guess so, nothing else to do around here.”

Michael and Kax just stared and laughed at each other.

***

Once their food was finished, they headed off back to their classes for the day. Michael was trying to draw up new plans for the ship he was designing and hopefully, get a basic shuttle built for testing soon. It was a long road because half the materials to create the alloy were not on their planet. He tried to test and see if parts of the alloy could be taken apart and stretched. The alloy was about three inches thick and if it was as strong as he believed it was then stretching it out to half an inch should protect the same and from there be able to cover most of the side or front of a small shuttle craft. But how was he going to spread it out there was no way to stretch it out. He looked at the item data files of when it was half transported. He thought long and hard on this seeing what could be done. Going through file after file data after data. Finally, it hit him. He could send it through the transporters one more time but once it was broken down use the computer to modify its patterns to reappear in the shape he wanted. he hoped it would work if worse came to worse he would lose the alloy and would have to stop testing for the time being but if it worked the rewards would be too great. He grinned and very large grin and continued with his work.

He took the alloy to the transporters pad and went over to the controls. He laid out his notes about what measurement he needed next to the controls and then headed turned on the transporters. He looked in the computer data files to see what they had for the styles of ship parts. He kept looking till he found the one that matched the basic front of the shuttle craft they were more than likely going to test this on. When he had the pattern he wanted to be picked out he set the pattern readings then turned the transporters on and waited. As he worked on with the transportation he thought he heard footsteps on the other side of the domed area. He picked up his head and looked for a second to check nothing. He put his head back down and went to work, brushing it off as just paranoia because he was in a locked and secure room.

Chapter 39

Days went on. All were adjusting to their new assignments. Kax's was a bit harder to place. Sure she was a test pilot but they now had to find something for her to test, eventually, they did. Kax headed to the testing hangar and looked at the small pod like the shuttle that is being built in front of her. She stood there watching it for a while, till a man came up to her. He cleared his throat and said, "Cadet Tillion please follow me to where you will be working."

She took her eyes off the gray and white shuttle and followed the average looking Squallite male officer to the office in the back of the hangar.

He sat down at his desk signals for Kax to take a seat.

She did her best to sit in the taller than a normal chair. Her feet barely touched the ground.

He had her file in front of him. he looked at a few pages. He looked up at her and said, "It was kind of good timing that you all showed up despite the circumstances. But we haven't been working on new ships for a while since we didn't have the materials but the Fleet Admirals have sent us some new supplies for joining in the war."

He sighed, looked down thinking about the war and what was to come. He looked back up and continued, "So we have just about finished the new shuttle pods constructions with the new tech and would like you to fly and see how things work so that we can work on making the larger ships."

She used her thumb to point over her shoulder and said, "Is that the pod outside there working on?"

He nodded, "Yes there finishing up the final touches, this model has guns on it and it is designed so that when a ship is so badly injured one can escape in the pod and still fire for one last fighting chance."

Her eyes widened, "That's suicide the purpose of the escape pods is to escape not attack you have no defense in those little things."

He shook his head, "Not with the new alloy we have just received we can use to cover the pods then the only damage that could happen to them is they get thrown off course."

Kax's eyes widened even more. She was ready to get out of the chair and leave but first said, "That's even worse going off course is so dangerous you may never get back, and there is so much unexplored space."

He sighed looking down at his desk, "That is a risk we have to take during the time of war. Most of the time when we send out the escape pods most don't make it home, but this way we have a last chance to save lives and these people have a chance to start a new life on a new planet."

Kax calmed down a bit, not so anxious to get out of her chair and replied, "You have good intentions, but we are also near Cassiopaean space. One of them could crash on one of their planetoids and then they would have our brand new technology."

His sigh grew deeper, "The Squallites have never fought in a war in space we have remained neutral ever since we had the war on our own planet between the tree people and the ones who lived under the ground. We lost a lot of great technology and people in that war and we as a people agreed to never fight again. Even if some of our technology falls into the wrong hands we will still have some of ours."

Kax relaxed a bit more and sighed, "Yes, a profound choice but you have a real war on your hands. You can either wage it with live weapons, or you may never know the pain of loss. I don't want people to die but if avoid it our life will become our weakness."

He smiled at her and said, "Are you sure you are a pilot and not a diplomat."

Blushing she laughed, "I just come from a wise family is all."

***

Going to class Skyler decided to take his time. There was only six of them in the class so he wasn't too worried, it's not like they could start class without me. He walked into the class fifteen minutes late. He saw the class just sitting around reading their textbooks with no instructor. He frowned looking at the mixed race class from the bottom of the lecture hall and said, "Hey I'm not one who cares to do work but where is the instructor?"

The red skinned female Modorlean looks up and said, “Be quiet and get to work it is the right thing to do.”

“A bit rude wouldn’t you say, I was just asking,” Skyler said.

The blue-skinned male Modorlean sighed and responded with, “My sister did not misspeak. It is better to just do your work and continue even if not all are here.”

“Now wait just a minute!” Skyler said.

A pale prism colored short haired girl at the top of the hall waved to Skyler. He just ignored the Modorlean siblings and walked up the stairs past the Sagittarian male and Human female and sat next the ridged forehead alien. He slid into the seat and closer to her and grinned. “So where’s the teacher?”

She laughed and answered, “He left and said to just finish up where we left off in the books.”

He laughed and shook his head, “Really now well then why are we sitting around here when we could go back to my ship and have our own private study session.”

Blushing she rubbed her tree like ridges. “I’m guessing the Alien thing doesn’t bother you?”

Leaning in close he whispered in her ear, “As long as you don’t poison and eat me when we are done I have no problem with that.”

She giggled shaking her head, “No we didn’t, the name is Jozie by the way and I would love you see your ship.”

Skyler got out of his seat, held out his hand, “Then let me show you the way.”

She took his hand and got out of her chair and head out of the classroom and head to the ship.

***

Skyler rolled over in his cabin bed.

Jozie rolled and cuddled the side of Skyler and smiled, “That’s was great haven’t had that much fun in a long time, Captain.”

He grinned and kissed her on the ridges, “You weren’t bad either, what race are you?”

"Classpian," She batted her eyelashes, "I'm just wondering, who's Kax?"

He frowned and replied, "What are you talking about?"

"Well I told you my name was Jozie but you kept saying Kax I don't mind, but you know other girls will."

He sighed and shook his head, "She's a Catillion that I really like she is so sexy and has the cutest nose great breasts and gorgeous strawberry blonde hair."

She shifted a little in the bed, "Does she know you like her?"

Shaking his head and closing his eyes, "No I haven't worked up the courage to tell her how I feel about her. She is such a good friend."

She plays with the small patch of blond hairs on his chest and said, "You could pick me up with knowing little to nothing about me, but you can't tell this one girl how you feel?"

"I love her; I have never told anyone that before. I could say I love sleeping with you and I love the way you did that thing, but nothing serious I don't know if I really can."

Jozie shifted and looked Skyler in the eyes and said, "Or maybe you're not ready to love her. You say your love her, but you are still picking up random women. Maybe you just think you love her because she's a friend and out of your reach."

Thinking about it, he shook his head, "No it is more than that, there is something about her my heart flutters when I see her and I just want to hold her and never let her go." She shook her head, then leaned in and kissed his neck, "Well, then maybe you do have something special with this girl but right now I am the only girl in this room."

His neck tickled from her kissed. He rubbed her shoulder and said, "I guess you want to go again?"

She nodded and said, "This time you can call me Kax."

He grinned rolling over on top of her and said, "And remember to keep calling me Captain."

She leaned up and passionately kissed him.

Chapter 40

Michael came by the ship in the morning to check on Skyler before school. He went to the door and was about to knock when the door opened and he saw the girl with the starfish forehead leave the room adjusting her uniform. Michael asked, "Hey is he in there?"

She zipped up her uniform top and answered, "Yup but he is going to be making a few video calls he said so your best to wait before you knock."

He smiled and nodded, "Thanks, I will wait."

She headed to the exit of the ship. He stood at the door and he heard Skyler talking. At first, he tried not to listen but he can't resist the urge.

"Glad we finally got time to talk," Skyler said to the monitor screen on his desk. The man on the other side replied, "We to I have heard the news about what is going on so I know why you are missing class, just not why you are not wearing a shirt."

Skyler laughed held up his index figure. He got up from the chair and grabbed his black undershirt off the floor and came back to the desk. "Am I better now, Captain O'Brien?"

"Much better, now how are things there?" O'Brien said.

"Things are ok, as happy as I ever am." Skyler sighed.

"Well everyone is doing what they can to get you guys back here. But congratulations on getting the Squalls into the war. That is something no one has ever done before."

Skyler rubbed his face, "Ya that was just due to the circumstances."

O'Brien laughed, "You're lucky this is all you had happen to you. The Cassy's are extremists and are not to be trusted, they could have blown your ship to pieces if they felt like it."

"I guess you're right, considering they are friends with the Squalls it is odd that there aren't many of them around?"

Very seriously O'Brien answered, "I'm not sure exactly why, but part of their friendship is not being near each other."

Skyler scratched his head in confusion, "This place just gets weirder and weirder."

O'Brien laughed, "Ya isn't that true. Hey, do you know a Commodore Sandy Munroe?"

Skyler's heart dropped and he stared dead into the monitor screen, "Ya I know her, that's my mother, why are you asking?"

O'Brien held up a sealed letter in his hand, "I had no idea she was your mother, I have been picking up your mail since Cane has been busy with all these negotiations. Do you want me to open the letter or wait?"

Skyler shook his head, "Rip it up. I'm tired of her stupid ways to try and contact me."

"I didn't know it was so bad between you to. I did wonder why she was writing to you she didn't seem to be your type; let alone the fact she is in the ground crew in the other fleet."

"Ya one of the reasons, I haven't seen her since I joined. She is not happy with my decision of joining and I really don't care what she thinks of my life."

O'Brien tossed the letter towards the garbage can. Looking at Skyler who he was now not sure if he was mad of just wanted to cry. He smiled and changed the subject and asks, "So any storms out there?"

Skyler laughed, "Constantly they come and go so wickedly, I'm not the only one who makes this cabin a-rocking."

O'Brien laughed and shook his head, "Well how else do you think the planet got its name?"

A timer beeped next to O'Brien. He looked at it and then at Skyler, "Sorry about this, but I got to go the afternoon class is starting and I got to be there, it was nice talking to you, keep in touch. Also, I'm emailing you your notes just because you're not here doesn't mean you can't still learn."

Skyler rolled his eyes back and said, "Ya I will read them, why can't this just be my vacation?"

"Because you're not old enough for one. Talk to you later," He hit a button in front of the screen and turned it off.

Skyler looked at the time and then put on his pants and jacket, then got ready to go. He stepped out of the room and saw Michael was standing on the other side of the sliding doors, "Hey how long have you been standing there."

Michael lied and answers, "Not long just got here, now come on we will be late for school."

Skyler looked at the clock on in the hall and saw was about ten minutes before the morning's first class and says, "Why do we have analog clocks on a starship?"

Michael looked at the clock on the wall and answered, "Turns out there more accurate in space than they ever were on Earth."

Chapter 41

Sitting alone in his cabin after another long day, Skyler looked at the ceiling at the picture of the galaxy. He loved space. It was his home, even the last few weeks on this planet he didn't miss home. What was there for him on Earth? His mother didn't want him, his father was dead, everyone else he would see in space. Space was his Babylon, waiting to be conquered.

There was a knock at the door. He frowned and said, "Come in?"

Michael came in.

Skyler way lying on the bed in his green United Galactic Forces issued underwear and frowned at Michael, "What are you doing here? It's Saturday, there is no class today."

Michael instinctively picked up Skyler's clothes that were scatter on the floor, dropped them on Skyler and said, "Remember you I and Kax were going to go for a hike up the red mountains?"

Skyler slapped his forehead and said, "Right I forgot about that, but I do remember saying something like no way, I'm not hiking on my day off."

Michael, "No you didn't, but I think you will change your mind when you see Kax's hiking outfit."

Kax came in the room in a pair of tan rolled up short shorts black tights and pink halter top.

Skyler moved his clothes down off his chest and said, "Hey Kax that's a nice outfit, when did you get it?"

She smiled, "Uh, the replicator. Only place I can find clothes that fit on this planet."

Skyler shook his head, "You think with the human and other alien population of the planet being about ten percent there would be at least one shop with smaller clothes?"

Michael shook his head, "There is no need with replicators and tailors all over the place. If you want organic clothes you have to be a Squallite."

Skyler rolled his eyes and proceeded to put on his jeans and black tank top.

Michael looked at Skyler. "That's what you're wearing don't you want to protect yourself against bugs?"

Skyler looked at Kax and then at Michael who is dressed like an old-fashioned African game hunter, "Kax is wearing less than me what's the problem?"

Kax pinched her arms and revealed a thin clear skin like covered her arms, "Bug proof skin."

Skyler looked at Michael, "And you Mr. Jones?"

Michael took his tan jacket off and pinched his skin.

Skyler rolled his eyes and went over to the replicate and has a set of the skin made. He tried to read the instructions and groaned when he unfolded it. "So what is it like invisible long johns?" Skyler struggled and tried to find the top of it.

Michael went over to him and helped him pull it apart, "Here Skyler just open it at the top and slip in, make sure to take your clothes off before you do it. I and Kax will be outside if you need us."

Skyler was left alone in the room trying to put on an item that was almost impossible to see.

Michael and Kax waited outside the room. They heard Skyler fumbling around in the room. They both tried not to laugh, but the urge was too great.

Eventually, Skyler came out the room fully dressed and ready to go.

Kax looked him over and said, "You're wearing the skin aren't you, or did you give up and are pretending?"

Skyler smirked, "I'm wearing it don't you worry."

Kax narrowed her eyes at him suspiciously.

***

An hour of walking through the town the trio finally reached the edge of the forest. Michael looked up from the forest's edge and pointed, "That's the red mountain was going to climb you guys ready."

Kax looked at the mountain Michael was pointing to and said, "Why is it called the red mountain when it clearly looks blue?"

Skyler glared at Michael, "You said we were going to climb a mountain and now an hour later we get to the mountain and it's not red it's blue and we had to walk here!"

Michael laughed at Skyler, "So little you know about the outdoors, it thinks you're spending too much time in space."

Kax laughed and replied with, "I don't care what color the mountain is I want to climb it!" She headed into the forest.

Michael reached for her shoulder. "Wait!" He said and looked at his watch, "Let's wait a few more minutes."

Kax and Skyler looked at each other in confusion.

Michael watched the road. After only a few minutes a cable car appeared, stopped and out from it appeared Dr. Hass.

Skyler frowned and looked at Michael, "You invited him?"

Michael smiled, "Yes he wanted to see more the planet and since we already agreed to go for a climb I didn't think it would be that big of an issue."

Skyler frowned at Dr. Haas and said, "No issue at all." He scoffed.

"How come all the cars in the streets have all these cables pushing and pulling them?" Kax asked.

Michael looked at the tracks and replied, "Well it's to keep cars from blowing away and hurting people. The Cables don't move we drive on them and go where we want a kind of like an Earth Cable car and street car combined, they run on peddling motion it's hard but a lot safer."

Skyler butted in, "Who cares about the stupid cars I didn't wake up early just to walk through town let's just climb this so-called 'Red' Mountain so we can all go home."

The rest of the gang laughed. Michael headed towards the mountain and turned around the said, "Come on everyone follow me."

Haas stopped taking holo images of everything and followed them.

Chapter 42

High noon and the sun was beaming down the group. Skyler looked around the hill and thought, *Why do we have to climb such a stupid mountain. What is the point it's just there and it's not even named right? Michael has the weirdest hobbies. Who is this doctor guy anyway why did he have to come?* Skyler swatted his arms around hitting his arms a few times. *Stupid bugs why are there so many and no one else is complaining.*

Not saying anything the gang keeps heading up the mountain. Kax's looked back at Skyler and said, "What's wrong? why are you swatting your arms around?"

Skyler stopped for a second remembering that she and Michael told him to wear that second skin, "No reason I just like exercising my arms while I walk." He rubbed his neck trying to cover a big red swollen bite mark on his neck.

She giggled. "That's the spirit keep your entire body active. By the way, the bugs on this planet are poisonous to Humans."

His eyes widened in worry. Trying not to let on he let out his inner panic, "Ya I know that."

Haas moved towards Kax and said quietly, "Um you do know that's not true, in fact, the bugs are very harmless the only reason they bite is to collect dead hair and skin cells for their nests."

She nodded, "Yes I know but he doesn't."

Winking and hoped the doctor would catch on. He moved away grinning in understanding.

Kax spoke up and said, "How much more to the top?"

***

Michael kept on walking, and not looking back at Kax, "We're not going to the top-" He could hear a sigh of relief from the two young ones. He continued, "-there is a spot up ahead that I really want to share with you, it will be worth it. But if you really want we could go all the way to the top?"

Skyler spoke up and said, "I am not walking all the way to the top that is just insane. If we wanted to see the top of the mountain we could have just taken the ship and the landed it at the top."

Michael shot a glare at, "NO that is rude. Trees are sacred here because we have so few and in the past they saved our people, you land a ship on this mountain you risk hurting the trees, I will not allow that!"

Kax was just as shocked as Skyler when she heard how passionate their friend was about the trees and of his people's home world.

Haas was off to the side taking 3D imaging of the different trees, "Well the good thing with all the hologram technology out there in a few years we could have this forest full again. If a tree falls in the woods and hologram will replace it."

Michael wasn't sure which of the two were being more offensive. He decided to ignore them and kept walking up the mountain.

A while later Michael stopped. They were there. Well close to where he wanted to be. Looking around for that special spot and he noticed it. He waved to the rest of the group.

They sighed in relief for they now feel they are making some form of progress. Walking a bit over the to the side of the trial and threw some trees he stopped. Looked around and while still standing started to take off his boots.

They all could see the large secluded hot spring It wasn't long before they began t take their clothes off.

Michael left his shorts on and took a dip in the pool. Skyler left nothing for the imagination and does a cannonball jumping into the pool.

Haas left his briefs on and slowly but properly got in one foot at a time sitting next to Michael.

Kax started to take off her top. Michael saw Skyler's peering eyes watching her. She stopped when she had clearly seen skyler as well. Her hands holding he shirt halfway up she stopped not sure what to do.

Skyler watched her waiting for her to finish.

Michael noticed her discomfort, "Don't worry about him he won't touch you."

"It's not just that I don't want him watching me." She said.

Without giving Skyler the chance to stop staring Michael shoved Skyler's head under the water and held it down. "Now's your chance quickly."

Kax took off her top the two remaining guys looked away. As she undid her shorts as Skyler struggled under the water. When she was in her black bra and panties she got into the pool Michael let go of Skyler.

Skyler gasped for air. "You should have warned me, you Electric bug!" He spat at Michael.

Michael frowned and responded, "Don't you think if I were electric everyone here would be dead by now?"

Glaring he snapped back, "Don't try and use logic on me you could have killed me!"

Kax cut in, "I wouldn't have let that happen as tempting as it might seem to wipe the universe of another male pig."

Thinking of a rebuttal, he stopped and thought and let it go. Looking at Kax, he said, "Sorry I didn't mean it to appear like that. You're just you are so damn sexy."

Keeping a firm face she replied, "Thank you, and what about Michael?"

He looked at Michael and shrugged, "Naw he's not my type."

They all burst out in laughter.

Enjoying the pool Kax leaned back stretching out her arms in the air and rolling her neck.

Skyler could not keep his eyes off her.

Kax had moved future away in the pool to be more private.

Michael tried not to look at Kax out of respect. He looked over at Haas who was already looking in his direction.

Haas looked into the orange eyes of the man next to him in the pool. He noticed Michael's disinterest in Kax and acted on assumption. He stretched and moved in a bit closer. "You don't seem that interested?"

Michael shook his head, "Naw those two always do these kinds of things I try to ignore them when they do."

Haas grinned, “Makes sense, your not interested.” He paused then continues, “Is there anyone you are involved with?”

Michael shook his head, “No I have my reasons.”

Haas still looking into Michael's eyes said, “Your eyes match my hair.”

Thinking that comment was strange he looked at Haas's bright orange upright hair and nodded, “I guess they do.”

Michael looked over at Skyler and Kax who were now playfully chasing each other in the pool. Michael began to question what Haas’ intentions were.

Haas leaned over Michael, placing his hand high on Michael's leg under the water.

Michael’s eyes widen, he tried to fidget away.

Haas leaned in to kiss him.

Michael pushed him off into the water. Shocked and scared he moved swiftly away.

Haas unsure of what was going on quickly regained his balance in the water and moved over to see what’s Michael was doing.

Michael had moved a distance away and was glaring at Haas. “What were you thinking!”

Haas moved to a safe distance towards Michael and responded, “I thought that is what you wanted?”

He just glared at Haas not saying a word. His hands and body trembling.

“I know my family history if that is what you want to know first.”

After sighing he responded, “That’s is not it at all I have no interest in your family tree or you in that way. I thought you were my friend?”

Haas took a breath and smiled, “I’m your friend and I meant you no harm or discomfort, I just thought you would be interested.”

He calmed down paused for a second thinking about how to reply to this, “I am sorry if I miss lead you, but I would still like to be your friend if you are interested.”

Haas nodded, “In this life you need as many friends as you can get.” He held out one hand.

Michael took his hand in friendship. He looked over towards Skyler who was still playfully having some fun chasing Kax around the pool.

Haas who was still looking at Michael said, "Not to trying to make you feel uncomfortable but if you're not interested in men why do you show no interest in women?"

He looked straight into Haas' eyes as serious as he could be, "I show no interest in either, not because I favor one over the other, not because I have no interest but for cultural and family reasons. Once I figured all of them out I will consider a relationship. Until then I am Asexual."

"Interesting you will have to tell me more about your culture sometime." Haas gave Michael a wink.

Michael gave a hesitant smile, *What is this guy up to?*

Chapter 43

"What am I supposed to do with all this stuff," Kax said out loud to herself. "Do I store it in the cabin or move it into Michael's cousins place, so many chooses I don't know what to do. I have bought all the stuff and now I have over shopped."

Sitting on the bed, she noticed a blinking message light on her computer screen. She got up went over to the computer and played the message. Hey, Kax it's Jake calling. Thought I would see how you're doing I haven't seen you around lately, were you on the ship that went to Squall? If so, let me know I would have called sooner but I have been busy with work and school. Call me back when you can, oh and Ron says hi.

She looked at the time stamp and saw he called an hour before she had gotten to the computer. She quickly hit the call return on her computer. Ring, ring, ring the computer went. She was worried that she had missed him.

Finally, the other computer picked up. Jake was on the other end smiling and waving at Kax. "Hey, Kax how have you been?"

She smiled and answered, "I'm trying to figure out what to do will all my stuff."

He laughed and tilted the screen to show all his bags of stuff, "I know what you mean, may I guess by the background you are on Squall?"

she nodded, "Yes I am sorry I haven't had a chance to contact you about anything. How long has it been?"

Jake looked at his computers calendar and answered, "Just about six weeks, since we last talked, you that busy? It is almost as if the Cassiopaean's are trying to keep us Squallites out of the war."

Kax smiled, "Are you trying to tell me something I don't know."

Jake shook his head, "To you I would tell all but in this case, but I do not know." He turned his head, "Oh yes by the way I got to show you something." Moving his hair back behind his ears, "Do you like them?"

She laughed looking at his pointed ears, "I thought you were going for the human look, not an elf?"

He nodded laughing, "The store only had elf I hope to get a human set made soon but because they are prosthetic I am keeping them coved so no one sees the seam lines. My old set broke, also these are regulation because they do not affect my hearing or vision."

Kax said, "They look lovely and through the screen I cannot notice the seam lines, is that all the progress you have made on yourself?"

"Well, I have been working out and have a meeting what the surgeon next week to talk about my options. It is a slow process. I am hoping they say I can go for a stapedotomy where they will take the staples out of my ear and replace it with a human stapes. It is mostly done for hearing the loss in humans but for me, that is the main thing I want to be done. Even if I physically change that is all it is physical. But with a stapedotomy, I can wake up and not hear electricity anymore and then there would be no way to turn back."

Listening to his story she smiled and replied, "Well then I hope you get it. As much as that is an issue for you. It is on the outside wouldn't you would want to be a human with this ability."

He laughed, "Ron said the same thing, his issue is his height he doesn't think it is believable for a seven-foot human he really wants his bone shortening surgery. I know there are tall humans out there and to me hearing the buzz of the wires reminds me of who I was. We both will go through the same surgeries over time but when there are so many on the list we have to prioritize them. He's jealous that I got mine before him."

Kax said, "Wow so it is a lot of work good for you guys I hope you get your ears done soon."

"There are few things they are working with that they are still researching that will help one day, like blood. That really bothers me Humans don't need to worry blood is all the same if they don't figure out a way to change out Alien blood to human we will have to be on hormones and other drugs forever. I worry that taking these pills will be a constant reminder of the fact I won't ever be one hundred percent."

She listened carefully listening to his story and said, "But once you go to the point of no return it won't matter it is better than nothing. Think of the pills as a reminder how far you have come and each day you are a little bit more you."

Laughed a bit, "That I guess, is one way of looking at it."

Smiling back looking at the time, "Just wondering since I don't know when I will be back how are we going to do these sessions if I'm not there?"

"Well, I and Ron were talking about that and well there are some things that can be passed on through word of mouth others need to be seen. If Ron was here now I would say let's get started but he has class early today. How is tomorrow for you we could talk in the afternoon?"

Kax looked at her computer's calendar and said, "Today is Monday and tomorrow is now, it won't work I am finally going to be testing out the experimental shuttle Michael helped design, but what about Friday I have half a day some pre-holiday planning stuff, shack-hog or something?"

Jake laughed, "Shacog, that's one of my favorites you should go to the festival and enjoy the food people make food that they only make once a year you will enjoy it."

Kax said, "Do you want me to send you any of the food through the transporters?"

He shook his head, "Naw, it is fine food doesn't taste so great through the transporters and there will be a small ceremony on Earth. Since Shacog is this week go to any store there and ask for a Rospip, pay whatever it costs I will tell you the story behind it. They only sell them on that planet and at a certain time of year. If they will not sell it to you get your Squallite friend to buy it for you. I don't think they will have a problem with you, though, you are one of the lesser known races and not many know what it is."

She got out her notepad and wrote the info down, "If it is only sold here then will it be safe to bring back?"

He nodded, "You should have no problem you have a private ship no customs if a Squallite does go through your bags then just tell him Shatoka and he will let you be."

Writing all these notes down her brain was confused, "Ok and what is so important about this Rospip?"

He laughed, "I will tell you Friday till then that is all I will tell you."

He looked at his computers clock, "I have to go now talk to you later, it was really nice talking to you."

They wave to each other and turned off the computer monitor.

She sat back stretching out a bit. Took a deep breath and thought of her life's situation. *Oh my, why do things have to be so complicated wish I was home things might have seemed hectic there, but I knew what I was doing.*

A knock came to the door. She sat up in the chair and said. "Come in." *I wonder who could be coming by so late.*

The door opened, Skyler came in.

Oh great, what does he want now?

Skyler came in and sat on the bed across the room feeling the bounce of the bed.

She spun in her chair to looked at Skyler sitting between all her shopping bags. "What do you want?"

Skyler grinned, "I think you know what I want."

She got out of the chair and move towards Skyler and said, "If that's all your here for then get out with that attitude."

He laughed, "Darn, I thought I would try that. No, I just thought I would come here and talk get to know you a bit more friend. Can't a guy and gal hang out without any sexual implications."

She rolled her eyes, "Not with you."

He laughed, "Kax why don't you like me?"

She sighed sitting back down in her chair, "Who said I don't like you? If I really didn't like you, why do you think I been hanging out with you?"

He shrugged. Looking at her and smiled, "I like you, you know that right?"

She rolled her eyes, "Yes, but only as a two-bit whore."

He glared, "What! No, I don't think you are a whore you're a lovely lady who is smart and strong and has a big heart. I like you as a person. You are a very nice and I know I'm not good enough for you and I wish I could live up to your expectations."

Flattered she replied with, "Thank you, but what are you up to."

He got off the bed and walked over the chair where Kax was sitting. He got down on his knee. Taking her hand and looking into her golden cat-like eyes and said, "Kax from the first moment I saw you I was in love you style your beauty it intrigued me. I know I act like a jerk from time to time, but you make me want to better myself."

She was unsure what to believe, nothing made sense. *Why is the womanizer Skyler telling her all these things?* Looking into his eyes, she can tell that he was being as serious as he could be. But for how long. Unsure what to reply to the green eyed boy in front of her.

She smiled and says softly, "I wish I could believe you but time and time again you prove to just be an immature chauvinistic boy." She could see the hurt in his eyes.

The only thing he said in reply, "I will change for you."

They both got up and she gave him a hug, "You are a friend, and there is a war going on. When we get back to Earth who knows what will happen to us we may not see each other."

Skyler sighed knowing he had lost. Placing his hand in his pocket feeling the box between his figures he said, "Well I guess in that case if we do get separated during in this war one of us will make sure we say goodbye."

She nodded her head, not noticing him playing with his pocket, “Yes I will not leave without saying goodbye to you.”

Moving his head to try and steal a kiss. He looked in her eyes instead and smiled. “I guess I will see you later.”

Their friendly embrace ended. He left, and she was alone.

Chapter 44

Skyler lay alone on his bed. On his back looking at the ring he bought. Feeling down never knowing if it was a waste. He wasn’t sure if it was the lack of sleep or the sting of rejection, but there was a pain in his stomach that made him so sick he wasn’t going to school. He wasn’t going anywhere. He started looking at the ring in the air.

The large .7 orange diamond stared back at him. Surrounded by pink and white twisted flower diamond pattern. He tried putting it on his figure, but it only fit half way. He admired the rose gold and sighed. He didn’t want it this way he wanted her to be wearing the ring. He spent so much money and time on picking this ring he felt captured her personality but now was never going to be hers. Taking a deep breath staring into the seemingly glowing jewels thinking and imagining what could have been.

Laying there still only his left hand moving in the air. He knew the store said he could take it back if she said no, but it didn’t feel right. This was the ring made for her and no one else. He could not return it not now not ever. One day they would be together and he would save this right for that day.

There was a knock at the door. He was too far into dreamland to hear it. It knocked again and finally the person came in. It was Michael.

He came over and said, “Nice ring who is it from?”

Skyler snapped out of his daze looking at Michael and confused on why and how he was here. He figured he had just lost track of time and answered, “The ring isn’t for me.”

Michael came over to the bed and looked at the ring on Skyler’s figure, “It’s a really nice ring must have cost a fortune. Did you buy that here?”

He nodded, “Ya, after our hike up the mountain.”

Sighing he looked at Skyler, "I guess she said no?"

Skyler sat up shocked, "No, and what makes you think she would say anything like that!"

He gave his friend a serious expression, "If the ring was for Kax I can think of a few reasons she said no. But also, you still have the ring so she couldn't have said yes."

He took the ring off his figure and sighed holding it in his hand, "I tried too. I tried to tell her I loved her, but those three words wouldn't come out. I managed to tell her I cared but not love. She told me she wasn't interested and the excuses there was a war. We are uncertain where our lives are going. So don't bother ruining our friendship."

Michael took the ring out of Skyler's hand to get a better look and said, "She has a point. Even if our lives go back to normal when we get home, next year she will be the fourth year and have more responsibilities we may not see her. You may not even see me. I was supposed to graduate in Jane I have no idea when I am now."

He shifted to look Skyler straight in the eyes, "I know you love her we both love her but were students in the time of war This career is hard to keep relationships in. As it is doing you think you really will be able to make it work?"

Holding back the tears. Skyler nodded looking at Michael, "Oh why do you have so been right, I wish you were wrong so much. I have never cared about anyone else like I care about her but, why does life have to be so complicated."

Michael wrapped his arm around Skyler. He looked at the ring then Skyler and said, "Take it slow I know you have liked her from day one but have your thought of what you're doing after graduation, where are you going to live and what will you be doing? Are you even going to be able to support a wife? Also, you always find more and more girls maybe you need to rethink and cut back. There're lots more you need to do before you settle down. You don't just buy a ring and expect the world to fall into place."

Skyler took the ring back and looked at it.

Michael shrugged and asked, "You can still return that right?"

Skyler nodded grabbed the box that was on the shelf attached to his headboard. "Ya, but I'm not going to. This ring reminds me of Kax it reminds me of her beauty and style it doesn't matter if she says no, I will give it to her one day even if it takes the rest of my life."

Admiring his friend's determination, he smiled, "You two might have a future together but, for now, you need to grow up. Now come on we're going to miss the whole day of school."

He put the ring back into its box and placed it on the shelf, "Ya, I guess I better go to school and learn something new."

Michael patted Skyler on the back and got up, "You will enjoy it Kax is a test piloting today on my design and after we can all go to the pub and celebrate."

Skyler got up out of the bed and smiled, "Never thought you would offer to take me to the pub but sounds like a plan."

***

Kax was in the academy's hangar. Nervous and excited for her first test pilot assessment. Wearing a padded blue uniform that felt rather bulky, but she knew it was for her own protection.

The ground crew prepped the fighter. A few engineers were still making their last minute adjustments. She sat in a chair that was off to the side watching them work. Waiting for someone to tell her what to do.

As she sat there she thought of all the things this fighter could do for the Earth and the Squallites during the war. This fighter was theoretically indestructible. This might be the deciding factor in this war. The fate of the war could all be decided in this one day.

She waited patiently watching the men work. She tried to stay focused, but it was boring waiting. They told her to be there early in the morning, but it was now close to noon she didn't want to rush them, but she could help but wonder, *How much longer is this going to take.* From there her mind drifted. She thought about last night and what Skyler said to her. *I wonder if he was serious. Even if he was will his mind change next week? He is cute but not sure where it can go. It would be nice to find out, but he probably will leave me for the next hot girl he sees.* Staring into nowhere she thought of all the times fun she had with Skyler the way he always made her laugh. There was a part of her that did like him, but there were red warning signs flashing all around him. *Right now he is not worth the effort. Knowing my luck, he will knock me up and take off to the other side of the galaxy and I will never see him again. Stuck with a mini Skyler. That would be cute baby Skyler with cat ears.* She laughed as her mind started to wonder.

A Squallite with dark red hair came over to her. He was confused by her laughing and taped her on the shoulder. "Cadet Tillion the fighter is ready for you."

She snapped back into reality and put her serious face on. She got up out of her chair turning to look at the mahogany hair color man and smiled, "Thank you I have been looking forward to this."

He led her to the fighter. She followed him and when she got to the shuttle a brief sense of fear came over her. Worried her body froze. She felt prettified what if this didn't work. She had flown many shuttles, ship and spacecraft before and nothing had gone wrong in the past, and that was in combat. She took a deep breath she was determined to become the greatest pilot ever and if she was going to be as good as her record said she already was there was no better pilot for the job. She took a deep breath smiled and entered the fighter, with no chance of looking back and the accepting the risk of all dangers that come with her career.

Chapter 45

Skyler got to class and looked at his small classroom of five. He was about fifteen minutes late again he looked around for the teacher.

Jozie saw him and waved him over. He went up the stairs of the auditorium and sat next to Jozie. She smiled and said, "I haven't seen you around for a few days?"

He looked confused and responded with, "What do you mean I have been in class all week?"

She laughed and said winking, "That's not what I meant."

He shook his head out of stupidity and laughed, "Oh well I wasn't sure you wanted to see me again."

She leaned and kissed Skyler on the lips, "I will always want to see you again."

He kissed back and with one hand one her shoulder and one hand on her breast. They learned in together. Kissing deeply.

A stern 'humph' came from the bottom of the room, it was the professor. "Cadets you do know fraternizing in uniform is an expellable offense."

Jozie pulled away from Skyler, "Sorry professor."

He glared at them and said, "Well since today they are testing out the new shuttle and this is a big issue and could affect the way of the war, so if anyone in class wants to go I will let you go."

Everyone in the room got up and left the room.

Skyler walked down the hall kissing Jozie. He leaned her against the wall kissing and rubbing her body. She moaned in enjoyment.

He said, "Do you think we have time for a quickie?"

She nibbled on his earlobe and said, "I'm always ready."

They quickly ran into the closest bathroom. Not bothering to go into one of the stalls he undid his pants.

She pulled down her nylons. Turning her to face the wall. Caressing her body and as he thrusts his pelvis. She moaned louder and louder.

Helping him clear his mind this isn't how he thought he would get his frustration out. It was one of the ways that always work. He turned Jozie around kissed her lips passionately. "You are so amazing."

She rubbed his chest smiling at him, "You are an amazing guy."

A message over the PA goes off, 'Launch is in fifteen minutes if you wish to watch please make your way to courtyard B.'

They pull up their bottoms. "Well, I guess that means we better get going."

She kissed Skyler one more time, "Ya, it's your girlfriend's big day."

He sighed, "She's not my girlfriend."

She giggled, "I guess not, but one day you might want me to put in a good word for you."

Heading to the door shaking his head, "Please don't she turned me down last night and well I don't want to talk about it."

They walked out into the hall together and she gave him a hug from behind, "Well she doesn't know what she is missing."

He smiled, "Ya, I guess you are right."

They get to the courtyard just in time.

Michael waved to Skyler. He was sitting on the second row of the bleachers. Skyler and Jozie went over and sat next to him.

Michael looked at Jozie and asked, "Who is this?"

Jozie leaned over holding out her hand, "Cadet Jozie- nice to see you again remember the hall Michael, Skyler has told me all about you."

Michael smiled at her and said, "It's nice to see you again Skyler hasn't told me about you."

She shook his head, "I can't see why Skyler wouldn't talk about me."

Skyler blushes in embarrassment.

Michael whispered into his ear, "Is she your girlfriend?"

Skyler shook his head whispering back, "It's not like that."

Michael nodded going back to watching the hangar doors. Haas showed up and sat next to Michael. "Hey did I miss anything?"

He shook his head, "No but the launch is about to start, oh and by the way you know Skyler and that's his friend Jozie."

They both wave at Haas.

Haas pulled out a silver compacts mirror like thing and said, "Am I the only one or do others like to eat popcorn and watch launches." Haas turned on the compact and turned into a hologram bag of popcorn.

Michael waved his hand to say no.

Skyler and Jozie, both grab a handful of popcorn. They look confused at the popcorn.

Jozie said, "Hey if this is hologram popcorn how come we were able to take it out of the bag and how come it smells?"

Haas smiled, "Simple friends, this device is my own invention the Popcornogram 300. I have added a butter odor admitted so it smells like real popcorn, Fooling the mind. The reasons the hologram lasts in your hand so far away is because when you put your hand through the bag the device sprayed you with a chemical that will wear off but temporary acts like a hologram reflector. When in range, kind of like a green screen effect."

She examined the popcorn in her hand and says, "So we have like a mini projector in our hands?"

Haas nodded, "Sort of more like temporary Nano holoprojector. That is so small they won't last long."

They both shrugged and continued eating there fake-corn.

The hangar doors started to open.

Skyler's eyes were fixated straight ahead this was the moment he was waiting for.

Jozie learned to talk to Haas.

Skyler waved his hands, "Shut it, the launch is starting."

The gang was quiet and watched as Kax drove the fighter out of the hangar and slowly flew it up into the air.

Skyler's eyes were glued to watching her work. Never really seen her fly before. He had seen her work but only from the inside, not ever on the outside. He watched as the fighter flew around and around gracefully. He was captivated by the way she piloted.

She flew it off into the outer atmosphere. There were two other friendly fighters that followed her. Once they were out of visual range wide screen was pulled out of the hangar so all could watch the video footage. The shuttle went off into space firing at her.

***

Kax looked at the view screen she saw the other fighters firing at her. She knew about the routine they were to follow her. She just had to keep the ship turned to the spot where the new alloy was. All was going according to plan. The ship was holding up well. Not even a dent. The mission was successful. She turned in ready to fly back with the other fighters. When she saw a spot showed up on her radar. It wasn't an Earth or Squallite fighter. It was a Cassiopaean. Quickly she hit the communication button the called headquarters. "Enemy ship in range." A shot went past her shuttle. *I have just been shot at they are coming at me.* The crowd watched on the screen. They had this all recorded, there was no denying that the Cassiopaeans had purposely planned this.

***

Skyler watched in horror on the screen.

He got up. Michael grabbed his arm pulling him back into his seat.

Skyler shot a look.

Michael said, "There is not enough time to get the ship ready we planned for this the backup will come, she I'll be safe, just wait."

Skyler didn't say anything, he watched as Kax was fired upon. She fought back as best she could. Skyler's heart was pounding he didn't know what he would do if something happened to her. She was the one he loved.

Finally, a flash zipped across space. Backup was here. A new looking fast ship flew and shot the fighter down. The Cassiopaeans retreated. The Squallite ships returned to Earth. The audience was relieved.

Skyler looked at Michael, "How did you know everything was going to be okay?"

"Like I said we wouldn't test something if we didn't have backup. Also, that ship has been waiting in space since the war began keeping watch we knew that someone would plan to do something sooner or later. Now we also have proof this was an unprovoked attack."

"So you mean Kax was set up?" Skyler said.

Shaking his head, "No not at all, we knew there would be something one day who knew it was today. Just be glad my design worked."

Skyler was still not impressed.

Haas learned over, "Michael, you're the genius who designed that new alloy. What is it made out of?"

Shaking his head, “I can’t tell anyone that info yet, not till it has been approved.”

Haas held back his glare, turning it into a friendly smile.

The fighter returned to the planet. Skyler was the first to get off the bleachers and ran to Kax’s side.

She climbed out of the fighter to wave to the crowd. Michael, Jozie and Haas walked over to the fighter.

Kax waved to the people, as she climbed down.

Skyler went running towards Kax grabbing her off the ladder and to twirl her into a hug. He thought about kissing her, but held back and just hugged her tight. Holding her close he whispered into her ear, “Don’t you ever scare me like that again.”

Her eyes widened at Skyler’s jester, wasn’t sure what she was supposed to do. Looking into his eyes, she could tell he was just as scared as she was up there. A tear came to her eye and she replied to Skyler, “I will do my best.”

He loosened his grip on her and brushed her hair back. Standing there just smiling looking at her. So many thoughts about him and her ran through his mind, like what would he have done if she was hurt or even died. Wanting to say the 3 little words that were on the tip of his tongue, but he knew her feeling towards him. Instead of saying anything directly to her he let go of her and said, “Let’s all go to the pub and celebrate, drinks are on me!”

Chapter 46

At the bar, Skyler had his arm around Kax. He went up to the hostess, “Table for five, please.”

Looking down at her reservation book, “Sorry we don’t have that much room right now maybe if you are willing to wait about an hour?”

Reaching into his pocket he grabbed out his wallet pulling out a fifty, “How much is it going to take to get us a nice table?”

The hostess took the money, grabbed a couple of menus and took them to a nice booth in the back.

Skyler sat next to Kax in the middle, Jozie on Skyler’s other side, Michael next to Kax and Haas next to him.

The hostess dropped the menus on the table and walked away. They all grabbed a menu.

Kax sighed shifting away from Skyler.

The waitress finished with their orders and walked away.

Jozie flirted with her eyes to Dr. Haas. She shifted out of her seat and got up, "I have to use the bathroom. I'll be right back."

Dr. Haas got the message and got out of his seat, "Ya, I have to use the bathroom too I'll be right back."

Skyler's blood boiled. He knew what they were going to do. Jozie was his girl.

Kax saw the anger in Skyler's eyes. She placed her hand on his leg and said, "So remind me why you want me?"

Skyler quickly jerked his head towards Kax. When he saw Kax's golden cat eyes his thoughts of Jozie faded. Kax was the girl he wanted and cared about. Kax was the women he truly wanted. He smiled, "because your strong willed and so sure of yourself. Your shine bright like the sun and light up my world. Your hair is just the right shade of my favorite pink wine. And you…"

Kax's eyes widened and put her hands up to stop him, "Wow, do you really mean all that?"

Skyler smiled, "yes and much, much more you are the only women who I want to spend my life with."

Michael didn't understand what was going on. He knew of Skyler's feeling but where was this all coming from?

Kax put her one hand on Skyler's cheek and kissed him on the lips. "You're very sweet. Remind me of how beautiful I am when being down ok."

Skyler went to place his hand on Kax's shoulder and pull her close for another kiss, but she pushed him away.

Kax smiled. "That's as far as you're getting."

Skyler laughed and joked. "If I tell you more will that get me further?"

Kax shook her head. "Not tonight because pretty soon I will start to not believe you."

Jozie and Haas came back from the bathroom with smiles on their faces.

Skyler looked at Jozie again and thought. *Sure she is hot and great in bed but is she's not really what I want. She's not my girlfriend, why does it bother me so much that she was with Haas. Oh well, Kax is the only woman I'll truly be happy with.* He looked at Kax again. She was looking at her menu so she did not notice the look of happiness on Skyler's face.

***

Into the night after lots of food and lots of drinking. Skyler was getting a bit too tipsy to continue a conversation.

Michael was worried since Skyler was the one paying. He figured he better get Skyler to pay before he was too drunk.

Michael carried Skyler home after they bill was paid. He took him to his cousins house it was a lot closer than the ship. He popped him onto the spare bed.

Skyler fading in and out of consciousness from being tired and drunk looked up at Michael and said. "Why Kax doesn't love me?"

Michael shook his head as he tucked Skyler into bed. "Not this again. Skyler, she's not interested just be happy with what you have. You can't have everything."

Skyler frowned at Michael, "like you? Are you happy with what you got?"

Michael knew this was just the alcohol talking, "go to bed Skyler your drunk." Michael grabbed an extra blanket and pillow out of the closet and made himself a bed on the floor next to Skyler's bed.

Skyler watched Michael and asked. "Why are in my room aren't their extra beds?"

Michael sighed, "This is my room and yes but it is late I don't want to disturb anyone there not set up. Go to sleep."

Skyler looked up at the ceiling. "Do you think Kax will ever love me? I'm so lonly without her."

Michael grabbed his pillow and hit Skyler with it, "I told you to shut up and go to bed. If you keep bugging her she will never love you so forget it."

Chapter 47

Skyler came back to his cabin after another long day in class. He went over to his desk and turned on his computer. He would have hung out with his friends like normal, but he had booked this time to talk to Fleet Admiral Cane. It was 2 a.m. on Earth and Cane made time to talk to Skyler.

Skyler made the call and waited for Cane to respond.

Cane didn't take long to answer the call, "Hey Skyler long time no speak."

Skyler ran his fingers back through his hair and smiled, "It feels like forever Cane."

Cane smiled. "How are you enjoying it out there?"

Skyler shrugged. "Alright, once you get use to all winds. Tomorrow is the last Saturday of may so Kax, Michael and I are going to the ceremony of Shacog."

Cane smiled. "That's good you're getting to experience the local culture."

Skyler looked down at his keyboard, "Would you believe it I kind of miss Earth?"

Cane shook his head, "That's understandable this is the first time that you have left Earth for an extended period of time."

Skyler smiled, "Good to know. I don't know how much more of this health food I can take. And you know how short I am, compared to all these giants."

Cane lightly laughed, "get used to it. Humans might occupy space on most known worlds but we are the minority and you want to be a captain you will have to meet a lot of them. You think being the shortest one is bad. On Pegitarius there are people with 6 eyes two in the front two in the back and one on each side. They are always watching you. It is disturbing, but they are great witnesses in trials no one can get away with any crime there. I and your dad got stuck on there once it was an awful adventure, but good memories were made there."

Skyler smiled, "do you have more stories about my dad?"

A humble smile crossed his face, "I have them all. I met him when we were in our 30's but he shared everything with me in time. I don't think I had much of a life before him. Anytime you want to talk about him please ask."

A small tear fell from Skyler's eye, "thanks Cane I will remember that."

Cane could tell Skyler was upset, "you should ask your friend Michael to take you to a place called Vaniles. Your dad and me never spent much time on Squall but we had a stop over there once and we went to this restaurant. I won't ruin the surprise but go with Michael no one else. And you will see what I mean."

Skyler smiled, "thank you, Sir I will definitely go there."

Cane looked at his clock, "I would love to talk more but it is almost 3am. I wish our schedules were better so we could talk more. But I have an early day I hope you enjoy your summer there."

Skyler looked at his clock it was barley 8pm, "I could always skip a day of classes to make it easier for us to talk."

Cane frowned, "Skyler you are the one who wants to be a captain and I am your superior officer don't tell me you are or want to skip classes. When you come back at the end of summer we will have more time to talk. Until then enjoy the planet and don't forget to bring back souvenirs. Who knows when you will be back."

Skyler laughed, "whatever you say Cane I won't skip classes." He crossed his fingers behind his back.

"You're just like your father. Good night Skyler."

"Goodnight Cane."

Chapter 48

Michael went and woke Kax before dawn. He knocked on her door, "come one Kax if you want to get a Rospip we have to go now."

Kax looked at the time and said, "it's a Saturday I don't even get up this early for school."

Michael groaned, "it's a special store only open at certain times and I have to take you. So we need to go now."

Kax got out of bed and quickly threw on a top and put on her jeans and ran a quick brush through her hair. She stepped out of the door. Looked as awake as she could. "I'm ready to go but your buying me breakfast when this is over."

They got to the store. Michael knocked on the shop door 4 times and the shopkeeper came to the door and said, "hello welcome please come in and look around."

The tall dark hair Squallite shop keeper looked at Kax and then back at Michael. "What is she doing here she is an outsider to our ways."

Michael looked at Kax and giving her a look as to say, 'explain to the man.'

Kax was a little nervous and shaking, "Shatoka I am doing the ritual of On-Mire and I am to be a part of the ceremony of Shacog and need to purchase a Rospip."

The man smiled and walked behind his shop counter, "good I am glad that the culture is spreading outside of our own race." He looked at Michael and said, "is there anything I can get you?"

Michael was looking at a wall of knickknack and shook his head, "no I'm good."

The man frowned at Michael, "your girlfriend here isn't even one of us and wants learn and embrace our culture. I hope by you saying no you have everything you need to participate in Shacog?"

Michael took a deep breath and shook his head. "No I don't I am kind of lapsed on my culture."

The man bent down and pulled out a medium black box and placed it on the counter. "This is for you. You have been spending too much time on Earth your accent is thick and you reek of humans."

Michael just glared at the man. Part of him knowing what the man said was true and hated himself for it.

The man reaching into the showcase below him and grabbed out a long decorated stick and handed it to Kax, "this is the basic Rospip but you are to make it your own. I suggest you add something from your own culture on to this since you are one of the few outsiders to do the ritual of On-Mire."

Kax looked at the Rospip in her hand and smiled, "thank you, Sir."

Michael walked out of the store annoyed with himself and shopkeeper.

The man leaned down and spoke to Kax face to face, "I can tell your friend is very uncomfortable with you learning these traditions. I am proud of you for it. Not many will say that to you. Do take this kit to you friend he needs it even if he rejects it."

Kax smiled and pulled her card out of her wallet and handed it to the man.

He looked at the card and saw it was a UGF student charge card, "you're a cadet, no wonder your friend has been around to many humans."

Kax watched him ring up the items, "He was born here but raised on Earth. That might be what your smelling."

The man smiled, "I have no problem with people like that just a lot of use lose our ways the further we get from home. You probably are the same to your race."

Kax took back her card, "I haven't been back to my home world since I was 14 so I probably am a little to human. I don't follow my worlds religion no more."

The man smiled and handed her a bag of her stuff, "don't lose sight of who you are that's one lesson you got to learn before you get to old."

She took the bag and nodded, "Thank you, Sir I will keep that in mind."

***

At the restaurant Michael was quite while they waited to order their food. Kax look was worried about Michael. She looked up from her menu and said, "Michael Skyler will be here soon if you have any personal issues you don't want to talk about in front of him you should speak up now."

He looked up from his menu and said, "I don't want to talk about with you or anyone."

She knew Michael was doing his brutey quite thing and would not put up with it, "your worried you're to human don't you."

He sighed and knew he was not getting out of this, "maybe I have. I thought I knew everything about my culture and I get here and have been feeling a bit out of place. I don't know as much as I used to know."

Kax put her menu down and smiled, "I think your father wanted it that way. From what I know of you two. Your dad seems to want you to be a human Squallite. Keep what you know of your culture alive but live as humans do. If he didn't don't you think he would have raised, you here."

Michael thought about it for a moment. Before he could say anything Skyler showed up.

"Hey guys," He swooped in and sat down next to Kax. He looked at the menu over her shoulder for a second then up at Michael, "hey buddy you know a place called Vaniles? We should go there sometime this week."

Michael was a bit shocked, "I know the place, not sure why you would want to go there with me but sure we can do that."

The waitress came over to the table, a tall young dusty haired Squallite. "so what can I get you three."

Skyler put on his winning smile and said, "are you on the menu because I could sure go for a tall drink of you."

Kax frowned at Skyler.

The waitress politely responded, "sorry I'm not and I don't think your girlfriend appreciates you asking me out."

Kax was about to say something when Michael spoke up, "fruit salad and a cup of oaka root tea."

Kax then said, "ham sandwich and orange juice."

"make that two," Skyler said.

The waitress wrote down their orders, "I'll be back soon with your food."

Chapter 49

Kax went to Skyler's cabin and knocked on his door.

Skyler got out of his bed and answered to door only wearing his boxers. He smiled when he saw Kax, "hey you finally change your mind about us?"

She looked behind him and saw Jozie in bed behind him, "what about her?"

Skyler looked back at his bed, "oh her she was just leaving unless you want her to stay."

Kax frowned, "I'm here because today is the ceremony of Shacog we have to get ready to go."

Skyler brushed his hair back, "oh right I forgot about that. Give me a few minutes and I will get ready. Come in and sit down."

Kax was reluctant but agreed to come in and sat down at Skyler's computer desk.

Skyler went over to his bed and shook the girl awake, "hey Jozie time to get up."

Jozie opened her eyes, she saw Kax sitting at the desk, "oh you finally got Kax into your room good for you. I will get out of here." She got out of the bed naked and started to put her clothes on.

Kax's face was beat red and quickly turned around in her chair.

Skyler put his clothes on and kissed Jozie goodbye. He turned back to Kax, "I'm dressed now you can open turn back around."

"You have been seeing a lot of Jozie lately haven't you?"

He nodded and sat down on his bed, "sort of, ya. We get along."

Kax shook her head and got up, "well it's good thing to see you have a girlfriend. But you do know when you have one you're not supposed to hit on other girls."

Skyler stood and headed towards the door with Kax, "Jozie isn't my girlfriend she's just a friend. She would be happy if you and me got together and doesn't stop me from looking at any other women."

Kax rolled her eyes, "fine whatever you two are. I am just glad you have someone to distract you. Now let's get going to the ceremony."

In the town square people were gathering for the ceremony of Shacog. Michael was waved to them from the second row. They wiggled through the crowd to get to him.

Michael handed Kax an orange robe matching to his, "wear this so they will know you are participating." He turned and handed Skyler a blue glow stick, "this is so they know you're just watching and that you are from Earth. Blue is the color of Earth."

Skyler looked at the glow stick, "I prefer green can I have a green one?"

Michael frowned, "No Green is for The Leo's. Stick with the tradition you are guest here."

Skyler took the blue glow stick and put it around his neck. He sat on the bench and watched the ceremony.

The bleachers were set up in a large circle and in the center there was a fire pit with orange rocks. The three elders were standing around the fire in lavish orange robes. They had ten-foot-long poles I their hands all decorated with leaves gems and other native materials of their land all uniquely decorated. Two elders sprinkled powder on the fire and the eldest of the elders slammed his pole standing up into the ground and a loud boom came from the fire. He then spoke, "ever since the beginning of our people they have celebrated Shacog it was the ceremony to give thanks to the tees for being our shelter and away for us to give back to nature. This is the week where we all give back to nature by the use of no technology, eat only food from nature and plant a tree with every meal to help keep our forests strong."

A group of other people in fancy orange robes came out and started handing everyone a package of seeds.

The High Elder spoke again, "these are the seeds you will need for the week. Do not waste a single seed."

Once everyone had their seeds. A group of young children came out dancing with their Rospip wearing traditional peach color robes.

Michael leaned over to Kax, "get up when I do, they are going by age groups here and follow what I do."

Kax nodded her head and waited for their turn. Watching the kids dance with their Rospip raising them up and down and shaking there sticks in random ways. Than it was the pre-teen's turn, followed by the teens and then it was Kax and Michael's turn.

Skyler watched Kax nervously dance trying to keep up. He gave her a light smile and thumbs up when she came around to give her some encouragement. Soon most of the people who were in the bleachers were up and dancing. Skyler was still sitting on the sidelines with the others who were watching. The dancing went on and on till just after noon.

Michael and Kax came over to Skyler. Skyler smiled at Kax, "you look good out there. Though I don't think orange is your color, you look better in purple."

Kax laughed, "thanks Skyler I will keep that in mind."

Skyler stood up and looked at the Rospip in Kax's hand, "can I see your dancing stick?"

"it's a Rospip and sure." She handed him the stick.

Michael handed him his too.

He looked at both of them. He saw Kax had added on a lock of her hair, a bell and her special division pin to it. "You can't put your pin on this don't you only get one?"

Kax took it back, "I have a few of them and if I lose them they will give me another. There pins and easy to lose. I would have added more but I don't have a lot of my stuff here."

He looked at Michael's, it had tick marks on the side, a piece of a material that matched his uniform, and few leaves. "I figured yours would have more things on it you have done this longer."

Michael took his back, "I just started another. The notches on the side are how many I ceremonies of Shacog I have been I but this is a new Rospip my old one is on Earth with my dad. I don't trust the transporters with it."

Kax's stomach began to rumble, "can we get the food I am hungry."

Michael nodded, "come one and let's go to the food pavilions."

At the food pavilions, there were dozens of different stands all selling different kinds of traditional foods. Michael took them up to the Koshlash stand.

"You two will love Koshlash it is like a stew but so much better," He got them bowls with lids. "And then let's go to the bread stand. Like anything you see feel free to get it. I just know you two will love this stew."

They made their way to the bread stand. While Michael was getting them some rolls Jozie can up to Skyler. "Hey Skyler I thought you would be here."

Skyler smiled, "Ya I'm just getting some food and then were going to sit down."

"Well when you have your food you should come over and sit with us."

He looked over her shoulder and saw dr. Haas from a distance, "you're with Haas?"

She nodded, "On my way here we bumped into each other and decided to go together."

Skyler awkwardly smiled, "that's great ya I don't see a problem with that see you in a bit."

Jozie walked back towards her table.

Skyler looked around for where Kax and Michael went. He saw them in the distance and walked over.

Kax was picking out desserts. Holding two trays, "we didn't want to disturb you while you were talking so we moved on. We got you a try so you don't have to hold your stew."

Skyler put is stew on the tray and then took the tray. He looked at the odd assortment of food on the tray, "um what is all this stuff?"

A male's voice came up from behind Skyler and said, "you will like this it's the closest to Earth food tasting you are going to get."

Skyler turned around, "Danrik what are you doing here?"

Danrik laughed, "it is my culture I should be asking you what you're doing here. How are you doing? haven't seen you around."

Kax put a few more squares on his tray. He looked up at Danrik and said, "were not even together and she's telling me what to eat."

Danrik laughed, "well she's has good tastes so it's not so bad."

Kax went to put one more square on Skyler's tray, "you put one more square on my plate you will have to sleep with me. I don't think I can eat all this food. You eat all you want Kax but I don't even know if I will like any of it."

Her face pouted a little then she looked at how much was on Skyler's tray, "oh I'm sorry I guess I got a bit carried away." She grabbed a square off his tray and took a bite. "Whatever you can't finish I will eat for you."

He gave Kax a kiss on the cheek and took a bit of the square, "you are just the sweetest thing, know you meant no harm."

She finished the square and smiled, "I think I am getting use to you."

Danrik leaned in between the two, "sorry to break you to up but the rest of us are done getting our food so if you two are ready we can go find seats."

"I told Jozie and Dr. Haas we would sit with them."

Danrik patted Skyler on the back, "don't worry me and Kanrick will have no problem meeting your friends."

Kax frowned at Skyler, "Jozie's here?"

They moved towards the table.

"Jozie is here with Dr. Haas."

Danrik pulled Skyler back while Kax went ahead, "boy you're going to have to tell me what is going on with you and her. First I thought she was Michael's girl and then yours but you said she's not but that is not the signal I am getting from you to."

Skyler whispered to him, "I love Kax but she doesn't want me. I see Jozie on a casual basis were very open. She's also is seeing Haas I think and Haas likes Michael but Michael is Asexual, or something he has a name for it."

Danrik laughed and patted Skyler on the back. "Your funny, I'll tell you, Kax might not say it but she has a thing for you and she's jealous of Jozie. How do you know about Michael and Haas?"

"I saw them kiss the day we climbed the mountain." He shook in disbelief, "and naw Kax can't be she doesn't want me so she's not allowed to be jealous."

"Michael is taking after his father." He rubbed Skyler's shoulder, "your young and still have lots to learn about women."

At the table Jozie was sitting next to Haas, Kax was across next to Michael and Kanrick. Danrik sat down next to Jozie and across from his wife. While Skyler sat next to Kax.

"Jozie, Dr. Haas these are my dad's cousins Danrik and Kanrick," Michael said.

Jozie took her hand off Haas's leg and shook Danrick's hand batting her eyelashes, "nice to meet you."

Kanrick cleared her throat, "Jozie you seem like a nice girl but Danrik is my husband.

Jozie smiled, "that's fine I do couples too."

Kax almost spat her drink.

Kanrick gave an unpleasant glare.

Michael turned to Haas, "hey Haas remember you asked me about taking holo-pictures of my cousin's house now's the time to ask them."

Haas's eyes picked and handed Danrik his card, "I am a Doctor of robotics and I specialize in holograms. I have never been inside a real Squallite home and would love to see the inside of your home and take some Holo-pictures for my research."

Danrik shared a look with his wife. "That sounds alright. But not this week during Shacog no technology remember. But you can come over and Michael an show you around."

Haas smiled, "that's no problem with me I am here till the end of the summer but if I have to stay longer I can work that out with my boss."

Danrik smiled, "Ya come by sometime after work one day Michael will show you the way."

Haas held out his hand and shook Danrick's, "thank you so much sir."

Kax noticed Skyler picking at his food, "eat your food don't waste it."

Skyler picked up a piece of meat out of the stew with his fork and showed it to Kax, "Kax I don't even know what animal this is from it could be poisonous to humans."

Michael looked over at Skyler, "you might be a pain in the ass but I would not try and poison you."

Skyler took a bite of his food, "well it's not too bad. But if I get sick I'm blaming you Michael."

Michael rolled his eyes, "you blame me for everything that goes wrong in your life so is what's the difference?"

Kax picked up one of the chocolate like balls off Skyler's plate and put it in his mouth, "Don't blame Michael if you get sick blame me this time."

Skyler ate the ball, "mmm, that wasn't so bad maybe it will be worth getting sick."

Chapter 50

Michael helped Skyler into the tree house pulling him up by his hand while Skyler tried to climb up the tall tree.

Skyler got into the small platform like tree house and turned to Michael and said, "I thought that living in a tree house was only for those participating in the ritual why do I have to be here?"

Michael reached down and helped Kax up, "because there is no technology to be used this week and your living on a starship. Technically your out of a house so you're staying with me and Kax."

Skyler helped Kax with the final step into the tree house. "There is barely any room up here were going to be spooning the entire time. and your planet has storms all the time what if the tree gets ripped out and we die."

"That is the risk we have to take. Lots of people die every year during Shacog but we keep doing it to remind us of the dangers out ancestors went through."

"Also you have never argued about spooning with me before," Kax added.

feeling defeated, "fine but I'm sleeping next to Kax."

She looked at Michael and then back at Skyler, "ok but you keep it in your pants. If I feel it once I am pushing, you out of this tree."

Michael laughed wondering how this was going to end.

Skyler looked around, "hey what do I have to do if I have to use the bathroom?"

Michael looked down at the ground, "you can go off the side or climb up and down each time."

Kax face turned sour, "really won't that be gross when we do have to go back down for food?"

"A little but it will go back to the Earth in the end. For food we will be climbing from tree to tree. I will do most the for food gathering for you two because your too short. I struggle with it but I don't want you two to fall and hurt yourselves."

"So you mean to tell me I have to spend the next week outside living in a tree house?" Skyler said setting up his spot for bedtime.

Michael rolled his eyes, "Yes consider it pay back for making me put up with all the girls you bring back to the room."

Kax looked around at the other tree houses, "how come ours has a floor and a roof and others have 4 walls?"

Michael sighed, "This was all I could afford. The money is dotation to the council but

still the more you donate the better tree house you get."

"Wait you needed money. Dude you should have asked me I could have bought us a better place one that's weatherproof what if we wake up all wet one day." Skyler said.

"I don't think waking up wet is a problem for you," Michael got his sleeping bag laid out, "Skyler it is my culture my bill to pay. I am not going to ask you to pay all my bills all the time."

Skyler rolled his eyes, "sorry I have money but I could have at least paid for our upgrade my share of the tree house."

Michael started to get snappy, "it isn't about the money!"

Kax put her hand on Skyler's shoulder and whispered into Skyler's ear, "I think this is more of a cultural thing for Michael just let it be and be thankful I got us waterproof sleeping bags."

Skyler turned and gave Kax a hug, "you're so sweet sometimes."

Michael finished setting up his sleeping bag. "I don't know about you two but I am going to get some sleep."

Skyler looked over at Kax, "last chance to zip our sleeping bags together."

Kax laughed and got into hers, "Good night Skyler."

Skyler awoke in the morning hugging Kax's empty sleeping bag. He sat up and saw Kax leaning on the ledge talking to the neighbors. Tree was no sign of Michael. he got up and put his arm around Kax, "so sweetie did you sleep well?"

She shrugged Skyler off and said, "Skyler I am talking to the neighbors."

Skyler waved to the young couple. He stretched out his hand and said, "Hello, I'm Skyler Therris. Nice to meet you two."

The husband stretched out his hand and shook Skyler's, "my name is Mirik and this is my wife Tagerin. This is our second year doing this together, but we have been doing this our whole lives."

Kax spoke up, "wow that is nice, it's our first time, but me and Skyler aren't a couple even if he thinks we are."

Skyler laughed, "oh sweetie don't be so modest."

Tagerin laughed, "well I hope you two enjoy your week."

Skyler looked at her and asked, "you got one of the open tree houses too how are you supposed to keep the rain and weather out?"

She raised her arms and pulled a string, and a curtain came down. "Yours has them too. When it rains you bring them down and they will keep you mostly dry. Also if you two want to be intimate, but everyone will still be able to hear you."

Skyler grinned at Kax, "hear that we can be intimate."

"I told you before no and if I see it or feel it I'm going to push you out of the tree."

Mirik laughed, "you two really are just friends."

"Until the day she says yes."

"That day will never happen with that attitude," Michael said climbing back into the tree with a basket of food, "I am guessing I didn't miss much."

Kax looked at the fruit is in the basket, "we were just talking to our neighbors Mirik and Tagerin, they showed us there are curtains we can pull down to protect us from the rain." She pointing along the inside of the roof.

Michael looked up, "huh I didn't know those were there good to know."

Skyler looked at the food, "so I am guessing there was no Earth food?"

Michael frowned, "how many times do I have to tell you no. but you can try this it's called a ompac it's like an Earth apple." He handed the fruit to Skyler.

Skyler took it and looked at it puzzled, "it's orange. It's like a giant orange apple. Apples aren't orange. Oranges are orange."

Tired of trying, "That's right Skyler and for the next week you will be eating them. All natural native food. Is all we will be eating so get use it."

Skyler turned his head and took a bite of the fruit. It did taste like an apple and wasn't to bad but he wasn't going to tell Michael that. He wished he could have a cheese burger.

Chapter 51

Day four in the tree house. Skyler looked up at the sky hoping to see a rain cloud, "Dude this isn't fair, before we started this there was rain like every day now all were getting is wind. I want a shower I stink." He rustled his hand through his hair in frustration.

Michael groaned, "is all you do is complain? I haven't had a shower either we all stink and I am sorry this isn't a mansion with an endless supply of cheese burgers and women but this is what my people use to go though this is a learning experience try and be a bit more respectful."

Skyler took a moment to imagine a mansion with cheese burgers and women, "Michael I'm sorry I have been edgy but I am not use to this. There is not much space to walk around, it's hot then cold, the food is still new to me and I feel dirty I want a shower or a bath. Your ancestors could not have just lived in the same tree they had to have moved around or you would be tiny little tree people."

Michael sighed, "I am sorry I didn't give you more warning about this. There are a few tree houses with showers but there on the other side of the park and not sure if people will just let you use them. I am surprised it has been this long without any rain. Hopefully it will rain tonight or tomorrow. I am getting tired of living like this too. I wish I was back in the dorm trying to drown out your sex noises."

Skyler rubbed his face, "I am sorry buddy I thought once you were asleep you couldn't hear me."

Michael sighed, "I will tell you again I don't sleep none of my race does we go into a meditative sleep trance."

Kax hopped back into the tree house panting. Her hair was drenched and she looked at the dry guys. "Watch out there is a storm coming I was at the other side of the camp meeting people and it started to rain!"

Skyler and Michael quickly rushed over to the ledge and watching the storm cloud coming their way. They both smiled giving each other a quick hug. Breaking the hug Skyler took his black t-shirt off. Waiting for the rain to come.

Kax went over and pulled the curtain down.

Skyler grabbed the curtain trying to lift it back up, "what did you do that for we need the rain we haven't had a shower in a week."

Kax glared. "Really I have. The tree house 5 over has a lovely shower they let me use. I don't want the rain in here I am feline we hate water unless necessary."

Michael saw the storm coming closer, "Kax you stay in that corner and me and Skyler will be here keep your two curtains down and we will leave ours open. We stink and next time tell us there is a tree house with a shower."

Kax moved over the opposite and turned away from the striping guys. "You never said anything about it. You could have jumped around from treehouse to tree house on your own."

The rain came down in seconds. It might have been half in a tree and a shower next to another almost naked guy but it was the best damn shower Skyler had had in a long time.

Chapter 52

"Hey Michael you ready! Our reservations are for one," Skyler called up the stairs of Michaels cousin's house. He went the back to the kitchen and drank his cup of cocha tea.

Danrik sat down next to Skyler, "give him time. as long as I have known Michael he has always been late."

"Really? Mr. Punctual, he is never late. He picks on me when I'm late for class makes me get up earlier so we can make it there before the bell. He is always on time."

Danrik laughed, “it must be a macho act he puts on in school. Hey Skyler do you drink?” He got up and walked over to the fridge.

Skyler's face lit up, “I love to drink you got any beers?”

Danrik pulled two beers out of the fridge and handed one to Skyler, “there not brand name it’s an old family recipe hope you like it.”

Skyler took a sip of his orange colored beer, “mmm this is so good. Does Michael have the recipe?”

He took a sip, “Michael better have it this is his dad’s recipe.”

Michael came down the stairs, “don’t give him beer he won’t stop drinking. You know how annoying he is when he is drunk?”

Danrik laughed, “well if you were down here when he called you all he would have had to drink would have been tea.”

Skyler smiled, “you should have told me your family made such great booze.”

Michael frowned, “just finish your drink so we can get to Vaniles.”

Danrick’s eyes widened, “your guys are going to Vaniles? Wow you two really do have a love, hate relationship.”

Skyler finished his beer, “what do you mean it’s just a restaurant?”

Danrik shook his head, “oh trust me Skyler it is more then that whoever told you two to go knows more than what there saying.”

Michael and Skyler shared a confused look.

“Ok well I’m done my beer lets go find out what this place is all about.”

They got to the restaurant. On the outside of the place looked beat up and run down, not a friendly place to be.

Skyler was nervous about walking in, “Are you sure you want to go here?”

Michael opened the door, “You’re the one who invited me.”

Skyler followed into the restaurant, and was pleasantly surprised.

The outside had chipping paint, broken sign and blacked out windows. But on the inside there was a polished dark hardwood floor. Velvet curtains. A shining orange crystal chandelier on the center of the restaurant. Triangle tables with ancient Squallite designs on the top.

An older lady in orange robes with very detailed orange bead embellishments all over. Her long white hair and was put back half in a bun. "Your captain Therris's son. It's been many years since I have seen those green eyes."

It appeared they were the only ones in the place. *She remembers my dad? How would she know who he is anyway?* Skyler thought. "Yes but I never told you my last name the reservation just says for Skyler and Michael."

She smiled and brushed Skyler's hair back with her hand with long nails and covered with rings, "Well you weren't born when I met your father but you look just like him. You carry his spirit in you, your destined for greatness just like him." She turned and looked at Michael, "Sam Jones's son I have never had your father walk in here but I know your story all too well. You two boys are an interesting pair; I wonder what someone was thinking." She turned and walked away, "take a seat, I will be back in a moment."

Skyler turned his head to Michael, "that was a bit odd?"

Michael grabbed a seat, "your telling me. Who told you about this place again?"

"Cane, he said him and my dad dinner here years ago and I was to only bring you. It was the only time my dad was ever on Squall." He took a seat across from Michael at the triangle table. Not sure if he is supposed to sit on the same point as Michael or on the tip of the triangle. He tried to sit somewhere in the middle of the to to give Michael some space.

"You said Cane?" Michael adjusted his seat to give Skyler and him the most room between them, "I swear that guy is up to something he might be one of our highest commanding officers but he knows more than he lets on. I just wonder what his game is."

Skyler shrugged, "I don't know. But has he ever steered us wrong?"

Michael rubbed his chin, "You might be right."

A moment later the lady came back out of the room and handed them one large plate of spaghetti. They both looked up at her oddly.

"Ma'am not to be rude but we didn't order this and why do we have to share the plate?" Michael asked.

"It doesn't matter what you had planned to order," She put two forks down in front of them. "I will be back with your drinks."

"Make mine a beer!" Skyler called out as she walked away.

Michael looked at the food, "I don't think it matters what you say she has already figured out what we're eating and drinking."

Skyler took his fork and stabbed it into the food and twirled his fork, "well in that case let's dig in. We might as well enjoy this and if we don't we can grab cheeseburgers and a salad afterwards."

Michael laughed and put his fork into the plate as well. They twirled there forks and then pulled out. Some of them had the ends of the same noodles. Michael looked on the table for a knife.

The lady came out with their drinks, two glasses of sparkling water. "Here are your drinks, I trust everything is ok?"

Michael moved his fork up a bit more. "No it's not, can we have a knife to cut our noodles."

She shook her head, "sorry that's not how it works."

Skyler looked at Michael awkwardly, "ma'am were friends not a couple were not going to kiss."

She laughed, "I am not expecting you to that, the point is to work together. You figure it out." She made her way back to the kitchen.

Michael looked at the noodles. "We could try pulling and getting them to snap?"

Skyler looked at how the noodles were twisted. "Right now we have them twisted like a rolled up scroll. If we pull they will fly back in our face. If we just let this set go and one of us turn one way and the other turn the other. We can have them twist in an angle and then it would be easier to break. Or we both put it in our mouths and only one of us bite down."

Michael thought of the options, “this is one weird place, I wonder what Cane and your dad did?”

Skyler said, “let’s just pull I think that is the better option.”

Michael nodded and they tried it. It was not the best solution but over time they got it. A few times the noodles did fly back at them and they laughed getting sauce splashed all over them.

When the plate was empty they looked down at the bottom of the plate. There were old letters on the bottom of the plate. Michael looked in closer, “It is written in old Squall, Omaca umpa holta spekt yuletra.”

Skyler looked confused, “what does that mean?”

“My old Squall is rusty but if I am correct it is an expression that means,” He paused taking a moment to translate in his head, “you worked together now eat cake?’ What that doesn’t make sense.”

The lady came out with to plates with a slice of cake on both of them, “Here you go did you enjoy the challenge.”

Skyler’s mouth watered when he saw the white cake covered in white frosting with chocolate sauce drizzled on top with a dusting of caramel chips. He wanted to just reach out and just grab the cake right out of her hands, but he waited.

She placed the plates down on the table and said, “I think you will find this one a bit more interesting.”

Skyler who was just a second ago anxious to devour this cake now was not sure he wanted to touch it.

Michael looked at the cake, “I don’t think it is toxic.”

Skyler took a deep breath and then looked at the lady, “How did my dad and Cane deal with the spaghetti test?”

She put on a devilish smile, “they didn’t eat spaghetti they had a steak.”

Michael was intrigued by this story, “what was the challenge with a steak you would split it down the middle and share.”

She laughed, “that’s why you two got spaghetti. With those two it was always a fight for power they had to learn to compromise. You two need to learn to work together.” She took the spaghetti plate away and left them to their dessert.

Skyler went to eat his cake to realize his plate didn't have a fork. He looked at Michael's plate, "she only gave us one fork, and she gave it to me."

"Well I guess I will just have to use my spaghetti fork." He looked at the table and noticed that there wasn't one. *She must have taken the fork with her.* "Well it appears there is only one fork what do you suggest we do?"

Skyler wanted to eat the cake but he knew Michael probably wanted to eat the cake just as much. He swallowed his pride and handed the fork to Michael, "here buddy you take the fork, I will eat the cake with my fingers, I don't mind getting them sticky."

Michael rolled his eyes and took the fork, "thank you that was nice of you even if you added in the sexual innuendo."

Skyler shrugs, "hey I'm a nice guy, I would give you my right arm if you needed one."

Michael shuddered, "I don't want your right arm but why are you so nice to me I thought you didn't like me?"

Skyler frowned, "you're the one who doesn't like me. Michael even if your constant put downs, you are better to hang out with then my family."

Michael pushed the fork over to Skyler, "you have the fork you will need it. I should get my hands sticky for once."

Skyler took the fork, "how about we both get our hands sticky and say goodbye to this fork."

Michael laughed, "suit yourself."

They put the fork at the corner away from them and ate the cake with their fingers.

Chapter 53

The summer was coming to an end. Skyler was happy to be out of the tree house and back in his cabin. Just getting out of the shower he saw a light flashing on the computer. He goes over and turns on the screen and sees Cane is calling him. He answered the call. "Hey Cane why are you calling me?"

Cane sighed, "do you ever wear a shirt."

Skyler brushed his hair back, "I just got out of the shower. What is this about? We didn't have any scheduled time so I know this has to be a business call with me only having 2 weeks left here."

Cane nods, "you're right Skyler. Remember the orb I sent you to get when I first sent you out there. I thank you for bringing the Squallites into the war, but we still need the orb."

Skyler rubbed his face learning forward on the desk, "they won't give it to us I am sorry but I don't think there is another way."

Cane's eye went dark, "I can't express how important this is but I do not care how you do it just bring the orb to Earth. And I mean anything do whatever it takes."

Skyler nodded, "ok I will what I can."

Cane cut the call.

Skyler sat alone as his desk, *How can I get the orb. They said no and I can't just walk in and take it. Or can I?* He made a call to Dr. Haas.

Haas answered, "Franklin Haas here, oh hey Skyler what do you want?"

"Haas are you alone right now?"

"I am at Michael's cousins house right now but I can go outside and for a few minutes what is this about?"

Skyler got out of his chair and started getting dressed, "Holograms, I need a Hard light hologram projector or something similar."

"Listen I know you like Kax but if your wanting her I recommend a shapeshifter. Holograms are not the way to go."

Skyler could hear the door close in the background, "No, I would not be asking about that not with her or to you. I'm letting you in on a secret mission. Me, Michael and Kax were sent here not just for summer training but to get the Worm Orb. The Squallites said they would give it to Earth but they lied we brought them into the war but I have just been given orders before we go home I have to get that orb. I don't know how but I thought of you and your holograms. I think we should steal the orb and replace it with a hard light hologram so they won't even notice."

"I like your idea. I do have something that I think We can use. Who else will be involved in this heist?"

Skyler thought about it for a second, "not really sure. I know Michael would know how to get in there but I'm not sure he would agree to it. You know what when your done there get Michael, Kax and Jozie together and come to my cabin we can figure out a plan together."

After a few hours of thinking the gang all arrived. Skyler set up a few chairs he could find in his room for the guests. He hit the button on the door and let them in. "I'm glad you all could make it. I hope someone has caught Jozie up to speed on what this is all about. I wouldn't normally bring more people into this but I think she may be able to help."

They all walked in a took a seat. Jozie sat on Skyler's bed. Skyler went and sat down next to her. He looked at Michael, "so do you think you can get us a second chance with the council."

Michael sighed, "you were the one who made the appointment in the first place but I can try. Why do you think with more people they will let us have the orb this time?"

He put his arm around Jozie and said, "well we will give them one last chance to say yes. Then if they say no we steal it."

Michael's eyes bulged from his skull, "you want to steal one of my peoples most sacred items. Are you out of your freaking MIND!"

Skyler had never seen Michael so enraged but had expected it. He looked over at Haas, "were you able to bring it?"

Haas pulled out a small metal disk out of his lab coat pocket. He turned it on and a large roll of cheese appearing almost real.

Michael snarled, "you want to replace the orb with hologram cheese!"

Skyler rolled his eyes and turned back to Haas, "do you happen to have a Holo-Image of the orb?"

Haas shook his head, "No I don't but I figure once we break in I will be able to take a image and replace it. It will take long less than a minute."

Michael hissed, "Skyler I know you have been a jerk before, but this is going to far!"

Skyler sighed, "Michael this order is coming from someone higher than Cane. If you don't want to be a part of it I will take your resignation and you can stay here because they're not going to let you back on Earth if it comes out your refused to help in the war."

Appalled, Michael replied, "refused to help in the war I invented a new alloy for them, so they can have stronger ships what more do they want!"

Skyler looked Michael dead in the eyes, "I don't see you leaving? But I will tell you this if you don't want us to steal it you convince them to give it to us."

Michael raised his hand as to say something, but just as fast put it down. "No Skyler your right we need that orb. Let's knock the council's ego down a few pegs."

Skyler was confused by Michael's sudden change of attitude, but it was getting late they had to make a plan. "Okay are we all on board now?" Looking around and saw that they all were nodding their heads. "Okay good now here is the plan. Tomorrow Michael and me will go back in ask nicely one last time for the orb if that fails. We come back at night. Jozie I will need you to distract the guards. The rest of us will go upstairs. Michael will know the way and to where it is hidden. Once in the room Haas will replace the orb hand it to Kax. You three will sneak out the back way and I will go out the front. That way if anyone gets caught it will be me. I am willing to take all the blame for this. Any questions?"

Kax held up her hand, "why does Jozie have to distract the guard and why not me?"

Skyler looked at Jozie and smiled, "because Jozie will sleep with almost anyone regardless of gender or species. You won't."

Jozie tossed her hair smiling, "it's true I have no problem with my involvement in this plan."

Kax pouted her face, "who says I won't make out or sleep with just anyone test me I will do it."

Skyler raised an eyebrow at Kax, "okay then kiss Dr. Haas."

Kax determined to prove a point gets up and kisses Haas on the cheek, "There you go."

Jozie laughed and got up off the bed and went over to dr. Haas. She put her legs around him and sat on his lap. She leaned in and French kissed Haas rubbing her hands across his chest.

After a moment she stood up and smiled at Kax, “that is how it’s done. You don’t kiss him like he’s your grandma you kiss him like you want him to take you like a man.”

Kax sat back down and pouted, “sorry I’m not a whore like you.”

“That's why I didn’t choose you for that job.” Trying to make Kax feel better skyer said, “that’s one thing I like about you. Also that’s the reason I want you to take the orb out of the building you look innocent and no one would think you did anything wrong.”

Kax just sat there quietly not saying a word back.

Skyler looked at the group, “so everything make sense to everyone and we have this all figured out?”

Jozie sat back down next to Skyler and said, “what if they find out about the switch you all get to leave the planet I’m stuck here till my dad is posted won’t I get caught?”

Skyler leaned over and kissed her on forehead, “That’s another reason you are to distract the guard, because if we do get caught your innocent all you did was fool around with the security guard.” He looked around at the room one more time. “So does everyone have this all figured out.” He looked around the room and everyone nodded in agreement. “Well then I will be in touch.”

Chapter 54

Morning came, and Skyler was ready to go. Wearing his satin green dress uniform and medals. This was the Squallites last chance to say yes. He stood in front of the mirror hands shaking. *Dammit Michael where are you I can’t wait any longer.* He began to pace around the room with his hands behind his back. Finally, there was a knock at the door. He rushed over to the door and opened it. “What took you so long I’m going out of my mind waiting for you.”

Michael was in his full-dress uniform to, “well first off I had to wait for my marks to come in remember we were doing schooling, I passed. Then I had to call the Elders and they are willing to see us and give us one last chance.” He took a deep breath and said, “I don’t know how this is going to go but Skyler we have to be 100% professional with this. No loud outbursts, not like last time."

Skyler nodded, "I know. So, are you ready to go?"

Michael nodded and headed out the door.

Waiting or for the council to see them. Skyler and Michael sat on the bench outside of the office. Skyler's hands and feet were shaking he didn't know what laid behind that door.

Michael noticed and whistled a little tune.

Skyler turned his head and frowned, "what's that?"

Michael stopped and turned his head to look at Skyler, "Sorry it is a habit. My father used to sing to me when I was nervous and taught me to do it when he wasn't around. Will stop if it is bothering you?"

Skyler shook his head, "no I like it you can sing the song if you wanted."

Michael smiled and sang an old Squallite song to help calm his and Skyler's nerves.

The female elder waiting till the song was over before she stepped out of the office and called out to the boys, "Captain Therris and Lt. Jones we will see you now."

Skyler closed his eyes and took a deep breathe. This was the hardest thing he had to do in a long time. knowing the odds were against them he still had to try.

They walked into the office and took their seats in front of the council.

The high elder looked at the boys and said, "You two have been here twice before and we have said no what makes you think this time we will say yes?"

Skyler looked down and let out a small laugh, "well sir it's an expression on my planet, 'third time's the charm.' But really sir we're getting ready to leave and I thought I would give you one last chance to reconsider our offer."

The high elder smiled, "you humans never learn, no means no. You got us to go to war which my people have not done in almost 1000 years and you still want us to give you our orb."

Michael spoke up, "that orb was given to you as a sign of peace between the Cass and now you are at war if that orb goes missing they will not notice. They already see us as human sympathizers and you know why the Cass hate the humans. Please give us the orb and continue this bond of peace and friendship between Earth and Squall."

The high elder shook his head, "No, and that's firm. We have gone to war for our own people and we will help Earth where there are treaties and previous agreements to, but we are not their allies. Earth continues to degrade and enslave our people and we do not support it. We cannot stop people like your father from going to Earth but we can refuse to help the humans."

Skyler clenched his fist and held back the urge to scream, "I guess your minds made up and you do not wish to help us I'm sorry we are such a pain in your side."

Michael didn't want to lose, and he didn't want to come back that night and steal the orb he made one last desperate attempt to get the orb, "What if I get the humans to give the Squallites equal rights? I will go back to Earth and demand they do it."

The Elders laughed, "We will give you the orb when you do that but not before."

Michael smiled he thought of a great opportunity, "I can agree to that."

Skyler looked at Michael confused, "What we can't get the rights changed overnight?"

Michael leaned over and whispered to Skyler, "listen I have a plan I'll tell you later."

The female elder pulled out a piece of paper and filled out a few things and slid it over the table closer to Michael. "Fill this out."

Michael stood up and looked over the document only made a slight change, "when I take over as owner of the orb I want anyone who has committed crimes against it cleared. I know there have been many people in the past who have tried to steal it. When I become the new owner, their names are to be cleared."

The elders looked at each other and nodded. The high elder spoke up, "If you become owner of the orb. You still have to get the Squallites equal rights on Earth."

"I'll figure out a way your highness." Michael sighed the edited document and handed it back to the elders and sat down.

The high elder looked at the two boys and said, “well I think all is done here you two boys may go now it is a busy day.”

Skyler and Michael stood up and bowed before they left the office. Once out of the room Skyler walked close to Michael and said, “what was that about we were to get the orb now not when you do the impossible.”

Michael didn’t say anything just hurried out of the building. “Skyler just text the gang and get them ready I will tell you in your cabin.”

They hurried back to the cabin. Michael sat down on the bed while Skyler changed out of his uniform, “I don’t know when I will ever be able to give my people equality but when I do and you or any of us get caught for stealing the orb their names will be cleared. I just gave you a loophole.”

Skyler put on a pair of blue jeans and black tank top. “Cleaver just figure out how to do that and I will thank you from my execution.”

Michael laughed unbuttoning his uniform, “Squallites don’t execute people. They will probably if anyone gets caught will be thrown I jail for the rest of their life or exile.”

Skyler thought about it, “I’ll take the life in exile, your planet is boring.”

Michael frowned then saw the smirk on Skyler’s face, “maybe life in prison isn’t so bad for you.”

The two share a laugh, till they hear a knock at the door. Michael gets off the bed and answers the door. He smiles when he sees who it is, “Kax, Haas come in. where is Jozie?” he steps aside from the door to let them in.

Kax rolls her eyes, “Jozie saw a cute guy on the way over here and said she will be a bit late. But to text her if we leave without her.”

Skyler rolled his eyes, “well then let’s get ready for this. We have some time we have to wait till nightfall so there’s lots of time for Jozie to show up.”

Kax sighed, “so I guess the talk didn’t go well.”

Skyler sat down at his desk chair and laughed, “that’s one way to put it.” He turned his head and to Michael, “ask Michael what he did.”

Michael took a deep breathe, "I got us off for any crimes we get convicted of tonight."

Kax's eyes widen, "you told them were going to steal the orb!"

Michel shakes his hand, "calm down no I didn't, but in the event, I give the Squallites equality on Earth I become the new owner of the orb and anyone who commited a crime to do with the orb in the past there name is cleared."

Kax rolled her eyes, "Thanks for trying."

Haas sat down next to Michael on the bed, "hey buddy I think you can do it. You're already the acting first officer of this ship."

Michael laughed, "well let's just hope we don't get caught."

Skyler went over the plan one last time with everyone while they waited for the right time. All in dark casual clothes they walked off the ship. Skyler texted Jozie before they left to meet them there.

They walked down to the building Kax began to shake. Skyler put his arm around her, "hey don't you worry I will not let anything happen to you. You can always replace a Captain, but you can't replace a good pilot."

She smiled and leaned close to Skyler, "I'm cold not scared."

Skyler took his black zipper hoodie off and put it on Kax's shoulders. "you stay warm then."

Kax looked at him, "but now all you have is you under shirt are you sure your going to be alright?"

Skyler could see the building was close. He placed his hand on Kax's shoulders and leaned in and gave her a deep passionate kiss, "I'll be fine you just stay safe, and I love you."

Kax looked into Skyler's eyes and saw there was a deep going away sadness in there, "Skyler I…"

He put his figure over her lips and smiled as he looked into her eyes.

Jozie was already waiting near the door in the shadows. The group stopped in their path and waved Jozie over. She came over to the group, "so plans the same you want me go in first?"

Skyler nodded, "yes go in right now and get the guard away from the door so we can sneak passed."

She nodded and headed to the door.

The group waited a couple of minutes after she was in and they made there into the building. They could hear Jozie in the back with the guard. Michael lead the way knowing where all alarms were. They took the elevator up.

Skyler spoke to the group, "okay on the way back I will take the elevator and you take the stairs and stick with Michael."

They all nodded. The elevator stopped at the top level. They go off and Michael picked the lock into the office. Once in the office Michael and Haas go to the back of the office and crack open the safe. They saw the blue glass swirling glowing orb no bigger than a large baseball. Haas pulled out his holo camera and took a 3D image of the orb. Michael took the orb. Haas went over to the desk and typed a few things on his computer then pulled out his mini holo projector and pulled out a hard light realistic 3d image of the orb. He turned around and placed it inside the safe then closed it.

Michael walked over to Kax and handed her the orb, "put it in the hoodie."

She took it and said, "I didn't expect it to be glowing." She placed the orb up her left

sleeve and then placed her hand in the jacket pocket so no light could escape.

Skyler looked at them, "so we got it and ready to go?"

Michael reset the alarm, "you can start out Skyler."

Skyler opened the door and the waiting for the elevator. While Michael, Kax and Haas took the emergency stairs. Once down the elevator Skyler waited to make sure the rest made it down the stairs. Jozie came over to him. She fixed her top and her hair was messed up. He looked at her and said, "where's the guard?"

She smiled, "taking a nap I wore him out."

Skyler frowned, "Squallites don't sleep."

Her eyes widened, "no one told me that. Um, we better get out of here." She grabs his arm and tried to run.

Skyler stayed put, "not till they come out of the stairs."

"fine then I'm going see you," she kissed Skyler and ran off.

Kax saw Skyler waiting at the bottom of the stairs, "you have to go."

Skyler looked at her, "the security guard is pretending to be sleeping. I had to make sure you got out of here. Go now!"

Michael and haas ran out the door first and ran in opposite directions.

Skyler went over to Kax kissed her and placed his hand in her pocket and played with the orb. He pretended to put the orb in his pocket. Skyler and Kax walked out of the building together parting ways. As soon as Skyler walked out of the building a swarm of guards grabbed him. They pinned him against the wall and began to search him.

***

Kax ran as fast as she could. Not looking back worried about Skyler. She ran all the way back to the ship and into Skyler's cabin. The rest of them were waiting there. Kax panted and tried to catch her breath. Tears were running down her eyes. She put her face in Skyler's pillow and cried.

Worried Michael sat down on the bed next to Kax. He put his hand on her back, "Kax what happened, where is Skyler and orb."

Kax pulled the orb out of her pocket, "call cane and have this transported to him immediately, when they find out Skyler just pretended to take the orb from me they will be looking for the orb and know we took it."

Michael handed the orb to Haas. "What do you mean they searched Skyler is he ok?"

"Skyler knew that they were watching us, he kissed me and pretended to take the orb. They caught him, and I continued to run. I have no idea what happen to him after." She put her head back into the pillow and continued to cry.

Jozie sat on the bed next to Kax, "Michael, I will comfort her you go and check on Haas and that orb."

Michael nodded and left the room.

Kax sat up.

Jozie's gave her a hug, "I know you care about Skyler a lot. I just want you to know what me and Skyler have is just a fling there is nothing between me and him."

Kax wiped the tears from her eyes, "I know, I just hope he is ok. I knew that look in his eyes when he entered the building he knew he wasn't coming back."

Jozie held Kax tightly, "he will be fine, he is Skyler nothing can keep him down."

Kax started to laugh, "you're right, and I think we should call cane and let him know to expect the orb."

She got up from the bed and went over to Skyler's computer and called Cane.

Cane appeared, "Kax what is up? I don't have much time. Where is Skyler?"

Kax took a deep breathe, "the Squallites refused to give us the orb and so Skyler had a brilliant idea to steal the orb. We got the orb it is on it's way to you right now Michael is transporting to your office."

Cane turned his head to the transporter, "nothing is here yet but in this case I will stay and delay my meeting for this. So where is Skyler?"

Tears came to her eyes, "He made them think he had the orb, meanwhile I did, we all got away and he got caught. I have no idea where he is right now."

Cane took a deep breathe, "I guess I will need to bail him out."

Kax shook her head, "no not right now we need to know what happened to him first. If you call the station they will wonder how you know."

Cane nodded in agreement. Just as he was about to reply a red light came on his transporter. "well it looked like the orb is final coming in."

Kax heard a knock at the door and a loud voice come from the other side, "Squallite Police department open up." Jozie went to the door.

"I will call you back cane take care," Kax hit the off button and Jozie answered the door.

***

Michael entered the transporter room and walked over to dr. Haas who was busy transporting the orb and a piece of metal together. He looked over Haas's shoulders and said, "that is not Cane's coordinance, who are you sending the orb and what I can only assume is a piece of my alloy to?"

Haas hit send and turned around to look at Michael, "I'm so sorry to do this to you I was really starting to like you, but I am a double agent and I have people who will pay me tons for these items."

Michael shoved Haas out of the way and stopped the transporting and hit reverse to gather back the particle matter, "How dare you do this to me Haas all this time I thought you were my friend and turns out you're a thief!"

Haas desperate to get out of this kissed Michael passionately on the lips.

Michael shoved him off, "Stop kissing me! I'm not into guys or you! You betrayed me!"

Haas pouted his face, "Michael don't say that. Come away with me, we can split the money and work together."

Michael shook his head and started typing in Canes coordinance on the transporter, "I am not like you and sorry we could not be friends." He went to hit the send button when he heard a click and felt something cold and metal on the back of his neck.

"I'm giving you one last chance to change your mind. I like you a lot Michael do not make me pull this trigger."

Michael put his hands in the air and turned around slowly. He looked right into Dr. Haas's trembling eye's, "you know this is wrong and I can't let you get away with it. If you knew anything about me in any way you will let me do my job."

Dr. Haas tightened his grip on the gun, "If you knew anything about me you would know all I am doing is my job. I am sorry Michael but lovers like you are replaceable."

Michael closed his eyes and let out a high-pitched cry. Dr. Haas fell right to the floor. "I guess you don't know anything about me. If you did you would have put in earplugs." He pushed the body over with his foot and continued started again to transport the orb only to Fleet Admiral Cane.

Chapter 55

The Squallite Police stepped into the captain's quarters. In their hands they held a cuffed Skyler and were followed by the Three Elders. The police spoke, "Tonight the Worm orb was stolen, and we only found him at the scene of the crime. We did not find the orb on him and have reason to believe that he was not working alone and that the orb may be somewhere on this ship. We will release the prisoner once we prove that the orb is not on this ship."

Kax smiled in relief when she Skyler. She felt bad seeing him in handcuffs but was happy to know he was ok.

Jozie smiled and waved her hand in the air, "well this is the captain's quarters if it would be anywhere it would be here. But we are just the captain's girls we haven't seen anything." Jozie moved close to Kax and played with her hair, "he keeps two of us, so we don't get lonely."

The cops rolled their eyes and started treating the place apart. Kax got up and went over to Skyler and kissed him on the lips, "I was worried about you, um when you didn't come back you we have to take off in the morning is there still time to prepare the ship?"

He smiled, "yes go get Michael and tell him he has to get things ready if there is something he can't do you do it ok sweetheart."

She smiled, "I will see you later." She went to head out of the room and the male elder grabs her shoulder, "where do you think you are going?"

She looked up at the elder and said, "Going to see the first officer, we have take off in the morning and if you have our captain in handcuffs then the first officer must get us ready."

"This ship is not going anywhere till it is fully searched and no one leaves."

Kax pulled away from the elder, "all the crew is here and accounted for no one will be leaving. This ship has a schedule to keep you will just have to conduct your search faster, you know what the orb looks like more than these cops maybe you should help them."

The cops came over to the door, “let her go there is nothing in the boy’s room may we continue to search the ship?”

The high elder nodded.

Skyler sat down on his bed, “you know I acted alone and I don’t have it I never had it someone must have got to it before me.”

The high elder glared at him, “silence you will speak when spoken to.”

Kax left the room and ran down the hall to the transportation room. She didn’t have to go all the way because she saw Michael drag dr. Haas’s body down the hall. She ran over and picked up dr. Haas’s feet. “what happened to him?”

Michael smiled when he saw Kax, “turns out he is a double agent and tried to send my alloy to his client. I have his clients number I will turn it over to the authorities when we get back to Earth. Till then I am dragging his sorry ass to the brig.”

Kax’s eyes widened, “really? I knew something was odd about him, but I would have never guessed that. Oh, and by the way you Skyler is on board they are searching for the orb, hope you cleared the records. Skyler has put us in charge till the release him.”

They got to the brig and Michael typed in his code to open the door. They placed Dr. Haas inside and stepped out of the cell. Michael locked up. He turned to Kax, “Of course I cleared the records. Did you call Cane?”

Kax nodded, “once Jozie got me to stop crying that was the first thing I did. But come on we have a ship to get ready.”

Morning arrived sooner than they thought. Skyler still in handcuffs waiting for his name to be cleared. Jozie stayed to keep him company but she had to be going soon. the cops came back into the captain’s cabin and spoke to the elders, “I’m sorry but we searched everywhere and there is no orb to be found. We searched all transporter records, and nothing shows up. I don’t think this boy stole the orb.”

The high elder looked at Skyler who was laying innocently on the bed, “I have no idea what you did with the Orb, but we know you have it somewhere. But since we have no evidence, we are exiling you from the planet. You were the only one at the scene and we can’t prove any other involvement. You are the Captain and if anyone in this crew aided you they would be only acting under your orders. Leave this planet and don't come back until that orb is returned to its rightful owner."

Skyler smiled, "I can live with that."

The cop picked up Skyler off the bed turned him around and unhandcuffed him. They all made there way off the ship.

Skyler turned to Jozie rubbing his wrists, "oh Jozie thank you for everything you were amazing this summer and I'm going to miss you."

She kissed him and gave him a hug, "you were great to, maybe we will see each other again sometimes you were a great guy to hang out with."

Skyler put both his hands on her neck, "I'll miss you but till next time." He gave her one last passionate kiss.

She hugged him tight for a minute. They broke the hug and she waved goodbye as she left the cabin.

He sat down and rubbed his face trying to take in everything that had happened in the last twenty-four hours. After a few moments he got up and got dressed in his uniform and made his way towards the bridge. Once he got there he saw Kax and Michael running around trying to get everything set up. he cleared his throat, "Tillion, Jones it's time to get going. We have all had a long night and a long summer I think it is time we went home." They both nodded and took their posts. Skyler sat in the Captain's chair and got to play Captain Therris one more time.

Acknowledgements

Luke Maynard,
Who has been my rock, my knight
and a marvelously talented human.
Your guidance has brought me to this point
And
Tommy Wiseau,
Because of you I learnt to write so good.

www.ingramcontent.com/pod-product-compliance
Lightning Source LLC
Chambersburg PA
CBHW030816310726
48980CB00006B/517/J

* 9 7 8 0 9 9 5 9 7 9 4 4 4 *